THE PROTECTORS:

Eric's Story

A Novel

G. J. Moses

PAGE PUBLISHING, INC.
New York, NY

First originally published by Page Publishing, Inc. 2017

ISBN 978-1-63568-811-5 (Paperback)
ISBN 978-1-63568-812-2 (Digital)

Printed in the United States of America

CONTENTS

PROLOGUE

It was a chilly and damp night here in Philadelphia, Pennsylvania. The visibility was good owing to a cloudless night and a full moon, which lit up the surrounding terrain like a spotlight. It helped light the way for the small group of men and women who were running as swiftly as they could. There were eight of us trying to catch up with our friend who was just over a quarter mile away and almost out of sight.

We were losing ground as each second passed as he was much faster than all of us. We were in one of many parks making up Fairmount Park and had been running flat out for fifteen minutes fully equipped for war. We were not on any path, but running in a straight line as the person we were following was not veering from his course. Our breath was ragged, our hearts were racing, and the sweat was running down our faces in streams. We barely slowed as we ran through a small creek and up the near bank.

We would not catch up to our friend until he reached his destination where we would do our best to keep him alive, even if it meant our own. We owed him that, not just for having saved our lives at some point in the past but because he was our leader, our mentor, but more than anything else, he was our friend! The one we were following is the Lord Protector of the Brotherhood. We are members of the Lord Protectors, whose sole job is to keep him alive.

I am known as Doc, and this is my story.

DOC: THE BEGINNING

Who am I? I am Eric Davis, known to most simply as Doc. How did I get here? It all started many years ago. As I run, my mind drifted back to when it all started. I grew up in a normal suburban family in the Northeast in the town of West Chester, just outside Philadelphia. I was the middle child with one older sister and one younger brother. My sister, Tiffany, as a gift for my fourteenth birthday, had taken me by train to the Secaucus county fair, which is a small town in New Jersey, just northwest of New York City. It was a Saturday near the end of April, and the spring night coolness felt nice after being at the fair all day.

Tiffany, who was two years older than me, had always been my best friend. Tiffany was a very beautiful young lady with long black hair reaching to her waist along with a gorgeous olive complexion showing our Spanish mother's heritage. Tiffany had saved her babysitting money for the last three months so she could surprise me with this gift. What a sis, huh? We were there as soon as the fair opened, and spent the whole day having fun with several of our friends. I had a soccer game first thing the next morning, so my sister and I left just as it started getting dark.

It all happened after we got off the train and were cutting through the Sears parking lot, which was closed, but the lot's lights were still on, so we felt pretty safe. Our house was just several blocks away, and we were anxious to show our parents the giant stuffed bear we had won. Suddenly, we saw around a half dozen men come out in front of us from different areas of the edges of the parking lot. They were all headed in our direction. We looked at each other with dread

7

in our eyes. I looked behind us and saw another several men coming toward us. As the men got closer, we could see that they were very rough men of different nationalities and, from their sneers, had bad intentions. Yes, we were scared, really scared.

As they got closer, we heard one of the men say to the others, "I told you she was a beauty. We are going to have some fun tonight." I recognized the man who spoke as someone I had seen at the fair several times that day. The man spoke with a New York accent I recognized from trips I had taken to the Bronx with my father. All had some type of gang member shirts on. This was not looking good for us.

I pulled Tiffany behind me and waited as I knew running would not do us any good. I did not know what I could do to stop them, but I was going to do everything I could. My legs felt weak, and my skin felt cold. Tiffany was crying softly and hugging the stuffed bear very tightly. Two of the men stopped when they were about twenty feet away from us and pulled pistols out from the back of their pants. They pointed these at us and laughed when we cringed. The remaining four in front and the two behind us spread out to encircle us. They moved slowly and confidently like they had done this before. When they were several feet away, they stopped. There was one very big man directly in front of us that acted like he was their leader. I heard someone call him Terrell. Terrell must have been 6'3" and all muscle.

Terrell looked at me and said, "So, boy, what are you going to do, fight all of us? If the girl there is nice to us, really nice, we will let both of you go on your way afterward. Whatcha say, girl? You going to be nice, or do we just take what we want? I want some of what the Teddy bear is getting, a great big hug."

They all laughed at this, and I knew there was nothing I could do to stop them from doing whatever they wanted to. I was so scared, more for Tiffany, as I was old enough to know what they wanted. I knew that she would be raped and brutalized before they hurt her or even killed her as I doubted they would ever release us to tell the police. I knew I would attempt to stop them but would be taken care of without very much effort on their part. I expected to die at any moment.

Suddenly, from nowhere, I heard a different type of laughter, a chuckle that was low and deep but could be heard by all. A man came up between the men behind us and stepped in front of me. He was all in black and wearing a baseball cap that hid his facial features. But from the little I had seen, I saw that he moved with an animal grace with no wasted movement. And quiet! Even when he was just a mere few inches in front of me, I could not hear him move. Everyone was shocked. Where did he come from and how could he get there without being noticed.

The two men that were twenty feet away started looking around in a panic. The men closest to us pulled out some type of weapon, be it a gun or knife. Terrell pulled out a huge wicked-looking knife that must have been over a foot in length. Terrell swung it around like he had plenty of experience with it.

The stranger standing in front of me chuckled some more, turned toward us, and whispered so only we could hear, "Both of you, do not move, no matter what happens. I need to know exactly where you are standing. I am here to help." The stranger looked into my eyes and smiled. His eyes shocked me; they were red, deep blood red with black pupils and with no white showing. I shook my head in amazement as the darkness must have played tricks on me. When the man had looked at me, I could see his face clearly. He could not have been older than sixteen or seventeen years old. That could not be true, could it? He must be older than that. The man—should I say man or teenager?—shifted the hat so the bill now pointed backward. No sooner had he done that when he turned around to face Terrell again.

Terrell, who had been looking around, said, "So what do we have here, the lone ranger to the rescue? And what is it with the eyes? Are you high or something? One druggy teenager and a boy against all of us, well, that should make it interesting, at least for a moment anyway. Well, boys, it looks like we are going to have even more fun before we get to enjoy the young lady."

With that the man in black said in a calm voice that had a steely tone, "What boy? You mean this brave young man I stand with? Yeah, those odds work for me. I will take those odds any day of the week."

I stared at the man's back. Did I hear right? Was he talking about me? Was I the brave young man? I sure did not feel like it. As I looked at him, I was able to notice things I had not seen before. The man was Caucasian, about six feet tall, had what looked like a holster with guns that were slung low on each side of his hips, the sleeves on each arm held some type of objects, but I could not identify what. Around his waist in leather sleeves were half a dozen objects that looked like knife handles sticking out but were very thin with a little flair near the top. Finally, there seemed to be some type of object with a handle in a thin sleeve across his back, but it was all in black and blended well with his outfit. He was much larger than I first thought with his muscles being very well defined. He looked, well, solid like a piece of granite. Even in my fear, I noticed that this man seemed relaxed but poised on the balls of his feet—like a panther about to jump. But what could a teenager do against eight men? He was only several years older than me!

With that utterance from the stranger, Terrell walked forward until he was just inches from the stranger who did not seem to care. You could tell Terrell was unused to people not backing up in fear from his presence. I certainly was ready to as the stranger was dwarfed by Terrell. Terrell took his knife and slowly placed the point on the stranger's chest. "So, lone ranger, let's see how brave you are. If you move, my friends over there will shoot that boy. Got it? One inch and he dies."

With that Terrell lowered the knife a bit and pushed the knife so it went through the shirt and barely into the stranger's stomach and slowly started slicing upward toward his heart. The blade must have been very sharp as it cuts through the shirt and skin with ease. Even though the cut was only an inch or two at this time, you could see the blood flowing freely, but the stranger never moved. In fact, he did not seem bothered. When the stranger did not react, Terrell's face lit up in surprise. Even with the situation I was in, expecting to be killed at any moment, I was amazed; this man looked like he was waiting for something. But what could that be?

All of a sudden, a loud shot rang out. The two men that were twenty feet away flew up in the air going backward and dropped to flop on the ground before lying still. Was that one shot? Or two so close together that they sounded like one? The stranger, as if he had been waiting for this all along, grabbed Terrell's hand with the knife and twisted so hard that you could hear Terrell's wrist snapping. Before Terrell could even scream out in pain, the knife still being held in Terrell's hand, had been shoved up under Terrell's chin and out the back of his head. You could to see gray matter on the tip of the knife as Terrell crumpled to the ground, not to move again.

What happened next is still hard to explain. I had never seen anyone move so fast nor as deadly. The stranger, before Terrell's body even hit the ground, jumped forward and grabbed the one on the right of Terrell by his throat and squeezed tightly while bringing the man's head quickly down to his rising right knee, snapping his neck like it were a twig. Then he swung toward the left and, while turning, was throwing whatever was in his arm sleeves and legs with both hands. I later found out they were a combination of Hira and Bo Shuriken. They were thrown so hard that the man was lifted off the ground upon impact.

After throwing the Shuriken, and before they even reached their destination, the man grabbed both of the guns in his side holsters and shot them from the hip at the one man left in front on the left side. I did not even see him pull them; it was that fast. You could see the man jerk each time he was shot. The man looked amazed just before he collapsed to the ground. The man hit by the Shuriken was lying on his side, and it was obvious from the way he was sprawled that he was permanently out of action.

The man on the right dropped his gun and ran. The man in black ignored him and quickly glanced at us to confirm we were okay. He smiled just before he swung around to run toward the two other surviving gang members.

I turned to see that one of the men was running away while the other man was leveling a handgun not more than eight feet away. The fear and anger on his face was frightening, to say the least. Without even slowing or breaking stride toward the man with the gun, the man in black dropped his handguns to grab the handle on his back with his left hand pulling out a long Japanese-sword-looking weapon whose blade reflected the light of the parking-lot lights like a bright mirror.

The man with the gun swung his weapon to follow the man in black as he moved with a speed that was hard to put into words. With the sword tightly gripped in his hand and held toward the ground in a reverse fashion, the man in black turned to the right of the man, swinging the blade in an arc upward around midheight while turning his body swiftly in a tight turn. The blade sliced through the man starting at his groin and continuing up through his left shoulder and, in its travels, separated the man's right hand from his arm. The gun that he was holding, with the hand still clenching the gun, dropped to the ground and discharged loudly but, fortunately, harmlessly into the air. The man looked at the stump on his right arm in puzzlement with incomprehension of what was happening in his eyes just before his chest opened up and the blood poured through the great opening that appeared in his torso. As he slumped to the ground in death, I turned to see what happened to the men that had run away.

I could hear one of men screaming in terror as he was running away from us as fast as he could. I thought the man in black would follow, but he smiled at us and relaxed. That seemed strange until I saw two separate small groups of people also dressed in black emerging from the dark at either end of the parking lot moving quickly toward both of the running men. Both groups moved efficiently and, in a very short period of time, very deadly.

The remaining gang members did not make it very far before they were caught by the new groups. I watched in awe as I saw one man, well, I guess it was a man due to the breadth of his shoulders, run up and jump in the air just before coming down with the back of his upper arm on the neck of the man that had been by Terrell. I could hear the sound of the impact, and judging from where I was, I was fairly certain it was so hard. The man hit just stopped running and grabbed his neck as he dropped to his knees from the impact before rolling onto the ground. From the relaxed manner of the man who had delivered the hit and had stopped while waiting to confirm no further action on his part was needed, I did not expect to see the man rise again. The man was just too relaxed even to my eyes to believe he thought that the man he had hit would ever rise again.

The other man tried to run away from the newcomers coming toward him, but he was not near fast enough. I watched a slim figure that had long dark hair in a tight braid flying out the back of her head—there was no mistaking what gender she was with her lithe and slim figure—overtake him with ease. The woman was holding a large knife or short sword as she ran past the man and made a downward and then a forward gesture. The distance made it hard to tell for sure, but it looked like she made a quick stab into the man's chest. The man stumbled before collapsing onto his back. The man rolled frantically with both hands pressing against his chest. In just a very short time, he was lying quietly with no sound.

Who were these new men and women? Were they friends or foes? I felt like I was going to faint at any time. My sister was screaming and almost hysterical. The man in black with a concerned look on his face, walked up to Tiffany, took away the bear, and very softly said, "You are OK now. My friends are here, and no one is going to hurt you." With that he folded Tiffany up in his arms and let her sob against his chest. It was only then that I realized that he was still bleeding freely from his chest wound. I was going to say something when he looked at me and put a finger to his lips.

I watched as the new groups came up to the stranger. There were three in each group, six in total, and a mixture of all races. I was correct in my assumption that a woman was among them. Everyone looked dangerous, not the same as the gang that attacked us, but more organized, more lethal, like they had military training. They were all armed with some type of handgun in a holster slung on their hip or shoulder along with an assortment of other weapons, some of which I had never seen before but looked very lethal. They moved with a deadly cohesiveness that was frightening yet comforting to see.

The first of these, a compact man of medium height but with big biceps, was carrying a large rifle in the crook of his arm as he walked up to the stranger. You could barely see his features with the camouflage black face paint he wore. He said, "Lord, I am sorry for the delay, but we got here as quickly as we could."

The man called Lord replied without letting Tiffany go, "Iwao, my friend, your timing and shots were perfect. As always, when I needed you the most, you were there."

The rest of the new arrivals examined the men taken down by the man called Lord and verified they would not be of any future danger. Several kept watch, looking around for any sign of trouble. I watched in amazement as they went about their activities. You could not miss the feelings of friendship these men and women had for the man and he for them.

After ten or fifteen minutes, Tiffany was finally able to compose herself, looked up at the man holding her, and asked who he was. That was when I learned that the man's name who saved us was actually Christopher Wilson. It was not until much later that I found out why they called him Lord. Chris informed us that he and his friends were in the neighborhood on business and, once they saw what was happening, stepped in to help. I shuddered to think of what type of business it was being dressed and armed like they were.

Chris looked at me and said, "We couldn't leave such a brave young man and woman at the mercy of those thugs." Looking again at Tiffany, he proceeded to tell her that people like these prey on others for fun and the only way to deal with them is to eliminate them. Chris put his finger under Tiffany's chin to raise her eyes so he could look directly into them. "Young lady, good things are going to happen to you. Do not let this event change that. Do you know why I know that? Because I saw two very special people tonight. A brave young man that was ready to risk his life standing up to these bullies in an attempt to protect his sister even when he knew it was probably hopeless. I also saw that you never made any move to leave your brother even though you knew what was going to happen to you. Brave, loving individuals like yourself are destined for greatness, and I am honored to have had the opportunity to meet you. I hope that you two will allow me the honor of being your friend."

Tiffany smiled, wiped her eyes, held out her right hand to Chris, and said, "I am Tiffany, and this is my brother, Eric. We wish to thank you and would like to be your friends."

We reached a point where I could hear their conversation and something made me stop and hold Tiffany back. I was curious to see what men like these talked about after the fight that had just been fought. I was surprised to hear my name mentioned. Chris was telling the medic, "Roy, did you see them? That young man, Eric, impressed me with his courage. Eric stood his ground and did not give that big jerk an inch, not an inch. Eric is going to be going places. So will Tiffany. Both of them were so very brave and I am glad we were able to get here in time."

At this time Chris flinched and looked at Roy with humor in his voice while saying "although I am not sure I will survive your butchery." Roy looked up at Chris with a frown and said, "Well, this would not have happened if you would have just slowed your ass down so us mortals could keep up with you. Another few moments would not have mattered." At which Chris laughed while patting Roy softly on his shoulder. It was an amazing sight and you got the feeling that they had been through this same conversation many times before.

We continued walking and as if he could sense our presence, Chris who had not been facing us, turned with a smile on his face and asked how we were doing. I still remember to this day how that smile made everything that had happened in the last few hours seem so distant and made me feel that I was as safe as if I was home in bed.

I let Chris know our plans where upon hearing we were leaving, stood up, with Roy grumbling while he followed suit while stopping his stitching, and shook my hand. Chris looked me in the eye and said that friends do not forget each other so stay in touch. With that, he pulled Tiffany to him and gave her a hug, a tight hug even with the bear. Chris looked Tiffany in the eye and said not to worry, she would get over all this as time goes by. Tiffany told Chris that she was not concerned about herself but for him, that she felt bad he had been hurt saving them.

Chris put his hand on her cheek and said, "Tiffany, it was my pleasure—it really was. Life is made up of events in your life that you will think on for a long time to come. Some will be bad, some will be good. Making two new friends such as yourselves will definitely be one I will remember with great fondness. So do not worry about me, I will be just fine."

Tiffany then hugged Chris even more tightly as Rod looked on with apprehension at the stitches. Just as Tiffany was releasing Chris, she stood up on her toes and kissed his right cheek while caressing his left. "Thank you from both of us. I hope we will see you again," whispered Tiffany. If I did not know better, I would think Tiffany had a new crush. Nah, the pink in her cheeks was surely due to the night coolness, not from her blushing. And, unless my eyes deceived me, Chris was blushing as well. But then again, with all that had happened tonight, I was most likely mistaken, yeah, that must be it.

With that we thanked all of them once again and started to leave. Just as I was about to turn, I remembered what had been bothering me. I asked Chris why did he let Terrell cut him with the knife. Smiling, Roy looked up at me.

Roy said, "Son, I can answer that one for you. The Lord was waiting for us to take out the two armed men that were the furthest out. They were the real danger being so far from him. If they had been just a few feet closer, the Lord would have taken all of them on when you first saw him. But he couldn't guarantee it, they were just too far out. He did not want to take a chance that they would get off a shot at you two before he could get to them. That was why he did not start the fight until we got here and Iwao could take them out. He was concerned for your safety. And he needed to keep all their eyes on him and not see us when we arrived. And how better to do that than to allow them to do superficial skin damage thinking they were in total control?"

I looked at Chris, and he just shrugged. I looked at Tiffany, and I would swear she blushed even more.

I grabbed Tiffany's arm and we walked away arm in arm with Teja and Andrew by our side. I was not surprised to see Tiffany glance back several times in Chris's direction as I also did the same. Surprising, Chris had not sat down but continued to watch us as we walked away. I may be wrong but I believe he only had eyes for Tiffany and mirrored the same look Tiffany had when she glanced back.

Boy, it was an interesting night in more ways than one. I left there knowing that I had met a man that was very unique in this world. I wanted to do something more than words to thank this man and friends for all they did for us. We would not be alive but for them. But how? Then it came to me. I remembered Roy and what he had been doing. How Roy looked a bit uncomfortable while working on Chris. It was then that I knew what I wanted to do to thank Chris for all his help, for saving me and my sister. I would become a doctor and be there when he needed me.

Yes, I know, I was a fourteen-year-old boy with average grades and had not thought much past the next week ahead let alone what life career I wanted to do. But there was something about this man that gave me inspiration. Was it the man himself? Was it the desire to be a member of the special group that hung around him? I do not know but I made up my mind that night that if Chris needed a doctor, a really good doctor, I would be that for him. Not today maybe but soon. I was determined that I was going to be the best damn doctor in the world, for my new friend, Chris, the Lord Protector of the Brotherhood!

TEJA FOSTER AND THE PROTECTORS

Tiffany and I along with Teja and Andrew settled into a booth at Denny's. Teja sat to my left with Tiffany to my right and Andrew across from me. Teja Foster was her full name. Teja was a thin medium colored African American in her early twenty's about five feet and six inches. Teja was average in height but that was that was all that was average about her. Teja was a very striking woman and commanded a look by anyone near her, man or woman. You would call her gorgeous even though she had a very thin pale scar on the right side of her face. The scar ran from her eye socket to the bottom of her earlobe. Her torso was muscular and well defined. Her legs covered in tight blue jeans could not hide the fact that they were long, strong and sleek. Teja's dark hair hung to the middle of her back and was bound with a leather braid that did nothing to hide its fullness. Her movements were graceful and beautiful to watch.

Andrew Robinson, who was sitting across from me, was a Caucasian also in his early twenty's with a dark complexion from being in the sun so much. Andrew was around five feet and ten inches, brown colored mustache and goatee, wide shouldered with a broad regal nose that spoke of his Italian heritage. Andrew was solidly built and moved with a grace that belied his bulk. Both Teja and Andrew were quick to smile and laugh.

We were sitting in a Denny's after a night that I was sure both Tiffany and I would never live through. The two that we were sitting with were part of a group that had just saved us from certain death. Teja and Andrew, whom we already considered our friends, were there to make sure we got home safely. The two had changed out of

21

their black outfits and put away their weapons, well, the weapons we could see anyway. I am sure they still had quite a few on their person. I do not think they ever went about unarmed. I had just finished talking with my parents, using the coin operated phone in the hall by the restrooms, where I let them know where we were and assuring them we would be home in a few hours. I did not tell them of our ordeal upon a recommendation from Andrew. Andrew said that our parents would not understand and would worry deeply every time either of us was out of sight needlessly. So now, Tiffany and I were sitting in rapture, as Teja and Andrew told us about the Brotherhood and most of all, Chris, the Lord Protector.

It seemed Andrew and Teja, both from the Philadelphia area, were part of a large organization called the Brotherhood. It was an organization of men and women who had come together to live in friendship and would join together against anyone who threatened or hurt any of their members or family. It was all started by individuals who were impacted by Chris in some manner and decided to stick around one another. As the number of friends grew, they decided to make it more formal. The organization was started in the late sixties and grew little at first but had been growing quickly as the word spread. The total organization now numbered five or six thousand and spread throughout the world with the vast majority in the USA. Membership was not easy. You could not be a member unless you were willing to support and fight for the group when needed. Everyone was expected to train and be a supportive member on a daily basis, not just when convenient.

Teja smiled and spoke of how at first she thought it was not something she could do but her admiration and love for Chris gave her the drive to make it happen. I asked Andrew why they call Chris "Lord"; do they consider Chris a holy man? Andrew shook his head negatively while laughing said, "Chris, a holy man? To that I can emphatically say no. We do it to piss him off mostly in good humor while respecting him at the same time."

I was puzzled and Andrew could tell. Andrew smiled and let me know that Chris prefers to be called by his name and does not like titles. They use the title "Lord" as there are quite a few named

Chris in their organization so they needed something unique when addressing him. It was actually Caleb who came up with calling Chris "Lord." Caleb has a very unique close relationship with Chris and would never do anything to insult or harm Chris. But that did not mean Caleb would not have fun at Chris's expense. "Lord," when addressed to Chris, explained Andrew, refers to the medieval times when Lords were around to protect the people of the land. Lords were leaders of people that were to be respected and depended on in times of trouble. That was how they feel about Chris, the Lord Protector of the Brotherhood. Of course Chris not liking being given the Lord moniker made it all the sweeter. Andrew informed us that it is hard not to laugh in Chris's presence when he hears Caleb chuckle when Caleb sees Chris cringe upon being addressed as "Lord." Well, if you could call Caleb's deep-throated rumple a chuckle, that is. And everyone knew why Caleb was chuckling, including Chris, who when hearing his chuckle always glanced at Caleb like he would like to throttle him.

Teja's voice was soft and sweet. It was easy to get lost in it as she described how she met Chris and became part of the Brotherhood. It all happened several years ago. At that time, Teja knew she was very beautiful and had grown up using it to her advantage. Teja had been setup on a date with a man who was supposed to help her get a modeling job with a famous agency. Teja was used to winding men around her fingers and getting what she wanted. Rarely, if ever, was Teja concerned for her safety. Teja and her date had gone to a party where she met several model agency scouts so she was having a great time and was not paying much attention to what she was drinking. Unknowingly Teja had been given a drug by her date.

Not much later, when she was being driven home, Teja could not keep her eyes open no matter how she tried. She must have fallen asleep or passed out only to wake up several hours later in a strange room with several men leering down at her. Teja could tell that several pieces of her clothing had been removed while she had not been conscious by the cool air on her skin. She tried to move off the bed but quickly realized that there were restraints on both her arms and legs. A quick panicky glance showed that her arms and legs had been bound with strips of cloth from her shirt.

One of the men, there were four in total including her date, had a knife pressed to her face. The man had tattoo's liberally spread over his arms. The man stared at her with contempt in his eyes. When he saw she finally realized the situation she was in, told her if she resisted, he would carve her face up. That she would never want to look in the mirror again. That if she wanted to get out of this unharmed, she should just go along with what they wanted. Teja begged for mercy and asked them to let her go. Teja pleaded with them and swore she would not tell the police or anyone what they had done. They all looked at each other, put their hands up to their face in mock alarm and laughed. Teja screamed and tried to get out of her bindings, the knots holding her right leg unwound and Teja kicked the man in the nuts. The man howled and with the knife sliced the right side of her face open. It was not until later she knew to what extent but she could feel the warm blood streaming down her face. Teja thought she was going to be killed and cried in fear.

The man lifted the knife to slice her left side when without warning, the door was kicked in with the door jamb being splintered and flying through the air. A man dressed all in black came barging in before anyone had time to make more than a surprised gasp. The newly arrived man grabbed the man with the knife by his throat and the belt at his waist. The man was quickly lifted high into the air. With speed hard to believe, the man in black spun around in a tight circle and threw the man against the far wall so hard that the top part of his body went through the wall into the other room. The sound of the impact was so loud in Teja's ears that she hunched up into a ball even tighter in fear. Teja could see that while going through the wall, one of the support beams had shattered and gone through the man's chest. It was obvious that he would not be slicing up anyone ever again.

The other three men raised their hands but there was no mercy in the man's eyes or expression. Teja tried to see his face but it was in the shadows or moving so fast she could not get a real good look. Silently he strode further into the room with surety and power. He lashed out with his foot to strike one man in the throat at the same time striking another hard in the chest with his open palm. The man struck in the throat gurgled and grabbed his throat to gasp for a breath. It was not to be. The man struck in the chest, looked down at his chest in amazement and back up the man that hit him before violently shaking and spitting blood out through his nose and mouth. He slowly sank to his knees where his head slumped onto his chest, not to move again.

The last man, Teja's date, dropped to his knees and begged for mercy. The man in black ignored the man for the moment and turned to Teja. The man undid the remaining strips of her shirt that bound her, picked her up in his arms with surprising gentleness, looked her in the eyes and asked her what she wanted him to do. Teja looked at the pitiful man on his knees, remembered how helpless she had been, being at the mercy of this man, begging for her life as he was now. Teja felt the blood flowing down her face, remembered the mocking when she asked for mercy, and whispered to the man in whose arms she was nestled in, "no mercy."

With those words, the man in black while still holding her, leaped into the air, twisted onto his side and wrapped both of his legs around the man's neck. As he twisted straight again, the man's neck snapped with a loud crack and the light went out of his eyes. Teja's date slumped on the ground never to rise again. The man in black landed on his feet and Teja only felt a slight jar.

Teja looked at her rescuer closely for the first time and was shocked to see who her rescuer was. The man could not have been more than fifteen to sixteen years old. He might have been young but there was no doubt in her mind that the person holding her was a man, a very powerful and mature man. Teja could feel the power of his arms and could not remember ever feeling such strength before. Teja could feel the man's arms pulsing from his blood flow and the warmth that generated in his arms. It was an amazing feeling. He was holding her so tightly yet gently and without any signs of strain. But that was not the only shock for Teja. His eyes were a deep dark red with only the black of his iris's showing. The most intriguing aspect of this man though was the gentleness and warmth she could see in his eyes and face. The man looked at her with such intensity and concern that it was evident for her to easily see that she was in no danger from him.

Teja knew how to read men's looks. Most looks Teja got were in lust and desire but this man's face and eyes showed none of that, just concern. Teja did not know why but she felt safe in his strong arms. Teja put her arms around the man's neck, snuggled so close to his chest that she could hear his heart racing and sighed. At this time, several others, also dressed in black, came into the room, but Teja could tell immediately that they know the man she was being held by. Teja, still feeling the effects of the drug, relaxed and left herself fall asleep in the warmth of his arms.

Awhile later, Teja woke, still in the man's arms. The man was standing now with half a dozen others dressed in black like him. The man felt her wake up, looked down, and asked if it she was OK. Teja raised herself up a little in his arms, a bit startled, her mind being still hazy. It was hard to pull the awful memories back to remember what had actually happened and how she got here. Teja did this without releasing her hold on the man's neck. Teja, still feeling very secure and comfortable, relaxed again in this stranger's arms as she did not want to let go of this sense of security. As her memories came back, she looked up and asked where she was and who they were.

The man said his name was Chris and the rest of the group were close friends of his. They had gotten her address from her driver's license, which they had found in her pocketbook, which was in the room Chris had broken into. They were now in an empty lot about a block from her apartment. Teja's injuries were not life-threatening, and they did not want to take her to a hospital without her permission. They decided it would be best to wait for her to wake up to find out what she wanted to do prior to taking the next step. They had just missed the police arriving when they left the scene, but as the neighborhood was used to gunshots and murder, they had decided it was best to let it look like a drug deal gone bad. Luckily, the man that had sliced her face had a lot of drugs on him, so it supported that assumption. They had stopped in this empty lot until she woke up.

Chris smiled and said her neighbors might not understand a group of armed men barging into her apartment complex. Teja realized it must have been a long while since the event and asked Chris if he had been holding her the whole time. "Yes, you needed some rest, and the few times I tried to put you down, you would not let go of my neck, so I decided to just let you continue to sleep as is," replied Chris. Teja knew she was not very heavy compared to others but still could not imagine anyone being able to hold someone in their arms for that long. What strength this man must have! With that, Teja smiled at the thought and snuggled closer. Teja felt even more secure from hearing and feeling his heartbeat, which was loud in her ear that was pressed up against his chest and, strangely, beating very fast. Teja, still trying to gather her thoughts, looked up into Chris's eyes and saw they were now a deep, beautiful clear hazel. They were so bright that Teja felt they could light up the darkness if he wanted them to.

Teja asked Chris how he had come to rescue her, and was she imagining it, or were his eyes deep red then? A man next to Chris, a man whom she later found out was named Jose Garcia, chuckled and responded before Chris could talk. With an amused muttering that sounded something like, "They always ask about the eyes first," Jose told Teja. "Our explanation is more guess than anything as we are not scientists, nor have we done any real research into the matter. But we believe Chris has developed a unique ability to speed up his metabolism. How we believe he acquired that ability is a very long story and better explained at some other time. That increased metabolism causes his heart to pump many times faster than normal. The increased blood flow increases Chris's senses exponentially along with much greater speed and strength. His blood vessels expand under the pressure, and because of that, the red eyes. But there is a price to pay for all that, which is best left unsaid at this time."

Jose continued his explanation with a tone and familiarity that suggested he had told this story many times. "As for how Chris was able to save you, Teja, we believe for the same reason. Again, guesswork here, but the only one we can think of. Everyone gives off a vibe or pheromone depending on their emotion. Well, we believe that to be true anyway but have no scientific facts to back it up. But in support of that hypothesis, have you ever walked in a room and could 'feel' the tension even if no one says anything, or you can 'feel' the love between two people even if you never met them before? Have you ever heard of the saying 'You can smell the fear on him?' When Chris is in a heightened mode, he can either feel or smell strong emotions, if close enough. Each emotion has its own characteristics. Fear, and there are many different types, is a much stronger emotion than any other so much easier to pick up. Fear of your life and rape are the strongest combination that Chris is able to identify. We had just come from another situation, and Chris was still in the enhanced mode. Your fear was so strong that Chris knew it was very close and very deadly with no time to waste. He sensed it from the building we were just passing. Chris ran into the building without speaking, and we followed. The rest you know. Does that help?"

Teja put her left hand up to run her hand over Chris's eyes. At the same time, her other hand came up to her own right cheek and felt all the gauze padding. Chris saw the question in her eyes and said, "I wish there was more we could do, but we are short of good doctors. We were able to stop the bleeding, but there was more tissue damage than we can repair. We can help you find a good doctor and a plastic surgeon."

"I want to keep the scar, a small part of it anyway, to remind me of what happened. Why I need to be able to defend myself. I never want anyone ever to have that kind of power over me again," Teja replied, looking up straight into Chris's eyes with determination and strength. "Can you help me?" Teja asked while still caressing Chris's face.

Chris chuckled and said he might know a few people that might be able to help out in that area. Hence, Teja joined "The Brotherhood" and, eventually, over time, became a proud member of the "Lord Protectors." And no one, ever since that night, had ever tried to rape Teja again. Well, none who was still alive anyway.

ANDREW ROBINSON MEETS THE LORD

Andrew picked up with his story once Teja finished. Andrew had a different story but one no less impressive. Andrew was one of the many draftees during the Vietnam War. It was the late '60s, and the Vietnam War was in full swing. Andrew was an army private stationed at Firebase Bastogne. Andrew was a boy at the time and was only looking to get home in one piece. No heroics for him!

Andrew told the story with a look in his eyes like he was reliving the event while he spoke. It was close to Easter and he had just received a package from home. The package contained homemade cookies from his mother. Andrew's mom had made enough for him to share with his entire squad. There were chocolate chip, almond and butter tarts, along with at least another half a dozen other types. Of course, Andrews's personal favorite was the butter cookies with the little strawberry jellied centers. They were so good especially the way the jelly melted in your mouth. Just as he was finishing his second cookie, all hell broke loose. They were under attack. You could hear shells falling all over the compound. Andrew relayed the following story with a pained look now in his eyes.

I grabbed my M14 and ammunition belt, which was never far away. The rest of the squad was doing the same and running to one of the four artillery batteries of Firebase Bastogne. My squad was assigned to the 175 battery. As we got close, we could see several of our companions that had been guarding the 175 were already down. Several looked injured and others, well, they must have borne the brunt of this well-coordinated attack. I was assigned to the farthest position out front with my bunkmate, George Wilson. George had grabbed his weapon at the same time as myself and was just a few feet behind me. George was a quiet man of average height and build around eighteen or nineteen years old but one you could trust your back with. We were slugging our way to our position when all a sudden, the ground exploded under our feet.

I do not remember much from then on for an hour or so. I remember waking up with severe pain in my wrists and a shooting pain in my back. I had difficulty opening my eyes and realized they were coated in blood. It was midday and the sun was bright. The pain in my wrists were from leather bindings. I was strapped to a pole hanging upside down that was being carried by several of the North Vietnamese Army (NVA) through the dense jungles.

Next to me was George who was being carried in the same manner. George did not look good. His face was a mass of purple and red blood clots. His left leg looked like it had been hit in several places by shrapnel and was twisted at an odd angle. I could not tell where we were but I did not believe we were that far from our camp yet. I based that guess on how quiet the NVA were trying to be. There seemed to be several dozen of them. I was afraid that I would never taste Mom's cookies again.

I looked over at George and saw that he was awake. I was very concerned for him as he was very pale and looked to have lost a lot of blood. George, when he saw me looking at him, strangely smiled. Very quietly he said, "Do not worry. My brother Chris was scheduled to visit me today." And then chuckled and shook his head like it was a private joke.

George said this with such certainty that I was afraid he was no longer thinking straight. Just great, now I was being carried away with a madman at my side. What else could happen? It did not take long to find out. I heard a loud bird cry just before the officer, who had heard George talking with me, came up and struck him with his rifle telling George in broken English to be quiet. I must be going crazy like George as I would swear that it was a robin call that I heard and there were definitely no robins in this area. The smack by the rifle caused a gash in George's forehead that streamed blood over

George's smiling face. Yes, I said smiling! And then George winked at me and mouthed "he's here."

Had he gone crazy? George always seemed to be pretty cool headed and this was unusual behavior for him. Was it possible he knew something that I did not?

Suddenly, I saw and heard a whistling noise. It was the noise you hear when an object is going through the air at great speed. The four men carrying us reared up with black arrows protruding from their chests. We were dropped and fell to writhe on the ground in pain. The pain in my back flared up like it was on fire and I could feel blood running down my side. My ears reverberated with the sound of gunshots and screaming.

I heard the leaves rustle and a man; all in black with two swords in his hands come charging into the NVA. How do I describe this? How can I explain the swiftness, the power, the deadliness of this man? The man was around six feet in height with dark brown hair. I saw him go straight into the main body of the NVA who fell down like they were stalks of wheat. The man twisted and jumped with astonishing speed. The NVA were trying to bring their weapons to bear on him but he was never in one place long enough. That did not stop them from firing in panic and many bullets came very close to striking us. Close, very close but fortunately, none did.

I saw the enemy officer that had struck George grab a few of his men and push them down on their knees so they could aim better. You could tell that he was going to have them shoot right into the middle of the melee to get this man even if it meant he killed some of his own men. They opened fire but the man in black did something I had a hard time believing. In fact, I have run the events through my mind a thousand times to verify what I saw actually happened. The man, while still twirling and fighting the enemy close at hand, was deflecting bullets that came near him with his swords. I could see the spark from the deflections. How? How could he see the path of the bullet? Even if he could, how could he do that while still fighting? And he was still fighting. I saw him jump over a stump in the trail right into four of the enemy. The man struck the closest soldier in the chest with the blade in his right hand so hard the blade stuck out

31

the man's back. The man kept pushing forward with the man still attached and stabbed the soldier standing just behind. Both soldiers were now stuck on the sword in a matter of a second or two. The bodies acting as a shield from the gunfire from the men down the trail. The man in black while doing this had used the blade in his left hand to swing to either side taking out the other two soldiers. The man stopped, looked at George and smiled. Here we are in the middle of the jungles of Vietnam with dead and dying all around us and this man smiles. To say I was incredulous is an understatement. It was then that I noticed the eyes. They were the deepest red I had ever seen, deep bright bloody red.

The man very quietly said, "Hi, bro, you left before I could meet you but I figured you would not mind if I stopped in on your little party." My jaw must have dropped to the ground as I realized that this man in black that just took out over a half dozen NVA could not have been older than fifteen to sixteen years old. George's brother must actually be his *younger* brother! I looked over at George and you could see the family resemblance. George looked at me and whispered, "Chris was never one for formalities," and laughed. The laughter caused George to choke and spit up blood but he continued to laugh nonetheless.

With this, Chris looked more closely at the wounds George and I had. I shivered from the look in his eyes. The red got even darker, the eyebrows grew closer together, the fists gripping the two blades tightened and he turned his gaze to the dozen or so NVA still left alive. He stared at the officer. Then I heard him say out loud "Caleb, the rest are yours but that officer is mine." Caleb? Who was Caleb? Who the hell was he talking to?

Then I saw the biggest man I have ever seen, rise up out of the jungle behind a half dozen of the enemy soldiers. The man literally grabbed several of the men and smashed their heads together. I swear he smashed them so hard that his hands met before he released the bodies to fall onto the ground at his feet. A dozen feet away on either side of Caleb, whom I assumed this man was, stabs of flame shot out to strike down other soldiers. The soldiers crumpled without a sound or in screams of pain but in either case, they did not rise again. The

NVA that were left were stunned. They were running around shooting but wildly and not hitting anything. Caleb pulled out several hand weapons and let loose on the men by the officer. Several went down in short order. The flames on either side of Caleb continued to rain death down on the enemy soldiers.

The officer and the remaining two men with him had stopped shooting just long enough to reload but were raising their weapons again to take aim at Chris when he went back into action. The officer was about 20 feet down the path with the pair of soldiers spread out in front of him. Chris sprinted to the closest tree only to use that as a springboard to push off to fling his body through the air straight down the path. You would have to have seen it to believe it but this man was flying and twisting through the air with his feet barely touching the ground he was moving so fast. The two swords were spinning around him so fast that it sounded like a buzz saw. Every once in a while you could see a flicker of light and hear a pinging noise as he seemed to be able to deflect the bullets that got too close. Not all, as I saw one bullet tear into Chris's thigh and throw him off to the side. But Chris jumped up immediately and was flinging himself at them again.

The NVA were firing on full automatic. Chris ran right into the middle of the two men and within a second there were another two bodies lying on the ground. The officer continued to pull the trigger on his now empty pistol and screaming at the top of his lungs. It was then that I realized it had gone quiet. None of the NVA was moving.

I saw Caleb standing along with two other men with rifles in a casual but alert position. The other two had similar builds but not the height nor breadth of Caleb. I know I said it before but Caleb was huge! It was then that I saw Caleb had been wounded in his left shoulder but he seemed to be paying it no mind. The two with Caleb kept their gaze roving the brush while Caleb watched the situation with Chris. I was amazed at the softness I saw in Caleb's eyes while he watched Chris. And did I tell you? Caleb and the two men with him could not have been older than eighteen or nineteen years old. They may have been young men but you could see the experience of being in rough situations was not something new to them. They frightened while reassuring me at the same time with the confidence and power they radiated.

I then saw Chris reach the officer. Chris's leg was very bloody but he seemed to be paying it no mind. The officer tried to pathetically strike Chris with the gun, which Chris deflected off handily enough. Chris dropped his swords and slowly picked up the officer by his neck until he was about a foot off the ground. The officer struggled to get his breath and grabbed at a knife in his belt.

These NVA soldiers may be smaller in build but they sure did not lack courage. None had run away and when all seemed lost, the officer continued to fight. Not that it did him any good. Chris grabbed the officer's hand and took the knife away with very little difficulty. You could see the pain and surprise in the officers eyes at the strength of this boy. Chris with deliberate slowness, pushed the knife into the man's chest while looking him in the eyes. Chris said very softly but all could hear in the deep quiet that now surrounded the area, "You mess with my brother, you mess with me. Now you must pay the ultimate price!" With that, Chris slowly pushed the blade until the handle guard rested on the man's chest and the officer's head flopped back in death.

Chris calmly dropped the body, stooped to pick up his swords, and slowly walked back over to where we were being released from our bonds. Chris knelt next to his brother, looked at his wounds whom Tyler was now bandaging, and said good naturedly "George, are you trying to give Mom and Dad a stroke? You know how they worry about you. How do you think they are going to handle this? Well, at least now maybe you will come home and stop traveling to all the hot vacation spots around the world." George, looking at his brother with love clearly showing on his face, said jovially "Yeah, well, Chris, you should have seen the girls. Wow! But I guess you're right, I guess it is time to go home. I am a little tired though, mind giving me a lift?"

I was amazed. I could see both had been seriously wounded and yet they both had time to make light of the situation. One thing was clear though, there was no doubting the love they had for each other. Several times I saw George try and crawl to where Chris was where

I believed he would attempt to help protect him even though any movement must have caused intense pain.

Chris looked at me and asked how I was doing. Caleb who had come over to introduce himself and his cousins Elijah and Tyler, started treating my wounds. Tyler had already bandaged Caleb's shoulder, which showed a good amount of blood had been lost but seemed to have little impact on Caleb. Caleb removed a large piece of shrapnel out of my back, which alleviated a lot of the pain I was feeling. Besides the back wound and the rope burns from the wrist straps; I was in decent shape considering everything that had happened. I was not going to do any marathons in the next several days but I did not feel as bad as I had felt just a few hours ago. Amazing what being released and able to stand on your own will do to improve how you feel. Of course, being with individuals like this helped too.

Elijah put a rough bandage on Chris's leg while the other two now worked on George. Once everyone was bandaged as well as could be, we all started moving out. We did not want to stick around to see who would show up. Chris had Caleb help me while the other two scouted out in front of us and retrieved the four bows they had used to take out the men holding us on the stakes.

Meanwhile Chris picked up George and cradled him in his arms. The wound on Chris's leg had looked serious so I was surprised that he could pick George up let alone carry him any distance. George had to weigh around 170 to 180 pounds but Chris picked him up like he was just an infant. And with the same care and love a mother would. It was when George was firmly in Chris's arms, just before we moved out, we were stopped by George. Looking around all the rescuers, George said, "Thanks." Just that, no more. And looking around you could see that no more was needed. Caleb just smiled and bowed his head, Elijah and Tyler stopped by to pat George affectingly on his back.

I was about to say something similar when with my mouth open, Chris looked at me and said with a smile on his face, "We know, no need to say anything. And just for your information, we would have come for you even if George was not with you. We do not leave anyone behind or skirt our duty as Americans. So if you and my brother are done, can we get moving before we draw more unwanted attention?" With that, while holding George in his arms, Chris squeezed my right shoulder. I cannot explain it but it felt exactly like a gesture my older brother would do to show his affection for me. I felt at that moment like I was with family.

Chris carried George that way through the jungle the entire six or so miles back to Firebase Bastogne. I was starting to learn that there was a lot more to this man. Not once did I hear a groan or complaint even though several times you could tell that he was in great pain and would like nothing better than putting George down.

Only after we reached the base and George was in the care of the medical team would he allow someone to look at him. Seems I found out I was totally mistaken again. Chris had not blocked all the bullets as I thought. Chris had a total of three serious bullet wounds and four minor wounds that just one would take down most men down. Besides his leg, one bullet was in his upper right chest zone and the other was in his left arm by his shoulder. Chris also had several shrapnel wounds he picked up when he went through the camp where he found out George was missing, which started him on his way to rescue us. These had not been visible due to his clothing being soaked with blood and we had all believed it to be the NVA's. The Doctors that worked on Chris was amazed he was alive let alone joking and goofing with us.

Caleb, who had never left Chris's side, told me that he had seen this from him before. Chris just refused to let his body pain centers override his will, not that he could not feel it or that he could ignore it all the time, but forced himself to have a higher tolerance than most. Chris pushed it to the side and concentrated on what he felt was more important. In this case, it was the well-being of George and myself.

Yes, this was no boy here but definitely a man, a man I wanted to know better. At this I asked about the red eyes. Caleb, who was sitting next to Chris in a chair with his feet propped on the windowsill, went on to explain. It was the same explanation that we already heard Teja tell us. But I distinctly remember Caleb looking at Chris with sadness in his eyes to say that the red eyes came only at a great price.

When I said that I can only imagine the level of pain Chris must feel when in the enhanced mood with all his senses being so sensitive, Caleb just shook his head like I had no idea.

While at the infirmary, I found out that the base had been hit hard but had not fallen. Chris said that he did not want to stick around as the base was poorly laid out and he felt it would not survive the next major attack.

It was after we had all been examined and patched as best as the camp medical facilities, known as MUST (medical unit, self-contained, transportable) could, that I learned the following. When Chris decided to visit George, Caleb, who had taken it upon himself to be Chris's bodyguard several years before, tagged along with his two cousins who also were not to be left behind. From the conversations that we had in the base's hospital, I was able to fathom that they thought of Chris like a brother and had been by his side for over four years now. Who makes men, and especially being at such a young age, insist on traveling with someone to Vietnam in the middle of a war?

It was only in a matter of days of being in Chris's company that I came to see what should have been obvious. Chris cared about people, really cared. You could see that from his behavior and the way he interfaced with the soldiers in the hospital and around the base. It did not matter if you were white, black, or Asian. He cared. You could see the love that these hard men, yes men, had for each other. It did not take long to know that Chris would not hesitate to make the ultimate sacrifice for his family and friends. Caleb told me several stories of the heroic acts that Chris did for strangers, just because he thought it was right. Chris told Caleb each time when he asked why, "Their need was greater than mine." Caleb told me that he had started an organization based on some of the attributes that Chris lived by. It was called the Brotherhood. Where all men, women and children could live with the knowledge that someone would be around to help and protect each other. No matter your race, politics or wealth. It was a small group of several hundred at this time but it was growing.

Just before Chris took his brother and me home, yes, he took me with them and no one in the US military seemed to want to stand in this man's way. I believe George and I being wounded had a lot to do with it along with the end of my draft was just a few months away. We were going to be flown by chopper to the Danang Air Base where we would then jump straight onto another flight to Japan prior to continuing on home to the United States.

Chris told the military command at the base that he had some recommendations in the layout of the camp. Chris offered to help with implementing them if they were interested. Chris let them know that he expected the NVA would return sometime soon and with the way it was currently laid out, he did not think it was very defensible. The commander of the base laughed saying what would a civilian teenager know how to setup a military camp? Oh, did I forget to mention that Chris and company were not part of the military? They were just civilians who flew to South Vietnam, trekked by land all the way to Firebase Bastogne from Saigon just to say hi and check up on Chris's brother. The trip alone would have been suicidal for anyone else. Do you know anyone who would have done this? Would you have done this? Would I?

While we were flying out in a CH-47 Chinook, I realized that my life up to this point had been fun but had no direction. I wanted more out of my life; it was time to become a man. I wanted to be like these men I have come to greatly admire. I wanted to be a friend of Chris, Caleb, Tyler and Elijah. If they would have me, I wanted to walk side by side with them. I knew it would not be easy but I was determined to make it happen. I wanted to be a member of this "Brotherhood"! With this final word, Andrew stopped having that far away gaze and looked at us with his contagious smile.

It was strange but Tiffany and I were reluctant to leave as we wanted to hear more about Chris. Especially Tiffany, she hung on Teja and Andrew's words every time Chris's name came up. I was a little surprised by how much Tiffany seemed to have taken to Chris as she was usually a very level headed young woman. But then again, with all that had happened tonight, I guess it was to be expected. It was several hours later with Teja and Andrew, Tiffany and I were escorted home. It was tough not to tell our parents what happened but we both thought the advice we had received earlier was correct in their judgment. Our parents would be sick with worry every time we went out, and that was not something we wanted to ever put them through. So once we got home for the next hour or so, we smiled, talked of the fair with Tiffany bragging on my throwing arm to win the bear.

When we were ready for bed, Tiffany and I spent a moment in her room quietly discussing everything that had happened that night. Where I was more animated in reliving the events, Tiffany was quiet and reserved. Soon though, we both could not stay awake. Before leaving, we hugged each other to reassure each other that we were OK and safe at home. As I was about to close her door, Tiffany quietly said, "Do you think Chris will remember us? Will he think of me?" I looked at Tiffany who was hugging her bear tightly and you could tell her mind was far away thinking of someone else. I do not think she realized she had spoken aloud. I quietly closed the door and left her alone with her thoughts.

ERIC GROWS UP

That night changed my world. I had made a vow to myself and I had every intention of keeping it. It was not as easy as I thought but I started paying attention in school. Surprisingly I learned that I had a real talent for learning. It seems that I was the one that had been holding myself back. It was definitely not due to the lack of training or effort of my teachers, in fact I found them to be very engaging once you showed a real interest in learning.

My parents, friends and teachers were amazed at my attitude change and grade improvements. I went from a mid C to B average to straight A's or better. Some of my friends did not like the change in me as I was not the laid back person anymore. I was driven and did not have time for foolishness. They wanted to hang with someone that mirrored their desire of living for the moment and making no plans for tomorrow. These friends moved on and at first I was hurt. But then I realized everyone tends to do the same thing. Hang with individuals that mirrored their own desires. While I lost some friends, I gained many others. I became more involved in school academic activities, spent most nights studying and joined the baseball and track and field team. I also spent several hours every day at the local chapter of the Brotherhood.

Who were the members of the Brotherhood, you ask? They were individuals and/or families from all types of races, wealth, ages and political ideas. There were around fifty members in this group. What were the rules? Only one. Help. Just one rule. Hard to believe huh? Be available to help the other members of the Brotherhood. Each member was expected to train to learn how to defend themselves in both unarmed and armed combat. Not just the basics but to a high degree. When a situation arises where a member of the Brotherhood or family were in danger, you were to assist. No matter the odds or risk. In the rare times when the Brotherhood was attacked by an outside group, you were expected to join in until that threat was eliminated. That usually meant an all effort until it was over. The Brotherhood does not make peace with an enemy only so they could have the same situation arise again at a later time. The Brotherhood fights until there were no more enemies left. No negotiations, no truce, no peace. You attack the Brotherhood, you better be able to wipe them out as that was what it would take to beat them. Needless to say, the Brotherhood was usually left alone.

I know your argument, I said the only rule was to help. And then went on to say you had to train and fight. Think on it, how could you help, if attacked, if you did not have the skills necessary to be able to respond appropriately? So you train so you could fight, so you could "help."

The chapter I was a member of was a group that I was proud to be able to call my friends in short order. We would meet at a local school gym where they brought mats and weight equipment. They also brought hand weapons of all types. The weapons brought were dependent on what type training was being done that evening. Knives for hand to hand combat, bows and arrows for silent deadly training and many types of weapons from around the world. Guns and explosives were limited to weekend training at a local gun club. Safety was always foremost on everyone's mind and carelessness was not accepted. Everyone here was either a family member or a friend. No one wanted anyone to get hurt so great attention was paid to safety. The oddest thing when I first started training was that they did not consider my age to be an impediment. They all treated me as an adult and with respect. It was an amazing feeling and made me more determined not to let them down.

Not that there was not a lot of pain from bruises, sprains, a few broken bones and most of all, bruised pride. I knew I was not in the best of shape but it took only a few sessions to realize it would take a lot to get up to the level of the rest of this group. Heck, after the first night it took me several hours just to catch my breath. Most members have been training for years and made it seem effortless. It was not! It was intense and only after four months did I feel like I was getting to a point that I was starting to actually enjoy it. And what a difference it made to my body. The training lasted for ninety minutes and every minute was very intense. There were no breaks, no time to rest before the next event, no bathroom breaks, no time for chatting, no time except to survive. Prior to the start of training, there were a set of instructors that would decide on what was going to be the main training agenda for that evening and who would be in what group. The object was to put you in a dangerous situation you may find yourself in and how to get out of it. How to fight a single individual or a group. The whole idea was to get you to a point where you did things automatically and did not waste time thinking about what should you do. Those seconds made the difference between living and dying.

It was here I learned that what Chris had done for me and my sister, was not unique. Most of the members I talked with had something similar happen with Chris being involved to themselves or a family member. There was never a night that you did not hear Chris's name mentioned. The stories were not limited to when he assisted by fighting but in other areas too.

I was told a story about how he had helped a group of children known as the "lost ones." The story spoke of a half dozen children of indiscriminate age whom no one seemed to be able to get through to. It was not that they were bad or destructive but they just did not care about anyone or anything. No desire to learn nor help or even associate with their families, they just ignored everyone. Everything that was attempted to help them was unsuccessful. The families were at a loss of what to do.

Chris was asked by several family members if he could try and see what he could do to help. Chris replied he would give it a shot but only if they agreed to all his conditions. The parents and one set of grandparents who were raising one of the children due to the death of the child's parents in a car accident, were open to anything so they agreed to give Chris a chance. Chris then laid out his requirements. Chris was to get one week alone with the children except for one, but only one, family monitor who was to be present at all times while he was with the "lost ones." It was imperative that no one else visit nor interrupt until the full week was over except for swapping out the family member. The family monitor was not to interface with Chris nor the children. Be there but not be there.

Chris took all the kids to his home and after a week, left with a group of children that to this day, are full of laughter and energy. Each of the children when they left Chris's house to be picked up by their families burst into tears and ran to hug their parents, grand-parents, brothers, sisters, like they had not seen them in many years. The families were overjoyed. What happened is still a mystery to all but the family members as one of Chris's final requirements before accepting the assignment was that none of the family monitors were to ever speak what of what they saw or heard. No reason was given for this but all the families involved believe this was to shield the children not due to the method Chris used.

All the rest of us knew was that by the end of the week, all the families involved had one member or two be a monitor at the house at some point. If any had an issue with what Chris did, it would have become widely known. But all, when asked, smiled and said that Chris lived up to his reputation and did the impossible. That not once did he lift a hand nor speak loudly to any of the children. But beyond that they could not say any more. But no one could miss the look of approval and admiration when they said Chris had done what they could not. And it did not go unnoticed that these families over the next few months grew even closer and more tightly knit. Whatever they had witnessed, they now used at home.

And the "lost ones" are still together today as a group. In fact, they have added several more. They were now an integral member of their families but thanks to whatever happened at Chris's house, they were also now family to each other. And when they found another child like they had been, they took that child under their wing. All of them, including the two new ones, adored Chris and were always hanging around him whenever they could.

Whether it was about his latest rescue or a prior event, there was a lot of discussion on the impact this man made on their lives. I heard some stories where Chris, due to injuries, was close to death and only through his unbelievable constitution did he survive. I became more determined in my goal to make sure Chris had the best doctor by his side, that being myself. I also found out what type of people the Brotherhood was.

That year, Hurricane Agnes, caused some severe flood damage in Pennsylvania. Several chapters of the Brotherhood were impacted. My chapter contacted the chapters affected and found out what they needed most. They brought the people in need the supplies requested along with carpenters, mechanics, electricians and many more specialties. They stayed for a week and then swapped out weekly with other individuals. Never relaxing until they had all the affected family members and friends back to a point they were notified no additional assistance was required. I also found out that since all were used to working together while training, this also translated in getting everyone back up and running in a much shorter time frame than I would have expected. No one demanded help, no one even asked for help, it was just given. This happened to all the chapters affected, not just the ones we went to. All chapters participated in some fashion. Remember, there was only one rule—help!

As time went on, the more I was honored to be a member of this organization. It was a long difficult year but I got through it. I was now lean and mean while being at the top of my class. You would not have recognized me from the boy in the Sears parking lot. Just prior to my fifteenth birthday, all this training was what enabled me to see my birthday cake with fifteen candles.

I had just finished a session at the local school library for a term paper when walking home late at night, I was accosted by four men who wanted to rob me. I was just twenty feet shy of a strip mall with people nearby who saw what was happening but turned away quickly. The two closest had guns showing in their waistbands and gestured at them to make sure I understood that they would not hesitate to use them on me. One of the two armed men told me to give him everything in my pockets with a contemptuous look like I was beneath them and that I was lucky they had not just shot me and taken what they wanted. From the way he casually rested his hand on the butt of his weapon I was sure he had done that sometime in the past, probably more than once. I am sure he would have done that to me but did not want to get any money covered in blood and since I was only fifteen, should not be anything to worry about. In fact, I would not be surprised that once he had whatever was in my pockets, that he would shoot me just for the fun of it and to leave no witnesses.

The four men were within arms distance of me and I am sure they were going to get a lot closer if I let them. I let my instincts drive my actions. All my training came to the forefront without any conscious thought on my part. Once I realized what was happening, I kicked out to my left where one of the two armed individuals was standing balanced on one leg with the other relaxed. My heel smashed into the knee of the leg he was balanced on. It broke his knee with a loud crack and which he confirmed with a loud scream. Without pausing, I continued on to hit the other armed member on the right with a hard chop to the throat where I could feel his cervical vertebrae shatter. While he was dropping to the ground, I followed up immediately with a spin and roundhouse with the heel of my right foot to the head of the individual whose knee I had just broken and was now lying on the ground. I could hear the skull crack with a loud snap. Both of the armed men were now out of the picture.

I did not relax but continued on with what I was trained to do. Press on until the situation had been resolved. I pushed forward with a roundhouse that started at hip level and added the power of a half rotation on my left leg hitting with my closed right fist on the chest of the man to my left. My knuckles transferred to me the knowledge that his ribs were broken at the minimum. I could see his surprise just before his eyes closed and he fell at my feet. From the paleness of his coloring and blood dripping from his nose and mouth, it did not look like he would rise again. The last individual went down when I continued with my rotation and swept my right leg low enough to take his feet out from under him. I then dropped on my knees next to him while driving my right elbow down to strike with all the

45

strength I could muster straight onto his nose. I felt more than saw the impact. It left no doubt in my mind that I would not have to worry about him again. This was all done in less than a moment and before any of the four men could react.

I did not relax until I had a chance to check my surroundings. Part of the training I received was not to get overconfident just because the immediate situation looked to have been resolved. What was lurking around the corner? Were there any others that you were not aware of? So for the next several moments, I checked the area until I was sure that I was alone. All the people that had watched me being surrounded were nowhere to be seen. Amazing huh? I checked the four thugs and confirmed that they would not be robbing anyone again. I felt sick and wanted to throw up as I had never wanted to take a man's life. But I knew what might have happened if I did not defend myself. I had been down this road before.

I reviewed the incident and realized I had passed a test that can never be given until you encounter a real life situation. I shook my head in wonder at how much I have changed. I could never have imagined being able to fight off one let alone four with such success. Now I owed Chris once again indirectly. Because of his actions that night, he allowed me to save my own life tonight. I knew I had a long way to go. But I also knew the only thing standing in my way of accomplishing my goals was myself. My voice cracked as I called the police to report the incident from a local phone booth. I could imagine their surprise when they find out that a fifteen-year-old took out four men in their twenties. I then remembered Chris's earlier statement about me a year ago and smiled.

ERIC SEES CHRIS IN ACTION AGAIN

It was awhile later that I got to see Chris in action again but not the way I would have expected. It was at a Brotherhood event at a members' farm that was located about an hour and a half northeast of Philadelphia. The farm was a little over one hundred and twenty acres that had been in the family for generations and contained several historic homes and a barn dating back to the early 1800's. It was really beautiful, quiet and pristine.

Things had been hectic and tiring but exciting at the same time. So this event was a welcome break that I was looking to be able to take moment to relax. It was rare I got to spend time with Tiffany anymore so it would be good she was also coming so we could catch up.

There were around thirty families that came to the event that was more of a picnic than anything else where everyone brought their wives, kids, grandmothers, and anyone that wanted to get away for some fun. Everyone brought their favorite dishes and desserts. Hot dogs, hamburgers, beef ribs, fried chicken, pork chops, baked beans, potato salad, coleslaw, corn on the cob, baked potatoes, apple and cherry pies were in abundance but there were many other unique dishes. Sichuan and Hunan dishes, moo shu pork, and other Asian dishes complete with chopsticks.

Everyone brought whatever else they needed to just get away and enjoy being with close friends and family. They brought badminton sets, footballs, chess games, checkers, and dominoes of course, and believe it or not, the biggest hit was with the three games of twister. And to top it off, several even brought their guitars and harmonicas.

It started early in the morning and was scheduled to end late at night. The area was dotted with fire pits so of course the coup de grace was everyone had brought marshmallows to toast. The fire pits were left over from the revolutionary war and around the field there were even an old 4-pounder galloper here and there. It really was a beautiful place and the climate did not disappoint. The weather was just awesome. The sky was blue with only a small cloud here and there, the temperature was in the mid to high 70's with very low humidity. The area where the event was being held had been freshly mowed just for this event and was a beautiful green carpet.

Everything went well for the majority of the day. The kids were running around, several games of football were in play, badminton in the air, and lines in waiting to play twister. Food and drink everywhere. No alcohol as the family on whose farm we were on was concerned that it would not be appropriate with all the children around and serious concerns that someone would get hurt. It was no big deal, we had nothing against drinking but understood and respected the wishes of the family hosting the event. No one could have predicted the events that occurred.

Tiffany had come along with me and by this time it did not surprise me that she quickly left my side to sit with someone else. Can you guess who? Yes, she still had a crush on Chris. I wondered when that would end as I figured she would grow out of it but as long as she was happy, no harm done. I was a little surprised but Chris also seemed overjoyed that Tiffany sat with him. In fact, I do not think the two of them paid much attention to anyone else but only to each other. Well, it was really good to see her so happy and hear her laughter mixed with Chris's. Who would have known? It was those two going to sit on a blanket by a well situated off to the far right edge of the field where the accident happened that opened my eyes to just how powerful Chris really was.

When Chris and Tiffany went to sit by the well, followed by myself and Caleb, they were followed by a large group of children. Chris was very popular with all the children as he always remembered their names, never talked down to them and was open to playing any game they wanted. In fact, it was widely known that the kids thought he was more of a child than an adult. But there was a special group of children known as the "lost ones" who had a very close relationship with Chris. So it was no surprise that they were all here at this event. It was one of the "lost ones" that had the accident and opened my eyes even further into the depth of Chris's commitment to his friends.

One of the "lost ones" nearby was named Cathy. Cathy went by her nickname of Kitten as she was very small for a girl of six and had long beautiful fluffy brown hair hence her nickname. Kitten was playing on top of the well and had gotten into a large bucket that was sitting on a set of old brass hinges. The bucket had a large metal handle that was attached to a very old long thick rope. The rope was looped in a circle on a stanchion off on the right of the frame holding the bucket. The length of the rope indicated that the well must be several hundred feet deep as the rope at one time must have been used to lower the bucket into the water at the bottom of the well. But how deep the well actually was was unknown as the well had been sealed up with wooden boards a long time ago.

Kitten was playing in the bucket when Mary, her mother and who was watching her from several yards away, became concerned and told her to be careful. Kitten laughed and jumped up high while giggling loud her delight. It was her descent that caused the accident. When Kitten hit the bottom of the bucket her foot punched through the bucket where the bucket then ripped out the hinges holding it up. The bucket dropped and crashed down through the boards covering the well. Kitten's laughter turned quickly into a scream. You could hear Kitten's screams coming from inside the well fading as she dropped.

I had been sitting by Tiffany when Chris, before the scream had barely started, moved with a speed hard to believe. Chris jumped up onto the top of the well and without hesitation dived down feet first into the well. And then calamity visited upon calamity. The boulders that made up the wall around the well collapsed. Several that must have weighed a hundred pounds each fell into the well. Tiffany and I raced to the well with dread in our hearts. We peered down in the dark to barely see that several of the boulders were about forty feet down stacked on top of each other with no visible support except what looked like an arm that ended in a hand gripping the wall. And there was no mistaking the cry of a little girl echoing in the depths of the well. Kitten was still alive, but how and for how long, was the question. Tiffany and I were soon joined by Caleb and Mary with several of the families' seconds behind.

Mary was yelling terrified into the well for Kitten with Caleb doing the same for Chris. There was a quick response to Mary for help from a crying Kitten. I was opposite Caleb and was trying to see what was holding the boulders up. It was only after hearing a whisper of "Caleb" that I realized it must be Chris keeping the boulders from crashing to the bottom of the well. I could just make out the back of his feet pressed against the walls.

After careful examination, I could see that Chris was facing down stretched out holding onto the walls with his hands and feet with the boulders on his back and legs. The boulders all together must weigh close to several hundred pounds. I do not think even Caleb could hold those boulders up for long, if at all. How long could Chris hold on? What I did know was that if the boulders got past him, Kitten would not survive. I could not see Kitten but I guessed that she was still in the bucket and that the rope was some-how keeping her from dropping to the bottom. How I had no idea at the moment but I was soon to find out.

Caleb had Andrew and Elijah pull up several pickup trucks with winches on them. They strapped several ropes together hoping to be able to strap them around the boulders and pull them up. But the problem they encountered was there was no way to get down to Chris without possibly raining down the rest of the boulders. While they had been getting the trucks, the others started clearing the boulders that surrounded the well. It did not take long until all loose boulders that they could safely reach were moved to a safe distance away. All this was done while everyone else concentrated on getting Chris and Kitten out of the well.

Caleb attempted to snake a pair of ropes down to Chris to wrap around one of the boulders but Chris could not release one of his hands to connect them without endangering his hold. Caleb then had Abigail, who was the lightest and smallest of the Brotherhood here today, gear up and get ready to climb down the well to try and place the ropes around the boulders. Everyone knew that time was limited, no way Chris could last much longer.

Abigail started her descent carefully and slowly. It took a good five minutes that seemed like hours before she could reach Chris. All the while Kitten's mother, Mary, kept reassuring Kitten that she would be free soon. Hearing Kitten's crying echoing up the well was hard to hear and frustrating not being able to do anything to help. The strain for everyone was starting to tell, some were pacing, some were crying, some were slumped on the ground.

Abigail was able to get the rope around one of the boulders and gave the signal to start raising very slowly. Caleb had Andrew start the winch when there was a shout from Chris to stop. Chris, grunting out the words and there was no hiding that he was in great pain, let Caleb know that the rope connected to the boulders was also wrapped around his waist. When they attempted to raise the boulder, as the boulder lifted off Chris, it tightened the rope around Chris's waist. Chris could barely breathe and asked that the boulder be lowered back onto his back. Chris proceeded to tell them that when they attempted raising the boulder it also started the bucket swinging and almost tipped Kitten out. Kitten was still stuck in the bucket with her leg sticking out the bottom and if not for that, would have fallen out.

I looked at Caleb in fear as Chris could not maintain the weight much longer. Once he lost the strength to hold them up, both he and Kitten would plunge to the bottom of the well and be crushed by the boulders.

Tiffany was gripping my arm in fear. I was going to say something when I looked at her face where I saw stark terror in her eyes. I had never seen her like this before, not even the night we met Chris.

I asked Caleb what I could do. Caleb looked at me with a look similar to Tiffany's, and I could hear the desperation in his voice when he said that he had no idea besides attempting to dig another well besides this one to try and come in from underneath. But we all knew that would take too long, that Chris could not last that long. And that was confirmed when Abigail climbed out of the well. Abigail joined us and we saw that her hands were covered in blood. Before we could ask, Abigail said one word that explained everything "Chris's."

Abigail explained that when she had reached the boulder that was on Chris's back, she could see that there a jagged edge that had dug into Chris's back. Chris was bleeding pretty badly from this wound, which we were sure was not the only one. We had no doubt that Chris was in enhanced mode, which meant he was pumping blood through the exit wound even more than normal.

It was not talked about but everyone started preparing for the worst. All did not believe that Chris could last more than a few moments. Abigail explained, using the flashlight she had carried with her, she could see Chris's blood all over his back and soaked into his clothing. Tiffany was crying heavily and she definitely was not alone. Most, if not all, of the "lost ones" were doing the same.

It was at this time we all heard the noise. It was a low grinding noise, faint like a stone on stone. It was not constant but would be there for a second or two and then stop for another few seconds. Then it would repeat all over again. What could it be? Was the wall inside the well collapsing in? Was Chris losing the battle to hold the boulders? Was the end near?

It was getting to be midafternoon and the sun was bright over-head. Andrew had a dozen cars ring the well with their front ends facing inward to try and put some more light into the well. There were several hand lights available but not much else. The whole event had been going on for close to thirty five to forty minutes. Abigail was about to go down again to see if she could find another way to get the boulders off of Chris. It was Tyler, who had not left off peering into the wells since this all started, startled all of us all by yelling out in explanation. Tyler stood up straight, looked at us with bugged out eyes and said he must be seeing things. When we asked what he saw, he shook his head but he would swear that Chris was slowly inching his way toward the top of the well. Everyone wanted to take a look but Caleb kept it limited to Abigail, Mary, himself and of course, Tyler.

It was in amazement that after a few intense seconds, Abigail turned around and confirmed what Tyler had seen. Abigail said it looked like Chris was slowly inching his way up without ever releasing his contact with the walls. Inch after slow inch, Chris was working his way upward. Caleb, after intensely examining the situation, had Andrew and several others dig around the well on one side to create a gentle slope at the edge of the well. Caleb was emphatic in saying to make sure it was gradual but it needed to be able to take the boulders on Chris's back out of the immediate area so they could surround the well with men to assist lifting the two out. So Andrew led the effort to dig the sloping pit to take the boulder out around a dozen feet away from the well.

We all watched in silence as we listened for any failures on the walls, any slippage from Chris, anything out of the ordinary. Really, did I say out of the ordinary? Everything here was out of the ordinary. Mary kept talking to Kitten, soothing her while telling her to stay as still as possible, that Chris was going to get her out soon. Kitten, a young lady of six, scared out of her mind, surprised all of us when she whispered broken by sobs to her mother "Mommy, if anyone can save me, Chris can. Only death will make him stop trying as he is my friend, my family. He told me that when we were in his house." Mary turned to look at us with her hands covering her mouth and tears flowing from her eyes. Mary turned back to the well and said to her daughter, "Yes, my dear, only death would make the Lord Protector fail, no different than when he helped me."

It was another ten agonizing minutes before the boulder on Chris's back was level with the top of the well. The boulder on Chris's legs was even more impressive in size than the one on his back. But it did not look as jagged and, hopefully, had not caused as much damage as was now clearly evident on his back. Caleb had half a dozen of the brawniest men ringing the well. Caleb had three of them grab the boulder on Chris's back and slowly raise it until it was raised no more than an inch or two off his back. This was not easy and you could see the strain and anxiety on each of the men's faces. You could now see that when Kitten had fallen into the well, and the boulders had collapsed, the rope followed and had wrapped tightly around the boulder and then Chris who had followed so closely behind. The rope was wrapped twice around the boulder and intertwined through Chris's leg and his torso.

They were not going to be able to remove the rope without potentially losing Kitten so Kitten had to be removed first or the rope was stabilized. The boulder on Chris's legs was even more entwined in the rope than the one on his back. And as Chris's back came into view of the lights, the damage the boulder had caused was now obvious to all. There was not a person there that did not gasp in horror to see the amount of blood and the ragged gash that ran down his back. Chris's shirt was torn and mixed in with his torn skin into a horrible twisted lump of cloth, blood and skin. I was shocked, anyone with this amount of damage should be. well. it was not something to dwell on at the moment.

It was at this time that an ambulance and two fire trucks arrived. They were assisted by other members of the Brotherhood and soon were ready to assist. It was Caleb who came up with a plan of action that looked best to get Kitten secured so the boulders could be removed off of Chris.

Caleb had Chris brace himself and extend his legs as wide as possible without losing any traction. Then Caleb had a one of the ladders from the fire truck held aloft over the center of the well by six of the brawniest men there, three on each side. Caleb had one man and one woman who were the lightest there besides Abigail but were renowned for their upper body strength lay on the ladder facing the center. Abigail was securely linked with ropes that were run through the center rungs of the ladder. Now they were ready to try and get Kitten out.

Caleb verified that men holding the boulder were ready and aware of what was being attempted. Once confirmed that the boulder was secure, Abigail was lowered upside down by the two on the ladder. Abigail was lowered down between Chris's legs where she could reach the rope that was holding Kitten. Abigail, keeping the rope attached to the bucket holding Kitten centered so it would not swing or bang the bucket against the walls, pulled up on the rope along with the bucket to create enough slack so she could give it to others that ringed the wall. The plan was for these individuals to reach in and around Abigail and pull Kitten to safety.

Slowly they were able to pull the rope up while Abigail kept it straight. They had Kitten near the top of the well when Chris slipped down a few inches. Abigail almost lost her position and her hold on the rope. It was only with sheer determination she was able to hang on. Within a moment they had Kitten raised high enough and it was decided that Abigail would have to grab her around the waist with one free hand while still holding onto the rope as the others could not do so without pushing against the men holding the boulders. When Abigail felt that she had a solid grip, she let go of the rope and grabbed Kitten with both hands. Abigail had to free Kitten's leg from the bucket, which was not as easy as it sounds. But finally with Kitten's leg freed from the bucket and safely in her arms, Abigail let the bucket go where the bucket dropped and swung against the wall.

Several things happened then. Abigail was lifted up where she leaned to the side to hand Kitten to Mary but while doing this lost her stability and swung into Chris's legs. Chris, between the bucket dropping and Abigail hitting his legs, lost his footing. Chris's feet dropped into the well while he frantically grabbed at a rock projection to keep himself from following. Abigail meanwhile was pulled up and out quickly by the two on the ladder with assistance from others who were holding the support ropes off to one end of the ladder.

All these activities happening all at once pushed everyone several feet back off balance and away from the well. The men holding the ladder on the left side lost their grip and the ladder fell off to the side only now being held onto by the men on the right side. The men holding the boulder on one side were pushed back by the ladder where they lost their grip and dropped the boulder. With their hold released, the boulder dropped to join the other boulder that was still entwined by rope with Chris. Chris was pounded against the side of the well by both of two heavy boulders. After the crushing blow, the boulders then swung freely, which weighed in on the precarious grip held by Chris.

Chris, barely hanging on, looked first at Caleb and then looking directly at Tiffany where he smiled just before weakly saying "Kitten's safe, thank you all, good-bye my friends." With that Chris's eyes slowly closed and his grip relaxed. Tiffany fainted dead away and would have dropped to the ground if I had not caught her just inches before she would have hit the ground hard. I lowered her down gently and looked back toward Chris expecting to see he had disappeared from view.

Just as Chris had started to drop, Caleb screamed and jumped onto the top of the well with his legs spread across both ends, standing on what was left of the well above ground. Caleb grabbed one of the boulders in desperation and was barely able to stabilize it without falling in himself. Caleb stopped the boulders descent but seeing the strain in his face you knew it would not be for long. Chris was hanging limply by the ropes attached to the boulders. Chris was a dead weight and not moving.

Within seconds, men jumped into action. Soon there were another half dozen men reaching down to secure both boulders with Chris attached and pulling them out of the well. Seeing Chris hanging limply by ropes with his head rolling around with no control was frightening to watch. Caleb collapsed in exhaustion on the ground taking in long deep breaths. The boulder on Chris's leg was carefully cut away and rolled down the slope created earlier. Then they removed the last boulder and freed Chris from the ropes. Chris was placed onto the stretcher where Roy and the paramedics started frantically working on him. I was about to join them but Roy shook his head which he inclined toward Tiffany. They quickly cut the clothing from Chris to see the extent of the damage. It did not look good, not good at all.

Chris had taken much more damage than we realized. Besides his back, Chris's chest, waist and legs were crisscrossed with rope burns and it was obvious that he had taken additional damage when he first jumped into the well. It would not be surprising to find out he had several cracked or broken ribs. Chris had a big welt on his left temple that would require several stitches along with serious scrapes on his arms and legs.

And then there were his hands. They were torn and bleeding from his climb up the inside of the well. His fingernails were splintered, broken and bloody. Worst were his eyes, they were closed with blood leaking from the corners. It was a clear indication he had reached the end of his endurance. The paramedics were not overly optimistic but they were silenced by Roy. Roy told them forcibly to never count Chris out, that as long as he was breathing, there was always a chance. The paramedics, chastised, went back to work with a fervor.

When a miracle was needed, it was provided by one our youngest. Kitten, who had been placed on a second stretcher, demanded her mother pick her up. At first the paramedic attending her and Mary both refused. It was obvious that Kitten's leg was broken and would also require stitches where the bucket had snagged onto her leg. But there was no denying Kitten. They tried moving the stretcher over to Chris but Kitten was insistent they pick her up. Kitten screamed and carried on until Mary and the paramedic in tow finally picked Kitten up and carried her to stand by Chris's stretcher. Kitten leaned out of Mary arms to put one of her hands on Chris's face and whisper into his ear. We all stared in amazement when Chris slowly opened his bloodshot eyes to look at Kitten with a smile on his face and whispered back "I love you too."

How? How did he hear Kitten above all the pain, the trauma his body was going through? And then I remembered what I had been told the night I first met Chris, "Their need was greater than mine." Kitten smiled, gave Chris a pat on his face, before allowing her mother to put her back on the stretcher. Meanwhile the paramedics working on Chris, got over their surprise, shook their heads in wonder and started loading Chris into the ambulance.

Chris, weakly, very weakly stopped them. Chris pointed at Tiffany whom I was holding up against a low grassy mound near the well. Tiffany was just starting to recover. Chris, in a low weak voice but one that still commanded attention, "I will not leave while one is down. Bring her, Kitten and Mary along. Otherwise I stay." No one was about to argue and as I helped Tiffany into the ambulance I saw Chris whispering to Caleb. I was not surprised since there was very limited seating and most space would be occupied by the paramedics, that Kitten and Mary took one stretcher and Tiffany slid in tightly next to Chris, very tightly on his stretcher. Did I see a smile pass between the two of them just before the doors closed?

And with that the ambulance sped away with several protectors preceding and following. I was surprised to see Caleb was not one of them. The fire crew started working on putting a cap on the remains of the well with plenty of assistance. But as the rest started back to gather their belongings to leave, I found out why Caleb stayed behind.

Caleb with his loud baritone voice yelled out "No, damn you, no, don't you dare! Do not sully this day with sorrow and sadness. Do not let Chris find out that you let sadness for what happened grab your hearts and mind, not over him. Is that how you respect him and everything he has done for you, for me, for all of us? If you want to honor Chris, then lift your hearts up and see what he did today, which is no less than what he did yesterday, the day before, last week, last year, and so on. How many times has he risked his life for one of us? How many times has he told us that it was all worth the risks and pain because he gets something that he treasures more than life itself? Your friendship, companionship, and knowing that he was able to make a difference. So do not soak yourselves in sorrow that he is injured and fighting for his life. Rather raise your hearts and spirits knowing he did what he has always done. What he wants to do. That he was able to make a difference, that one person, a precious little girl, will see her family tonight because he was where he needed to be at the right time. See it from his viewpoint. See what Kitten saw before she left. Did you see that young lady's smile? Did you see Chris's smile? Do you know why? Because she loved Chris and Chris loved her. Everything else is immaterial. Both will get past whatever happens because they have each other, they have you, they have all of us. They are strong because we are strong. So put your sorrow away and do what we came here to do. Now, let's have some fun!"

With that Caleb paused and looked around. No one could miss the emotion and concern in his face. And with a final shrug, a smile now starting, he growled out "I do not know about you but this has all left me starving, so who is up for cooking some ribs?" After which, Caleb slowly chuckled and rubbed his stomach.

With that, everyone's spirit rose and slowly the smiles, the grins, the laughter started to appear. And everyone slowly started going back to the fire pits, the football games and twister games. I saw Caleb smile and shake his head. I walked over and asked what Chris said to him before he left. Caleb with a twinkle in his eyes said, "I already told you. I told everyone. Did you not listen?" And with that he laughed, slowly at first but soon in a full deep throated roar. I looked at Caleb in wonder and knew that Chris had not finished surprising me.

Caleb, seeing my deep inward looking stare, broke my concentration by asking me. "Eric, how well do you know Chris? Is it an idea of what you think he is or do you really know him? Answer me this. Who do you think is physically stronger, myself or Chris? I know everyone who sees me thinks that I am someone that could best Chris in physical strength. But strength is more than just being able to lift a heavy weight. There are many individuals that have the physical muscles to lift a certain weight, but it is the ones who can go the extra mile and bear the cost that comes with that extra mile who are stronger. I am strong and there are very few that I am not physically stronger than. But I am not in the same league as Chris. Think of what you saw here today. How fast he jumped into a situation most would have not even understood for many moments. And then he did the impossible. Chris, in an awkward position in an old well, held hundreds of pounds of stone on his back while injured and trying to keep a young girl from falling out of a bucket. All this for an extended period of time. And then when we could not find a way to pull both of them out in time, proceeded to crawl up the well with the weight while keeping Kristen safe. Who else could have done that? It was not just his enhancement. You saw his eyes at the end, his blood had no more nourishment left to supply his body. It was his will that overrode the pain, the physical weariness, the desire to just let it end. I would like to think I could do the same. I do not know as I have never been pushed that far yet. But he has been pushed there many times, many more that you can imagine. And do you know why? He shy's away when thanked, he does not like it when we try and honor him, he will not accept any award or gift for any action he did to help someone. So why does he do it? It is what I saw in him when I saw him sitting with that stray little dog the very first time. Chris does it because it is the right thing to do. That is all. Just because it is the right thing to do." Caleb turned and looked up at the sky for a moment that he was still looking at when he finished with "And I have been honored to be a part of his trip through life."

I waited a moment but realized that Caleb was lost in thought and to him I was no longer there. I made my way over to one of the fire pits where they were starting to roast some marshmallows. I thought about going to the hospital but figured that I should stay here. To honor Chris's request. Tiffany was not hurt and would be in good hands.

I was offered and accepted a stick with two marshmallows stuck on the end where I held it close to the fire while deep in thought. I liked it when the marshmallows are toasted brown and hot inside but not burnt. As I sat there I looked around and realized that many were doing the same as I. Reveling in the history of a man that we called friend. A man that showed us what everyone was capable of. Caleb talked of Chris's will but he did not talk of his own incredible will when he leaped to grab a hold of the boulders along with Chris all by himself and kept them from slipping into the depths of the well. Nor that he would have probably followed them in had he failed.

I smiled remembering how a man barely hanging onto life had time to think of others. Kitten, Mary and yes, my sister Tiffany. Yes, these were men that I could honestly say I admired, both of whom I was honored to call friends.

And that brought Chris's current condition to mind and I got a few stares when I chuckled as I remembered the smile on Chris's and Tiffany's face just before the ambulance door closed. Chris and Tiffany may have been tightly squeezed onto the stretcher but they sure did not seem to mind. In fact, if my eyes were not playing tricks on me, they were so very close together that there was actually quite a lot of spare room on each side of their stretcher. Much more than I would have expected being there were two adults on a stretcher that was not very wide to begin with. No, it must have been all the stress and excitement causing me to see things that obviously could not be true, yep, must be the stress playing tricks on me.

TIME FOR RECOVERY

It was the next day that I went to the hospital to check up on Chris. Tiffany had called home the day before to tell my parents that she was staying at the hospital that evening but that we should not come to visit until the following day. With Chris and Kitten both scheduled for one or more surgeries, it would be best not to bother them with visitors. So I was there first thing in the morning with others who were here long before the sun came up with a change of clothes for Tiffany along with a toiletry pack made up by our mother. Odd in that mom would have packed multiple sets of clothes like Tiffany was staying for more than a day but heck, mom was probably just giving Tiffany an option of what to wear. Mom was always considerate like that. Mom and dad planned to visit later.

It was really busy here when I arrived. Caleb I heard had been here all night. In fact, there were so many people stopping by all night that it was causing amazement at the front desk on just how many were making their way to Chris's room even though they knew Chris was in surgery. They would stop by and talk with Caleb for a few moments and leave with a promise to stop by later.

I was not surprised though. We all needed to know how Chris and Kitten were doing and somehow hearing it from someone else was not good enough. Everyone needed to see them in person or hear it from Caleb. Chris would be in the intensive care ward for a while and they did not have any plans at the moment for moving him to a regular room. It spoke volumes of how serious his condition was. Kitten's condition was not as serious and the Hospital expected to move her in the next day or two. Although they may find that harder than they think to make that happen.

One person, I should say child, who would not leave Chris's side was Kitten. The front desk nurse told me that Kitten was adamant that Chris had risked everything for her so the least she could do was stay here with him. Kitten's leg had been broken but, luckily, only needed minor surgery. Kitten's leg also required stitches where the bottom of the wooden bucket had torn into the section of skin where her leg had been stuck. But even with her leg in a cast, she would not leave Chris's side. And she did, most of it, sitting in the large recliner placed right next to Chris's bed just for her. The nurse, Carla, had a smile on her face when she spoke of Kitten and how she had run over everyone in her desire to stay in the room with Chris. Carla chuckled as she related how such a small little girl had all the doctors and staff eating out of her hand. If you knew Kitten, it was not hard to believe. She was such a wonderful young lady.

I was taken back a little when Carla asked me a strange question. She wanted to know if Tiffany was Chris's girlfriend. I updated her that Tiffany and Chris were just very close friends where she replied with her eyes twinkling at their corners "Are you sure of that?" Without waiting for an answer, the nurse rose to her feet to start her rounds while singing "You, My Love" by Frank Sinatra. I shook my head at her misunderstanding of how Tiffany and Chris had met and why they were such good friends. Girlfriend, really, get real!

Chris's room was a decent sized private room sporting a small table with a pair of chairs, a couch, a sink along with a small bathroom, which also housed a large shower. The recliner Kitten was sitting looked like it did not normally belong here as it was too large for the size of this room. George, Chris's older brother by a few years, was sitting at the table nursing a bottle of coke and a muffin. When I walked into the room, I heard Kitten quietly reading the story *The Little Engine That Could* by Watty Piper to Chris. Chris being asleep did not seem to matter to her so I just smiled as I quietly made my way into the room.

Ethan, Kitten's father, was also here but was currently out in the break room getting a cup of coffee per Carla. Besides the cast on her leg, I saw that Kitten also had bandage wraps on both her arms and a small abrasion on her chin. I walked past Kitten to where I could see the other person who had not left his side since the accident. My sister, Tiffany, was lounging on a couch trying to stay awake. It took her a few moments for her to realize that I was here at which she smiled and said good morning. Tiffany looked tired and there were lines of worry on her face but yet she still managed to be gorgeous. How she managed that being in a hospital room all night was a mystery to me. I quietly asked her if once Ethan returned, could we go to the break room to talk at which Tiffany nodded saying she could use some hot tea to soothe her sore throat. I could see that Tiffany had changed into some clothes someone had been kind enough to bring her and must have taken a shower at some time.

Ethan arrived at that moment and we took our leave. I watched as Ethan's face light up when he realized what Kitten was doing. He must not have been here when she started the book but you could see he was very proud of how she was handling the situation.

Tiffany and I sat down in the break room each with a cup of tea. The break room was a decent sized room down the hall that housed four small tables with several vending machines that thankfully one of which supplied hot drinks. No one else was present, which was nice as it would allow us to talk freely. I asked Tiffany how she was doing where she replied tired but okay. Tiffany looked at me and said that the past twenty four hours have been eye-opening, to say the least. I informed Tiffany it was the same for me too and that I was still absorbing all we had been through.

I did tell Tiffany I was surprised she was still here where she replied that she thought that she belonged here for the moment. Tiffany, with a smile, said Kitten told her she should stay too so who was she to argue. I laughed and said Kitten was an awesome young lady. It was hard to believe Kitten was so calm after everything that happened yesterday. Tiffany said I did not know the half of it, that Kitten was a young lady of amazing courage.

Tiffany informed me that when they first got to the hospital, the nurses and doctors had taken Kitten away with both her parents only to have them return several hours later with Kitten's leg in a cast and parents in tow. The orderlies also brought in a large recliner where they placed it next to Chris's bed so Kitten could keep her leg lifted and on a pillow. Tiffany asked Mary why was Kitten not in her own room sleeping where Mary chuckled and said Kitten yelled and had a sissy fit until they finally agreed to bring her back here to Chris's room. And the nurses and orderlies have shamelessly come under Kitten's charm so here they were. Mary had just shaken her head at Kitten in amusement.

Tiffany went on to tell me that after they had taken Kitten away, the doctors had taken Chris into emergency surgery, which had lasted over five hours. Tiffany rested her head on my shoulder and whispered she feared she would never see Chris again. The nurses and doctors who would stop by to check on her would not talk on how things were going with Chris. They would give her updates on Kitten but not a word on Chris. When she asked, begged would be more accurate, the looks of pity on their faces told her that they did not have much hope for Chris. And it was only after they came in to announce the surgery had just completed with big grins and said that it looked like he would make it, did it confirm her initial impression. Internally Chris was a mess and would require several more surgeries to put him back together. Externally he was not in much better shape so it was expected, if he survived of which half the doctors that have looked at him said they would be surprised if he did, he would be hospitalized for weeks if not months. Tiffany straightened up, smiled and told the doctors that doubted Chris would survive, they did not know Chris or they would never have thought let alone say that.

Tiffany continued on to tell me that Chris's parents, with George just a few moments behind them, had arrived shortly after Chris and Tiffany yesterday and had only left just a few moments ago to wash up. They had been gardening in the yard when they were notified and did not have time to clean up before coming to the hospital. So they were pretty dirty and needed a shower badly. They had washed up as best they could in the sink but there was only so much you could do there. They were reluctant to use Chris's bathroom with all the people stopping by so had asked if there was another shower they could use. The hospital eventually gave permission for them to use

THE PROTECTORS: ERIC'S STORY

the shower in an empty patient room located in another ward several floors up. Tiffany laughed when she told me that they were both supplied hospital gowns to use until George could go home to get them a change of clothes at which Mrs. Wilson, Ava as she preferred to be called, looked at Tiffany like they had to be kidding. No way Ava was going to be in Chris's room with all the people stopping by in a hospital gown. So Ava, with her normal practical sensibility, planned to just redress in her work clothes after cleaning them as best she could. As she said, you do the best you could, and that was why they made perfume in the first place. Tiffany chuckled when she related that part as she was reminded of how Ava had deliberately and slowly squirted a few sprays of her perfume before looking around daring anyone to complain. Everyone got a good chuckle out of that.

Tiffany went on to tell me that George had no plans to leave for the immediate future so Chris's parents expected to be in the clothes they had come in for the next several days. Tiffany had offered to go get them some clean clothes but they mirrored Kitten's statement that she needed to stay here too. Odd thing though, when Tiffany told me that, she blushed when I asked why.

Tiffany continued on with her story with a blush that got deeper when she noticed I was looking at her more closely. Tiffany smiled when she told that Caleb butted in at that time and said he would arrange to have several sets of clothes picked up for all three of them. Everyone laughed when Ava asked Caleb if he would personally be picking out her outfits. Caleb good naturedly and used to Mrs. Wilson's good natured banter replied "absolutely, do you prefer the black or white lace undergarments? Never mind I will bring both." Mrs. Wilson laughed and gave Caleb a huge hug in affection.

Tiffany spent most of the night talking with Chris's parents and found them very easy to like. Tiffany and I had met them many times before but it was almost always in a group setting. They seemed to like her also, especially Ava. I was surprised to see Tiffany shyly smile and lower her head when she quietly said that the two of them had spent hours talking about herself and Chris when at the end, Ava looked at her closely and said with authority "I approve." When Tiffany asked what she meant, Ava said she was just responding to a

65

question Chris had asked her several years ago. She said she could not answer it at the time but now she could. With that Ava had kissed her cheek and went to talk with Mr. Wilson. I asked Tiffany what she thought that meant. Tiffany replied she hoped it was what she thought it was but until she knew for sure, she was going to keep it to herself. Tiffany was quiet for a moment and must have had a chill because she shivered and hugged herself while giving me a great big smile. Tiffany did say she was very impressed with Chris's family on how close they were. To say they were tight was an understatement. Chris's relatives from out of town had been by already and more were expected later.

Tiffany asked if I had talked with Caleb yet this morning, to which I replied I had not. Tiffany then proceeded to update me on the events with Caleb who had come in much earlier. While Chris was still in surgery, Caleb had sat on the bed next to Kitten, who was in her chair alongside her mother, where he and Kitten had talked at length on what happened the day before. Kitten told Caleb how when she was falling she saw Chris coming down the well after her. Kitten saw Chris deliberately push off the wall and entangle himself in the ropes, which stopped Kitten's descent with a jar. Caleb asked Kitten many questions in regard to that issue to get to that final conclusion.

Kitten said in just seconds after she fell into the well, she saw the small amount of light from the top of the well darken to almost pure blackness. She saw a shadow that materialized into Chris in the center of the well. Chris grabbed the rope that was linked to the bucket, where he then took the rope and twirled it around his left arm. While doing this, Chris twirled his legs and then twirled his body once so the rope was looped around his legs and chest. Chris then reached out and braced himself against the walls with his hands and feet, where her decent was jerked to an abrupt halt. The light coming in from the top of the well framed Chris, which made his silhouette look like an angel, which matched how she felt at the moment. This was all in a matter of seconds since they had started falling down the well. Just as her decent stopped, she felt more than saw the boulders hit Chris. Chris grunted heavily, and they both slipped another dozen feet or so down the well before he found a hold that supported the weight on his back. Kitten could barely see Chris in the dark well, but she could hear him. Chris whispered to her, "Kitten, be brave, my young lady. I will get you out."

Tiffany told me that Kitten did not say it in those words, but Caleb was great at getting the information out of her where he could interpret what actually happened. Kitten was crying and in great fear the whole time as she had been swinging back and forth, which also included hitting the well wall many times. Were it not for her leg being locked in the bottom of the bucket, she would have slipped out and fallen down the well. It was when she smashed into the side wall just after Chris stopped her descent the second time that her leg was broken. Kitten said that as bad as her leg hurt, what scared her the most was the amount of blood that dripped on her. Even though she could barely see, Kitten was able to see the color and recognized the smell. As Kitten put it, it smelled just like steaks do before being cooked. Kitten knew Chris was hurt bad and was afraid for both of them. It was right about then that they heard Mary and Caleb yelling down the well. Caleb heard how even though Kitten could barely see Chris in the darkness as he was facing down, she did hear him when he whispered to her that she would be okay, that he gave her his word that he would get her out. Kitten said she was scared, really scared, more than at any other time in her life, but she believed in Chris. So Kitten closed her eyes and hung on praying for both of them.

Caleb, while glancing over at Kitten, informed Tiffany that Kitten finally realized after all of Caleb's questions, that Chris said he would get her out but never said he would get both of them out. Kitten looking straight into Tiffany's eyes while trying to hold back tears, interrupted Caleb at this time. Kitten asked Tiffany the following. "Chris did not think he would make it, did he? Chris knew he would probably not get out, but he came after me anyway. I do not know that I could ever be so brave as to be able to do something like that." Kitten then rose from her chair as best she could with her cast to lean into her mother's arms while crying softly, still looking at Tiffany, where she asked her one final question: "Do you think he was as scared as I was too?"

67

Tiffany slowly rose and walked over to Kitten, where she knelt, placing her hand on Kitten's arm reassuringly. Tiffany then replied, "Yes, I bet he was scared, really scared. But I know Chris and I would bet that he was more scared for you than for himself. So you must get better so you can help take his fear away, okay? Can you do that for him?" Kitten smiled and shook her head affirmatively.

Tiffany sat sipping her tea and soaking in the steaming aroma coming off her cup. I saw her eyes close and it looked like she would fall asleep right there. I was about to nudge her when she opened her eyes and smiled at me. Tiffany may have been young but our parents trusted her explicitly. When she had called the day before and explained why she was staying at the hospital, they said they understood but please keep them updated. My parents have met Chris several times and thought he was a good man. Especially so considering the changes they saw in me. When I had gone home last night, my parents were waiting for me and we spent the next hour or so going over the day. They were both very glad to hear that it sounded like Chris and Kitten would be OK from the last update they had from Tiffany. My parents informed me that they planned on visiting when Tiffany informed them it was a good time. It was crazy there now and best if they waited. Surprisingly they had not expected Tiffany to come home yesterday evening after she told them what had happened. There sure seemed to be something going on that I was missing. If I had tried to stay out all night, I do not think they would have been as ready to agree. I sure hope they treated me the same way when I was her age. I even hinted at that at which my mother laughed and said we will see. Again, something else was going on here that I was missing. Even my father seemed to be laughing at me.

Tiffany and I talked for a bit more when Caleb, Tyler, and Elijah entered the break room. They saw us and headed over to join us. All three looked tired like they had not slept since the day before and I would have been surprised if they had knowing their attachment to Chris. Caleb picked up a second small table and joined it with ours so we could all sit together. Elijah sat down on my left while Tyler and Caleb sat in front of us. Tyler looked closely at Tiffany and surprised both myself and Tiffany when he reached across the table and took her left hand in both of his. Tyler while holding her hand clasped tightly said they wanted to thank her. Tiffany, in puzzlement, said, "Why would you thank me? I have done nothing. It was the quick work of Roy and the paramedics who allowed Chris the time to get the expert care he needed."

Tyler, with a large smile but in a very serious tone in his voice, replied, "Yes, but it was you that made Chris's heart beat faster, much faster, when he needed it the most, when he had no strength to do it himself. Per the paramedics, it was critical in his survival. So again, we thank you."

Tiffany, whose eyes showed her confusion, looked at me while taking a sip of her tea with her free hand hoping that I could help her understand when it must have finally came to her. Tiffany choked on her tea and her face turned a bright crimson whereupon all three of the new arrivals burst into laughter. This only helped deepen the color on Tiffany's face. I looked at Tiffany in puzzlement. Tyler, chuckling, told Tiffany with all kidding aside, they were very grateful for her watching over Chris. That meant a lot to them and especially to Chris. And like it or not, Kitten had added her to her best friends list, which meant that she was now on the listing of the "lost ones" special friends list. That was going to mean a lot of practical jokes being played on her as the "lost ones" were famous for them.

Elijah asked what Tiffany and I would like at the coffee shop downstairs as he could not take the machine brewed coffee anymore. Tiffany and I requested teas with cream. Elijah did not ask Tyler nor Caleb but I was sure he already knew what they wanted. While waiting for Elijah's return, Caleb let us know that he had talked with the doctors and they had some good news to report.

The Doctor had just done a checkup on Chris and was surprised on how much he had recovered in the short time he had been here. When the doctor had checked on Chris when he had first arrived, he would have given Chris only a 20 percent chance of surviving due to all the internal damage. Now with the results from the last checkup, he raised that estimate to well over 50 percent, and he did not know why. The doc had no explanation why Chris, just overnight, was doing so much better. Almost like a miracle happened. Tyler with an even a bigger grin on his face, then asked Tiffany where had she slept last night. Tiffany blushed even redder than before, at which Caleb and Tyler burst out laughing. I looked at Tiffany in puzzlement where she signaled me later. And when I looked at Caleb for an explanation he gave me an exaggerated look like he had no idea what was going on. I sure was getting tired of being left out on all the jokes.

Elijah returned with the drinks with half a dozen hot blueberry muffins and we all took a moment to enjoy them. We spent a few moments going over Kitten's and Chris's condition and their prognosis. It was during this time that I noticed that Tyler who was staring at his hands, which were wrapped around his coffee mug was very quiet and looked like he had something on his mind. I asked Tyler if he was OK. Tyler looked up and smiled. Tyler said that he was reflecting on another time when Chris had done something similar. Tyler then started to tell us about an event that had occurred around a year after Caleb had decided to watch over Chris. Elijah, once Tyler identified the time period, smiled and shook his head in acknowledgement of knowing what event Tyler was going to tell.

Tyler proceeded to tell Tiffany and me that even though they had decided to follow Caleb in his endeavors to watch over Chris, they did not have the same passion as Caleb did. They had made that decision mostly because they have followed Caleb's lead all their lives, not because they felt any real sense of feelings for this young boy. Tyler and Elijah have lived next door to Caleb's family all their lives and being cousins only strengthened the bond between all three. Where one went, all three went. If Caleb wanted to watch over a boy, so be it—that was what they would do. But that did not mean they had come to love this boy nor had any real respect for him. That all changed soon enough.

Here is what Tyler relayed to me. As stated by Tyler, it was on a clear day just over eleven months after Tyler, Elijah and Caleb had started to watch over Chris while he was in their neighborhood, that they saw thick heavy black smoke spiraling up into the sky a few blocks from their home. They had been waiting for Chris as this was the normal time he would come through but he was unusually late. They were not in the area but the smoke looked to be close to where they lived. All three went racing to see what was occurring. As they got closer, they could hear the sirens and the roar of fire engines racing to the scene. When they reached the street they lived on, they saw that it was Tyler and Elijah's house that was belching the black smoke. They raced up only to be held back by the police trying to keep everyone away from the house.

Tyler stopped speaking for a moment to glance over at Elijah before he went on to tell me how he saw their mother sitting on the curb holding their youngest brother in her arms with several firemen checking them out. There was gray black soot all over their faces and clothes. Emma, their mother, was clutching their six-year-old brother, Wardell, close while rocking him back and forth. Emma was crying and yelling for Fajah. Wardell was sniffling and kept looking up at the house. Their four-year-old sister, Fajah, was nowhere to be seen.

Tyler ran up to his mother and asked what happened. Where was Fajah? Their mother said that when she was cooking dinner there was a grease fire. She knew better than to throw water on it so had thrown what baking soda she had on it but did not have enough to put it out. The fire spread and before she could get out of the kitchen, she was overcome by the smoke. She woke up outside on the ground.

Elijah picked up the story then without a pause. Their mother told them that the next thing she knew, she was lying in the neighbor's yard with Wardell sitting next to her with Necie bending over her holding her hand. Necie was Caleb's mother who lived next door.

Necie while trying to calm Emma kept taking quick glances back at their house. Emma followed Necie's gaze to see the smoke billowing out of her house. It took all of Necie's strength to keep Emma down when she started frantically trying to get up screaming for Fajah. Emma then related how Necie held her down and told her the boy went back in to get her.

Tyler asked his mother, "What boy?"

Necie, who had come over while Emma was telling Tyler and Elijah the events, told him that a boy, who could not have been older than eleven or twelve years old, was carrying Emma out of the house when she first arrived. Wardell was already sitting on the lawn. Necie

71

had come over as soon as she smelled the smoke. Several other neighbors were just arriving at the same time as herself. The boy, who must have also brought Wardell out, told her he was going back in as Wardell had told him that his sister was still in the house. Wardell had told him that Fajah was probably in her bedroom located at the top of the house. Elijah looked at Tyler and Caleb and they vocalized what they were all thinking, "Chris."

Just at that moment, the window at the top of the house, which was Fajah's room, was smashed out by a chair being thrown through it. Immediately following out the window was a boy carrying a young girl who facing him was holding onto him with her arms tightly wrapped around his neck and her legs wrapped around his waist while coughing heavily. Both had what looked like a pillowcase wrapped around their faces covering their nose and mouth. Heavy smoke followed them out. The boy was holding onto the top window sill while carefully working his way over using the window ledge. Once he was at the far end of the window and close to where the chimney rose up through the thick billowing smoke, paused as if in thought.

Everyone could see that he planned to make a jump across to grab onto the chimney. The fire crews raced to get their fire net setup to catch them if they fell or needed to jump. But that would take longer than they had as Tyler said you could see the window ledge was slippery under Chris's feet and he was having a hard time keeping his balance. The smoke was getting thicker and billowing around them. Another crew went racing to get a ladder set up but they were the advance unit and did not have one that could reach three stories up to the roof. There was ladder truck on the way but it was not here yet. The firemen were hosing down the roof to make sure that the fire did not spread there but it seemed to be making it slipperier. Firemen were yelling at them to hang on until they could get up there but the smoke was getting too thick.

Tyler said his heart was in his throat as he could not see how Chris could get off the window ledge with Fajah hanging on like she was. Caleb tried again to go into the house but was stopped before he could get very far. Tyler and Elijah also tried but they had no better luck. Elijah and Tyler looked on what they thought would be the last minutes of their sisters life. The little girl that had looked up to them for protection all her life. The sister that believed them when they said they would always be there for her. And here they were, watching her on a window ledge holding onto a strange boy fighting for her life. It hurt so much being unable to do anything.

Then, in disbelief, all on the ground got to see what no one would ever have believed the boy could do. The boy with a little girl wrapped around him and weighing him down, jumped over to the chimney where he used it only to push himself off to the edge of the roof on the front side of the house. Once there, he never stopped but continued on to jump to the right where while dropping grabbed the edge of the roof with his fingertips and used his momentum to swing him back toward the center of the house. He let go where Emma, and echoed by many others, screamed in horror. The boy dropped down one floor where he caught the window ledge of a bedroom window on the second floor with his toes and grabbing the top windowsill bricks with his fingers. Chris had done the last part while crouching down so as to allow Fajah to use his legs as support so she would not slip and lose her grip.

Chris's grip was precarious at best. Everyone gasped aloud at seeing a boy hanging some twenty feet up on the front of a house with a young girl wrapped around him hanging onto a windowsill only inches wide with only his toes and finger tips. And then both Tyler and Elijah joined in together when they said the next event will live in their memory for the rest of their lives. Chris, just a boy, being unable to hold on until they brought a ladder to him, jumped away from the house and did a double flip to the ground while wrapping himself around the young girl. Caleb continued on when both Tyler and Elijah were too choked up to continue the story.

Chris pulled the girls legs out from around his waist while in the air so they were no longer wrapped around his back just before he landed on his back with a thud that could be heard by all there. Everyone looked in horror as he slowly relaxed, which was when they saw Fajah, who had been wrapped up safely within Chris's embrace, look up at them with fear in her eyes. Emma ran to her and held her close. Elijah and Tyler who were right behind her, heard Fajah say she was OK in response to queries from her mother.

Fajah, who seemed to be suffering nothing more than being very frightened and some slight scrapes and bruises, asked Tyler and Elijah who was that man that had just rescued her. Not who was the boy but who was that man. Because when he first pulled her out from under the bed where she was hiding from the smoke, he told her that he was a friend of Tyler's and Elijah's and was here to help. Elijah and Tyler just looked at her in amazement before looking over at Chris.

There were several firemen kneeling over Chris with Caleb hanging around the edges. Chris was barely conscious. There was no doubt he had a concussion and a broken leg but no one doubted he had other injuries. Emma, while holding onto Fajah, walked over, kneeled and placed her hand on his forehead. Emma, weeping, thanked him profusely before she asked him why, who was he?

Elijah heard Chris, gasping out his reply, say simply, "Fajah's need was greater than mine." Tyler and Elijah looked at each other before finishing with both of them turning to Tiffany and myself saying that what he said next was why they would now would follow Chris to the ends of the world, with or without Caleb. Chris, barely able to move, looked up at them and finished telling Emma, "Why? This is what you do for family. You are family."

With that Chris fell unconscious, at which Caleb assisted the EMT's putting Chris in an ambulance that had just arrived. Elijah and Tyler then both answered together Fajah's question "Fajah, that man is Chris, our friend, our brother." Tyler smiled and said he finally learned what Caleb had understood earlier. Elijah shook his head in agreement.

We sat around for another half hour resting and discussing what was in store for the next several days if not weeks. Tiffany again surprised me when she notified all of us she planned to stay until Chris was released. For some reason, the others were not surprised but expected that from her. I guess they knew Kitten had asked her to stay.

It ended up that Chris was hospitalized for only a little over a week. Chris's constitution fascinated the medical staff and they ran more tests than normal to see why. They did not charge him for the extra tests, in fact, they did not charge him at all for any of the tests as long as they could run all the tests they wanted. It would be interesting to see what they found out but that would have to wait as we were all anxious to leave.

So it was on a Sunday, only eight days after the accident, that Chris was able to go home. It was amazing to see all the people in the parking lot waiting for him to get into his parents' car to go home. There had to be several hundred if not more. When Chris came out the front doors, there was a loud cheer with a chant of "Lord, Lord, Lord." Chris sheepishly waved and assisted by Tiffany, he gingerly got into his parents' car. Tiffany waved at me and then proceeded to get into the passenger side of the car to sit next to Chris. Huh? Why was she going with Chris? This was getting stranger and stranger all the time. I decided it was best to go home and get some sleep, my mind was too confused to make sense of all this. Where was Tiffany going?

ERIC MEETS CHRIS
AGAIN IN BATTLE

It had been several years since that event, which changed my life but I had made it. I was still heavily involved in the Brotherhood and looking forward to when I could use the skills I was learning to their benefit. I also spent every spare moment taking a medical course here and there at the local colleges. It was hard with everything else I was doing, but I had not forgotten my promise nor had my passion to make that happen lessened any. If anything, it had solidified and grown.

I had filled out muscle wise and was no longer lean. Still mean though, real mean when threatened. Several times in the last few years I have used the skills I learned through the Brotherhood and death was no longer a stranger to me. Nor did it hold the power of fear over me as it once would have. Brave? Or just confidence in your own abilities along with the love you have for others? Now I understood what the men and women who are in the US armed forces must already know and I only recently reasoned out. They have been doing this same thing for a very long time and they never profess they are braver than others. But no one doubts they will go places no one else would dare.

Tiffany and I had stayed in touch with Chris although for me it was very sporadic. It was amazing how far and wide Chris traveled. Tiffany had more contact than I did due to my busy schedule. I saw Chris mostly when he would stop in on one my training nights. Then I got to see how deadly he can be. I watched while he took on our best and proceeded to score hits with such speed that it left no doubt in anyone's mind what would have happened if he did not stop the motion before anyone was hurt. But as soon as he was done, Chris would show the maneuver to his opponent in slow motion so they could learn from it.

I learned from those there that this was normal for Chris to show up and everyone wanted a try at him as they always walked away a little wiser. I heard from a few of our best that the reason Chris was so deadly was that Chris did not work off of any set of moves, being either in attack or defense. That most martial art teaches different counter moves to any attack or counterattack. But what Chris did was react and let his body and mind determine the action needed for any given situation. And many of those times, it was not a move that had ever been used before so it was hard to defend against.

And his speed, well, let's just say, even in practice when not in the enhanced mode, it was something to behold. In the enhanced mode, it was indescribable. But Tiffany kept me updated and let me know whenever she talked with him or he showed up to take her to lunch or the rare dinner. Tiffany was a chatter box at those times and you could hear the excitement, and maybe something more, in her voice. Tiffany would be in such wonderful spirits for days after these events. I kept wondering how long does a crush last?

Next time I met Chris in more than a training session was when I was on a training mission during a summer break. I was with several others from my chapter and we were working with a brand new chapter out of Arizona.

Cross chapter training was frequent as you never knew when you would need each other's assistance. Along with developing the cohesiveness between chapters, it also built a long term bond of friendship.

There were three of us patrolling the neighborhood when we saw some activity by a recently abandoned building on the south side of town. We were only a few miles from the border between the United States and Mexico and the area was well-known for drug trafficking as well as a crossing point for migrants gaining illegal entry into the United States. We had no beef with migrants as we understood the need to do what you can to take care of your family. We would do the same if we were in their shoes.

But drugs were bad news for all and not something that we wanted around our kids. So if it was just migrants using it as a rest stop or to stay in for a while, that was OK with us. But if it was being used for drugs, we wanted to check into it further.

The building used to be a very large warehouse being only one floor made out of concrete blocks with plenty of skylights. It had been abandoned just the year before so it was still in pretty good shape. Our goal was just to check it out and be sure that there was no dangerous activates going on that could impact our neighborhood. Hopefully it was just migrants or even local kids having a party.

We spread out to take up positions around the warehouse when we saw a group of several armed men enter by one of the side garage entrances. When the door opened, we could see more men inside. It was obvious something was transpiring inside and these men did not want anyone snooping around. They were definitely not migrants or kids having a party.

After further recon, we could identify at least a half dozen guards armed with automatic weapons guarding the perimeter. Most looked like they were carrying the US AC-556, but one or two were carrying the Russian AK-47 with one fellow carrying an 80.002 for extra firepower. You definitely did not want to get on the wrong side of these weapons.

I know, you are wondering how we could recognize the weapons so easily. Knowing what type of arms was not unique in the Brotherhood as we memorized all types of weapons so we would know what we might come up against and then how best to counter it. Knowledge like that had saved Brotherhood lives countless times.

The guards were definitely not professionals as they all wore their own style of clothing and half were unshaven. We watched as they shot at a passing deer laughing as it panicked and ran into a tree before running off. It was obvious that whatever they were doing was not something we could allow to continue. We were not the police nor government authorized to take any action but we did not want criminal activities in our neighborhood. The new chapter may not be in the best of neighborhoods but that did not change the main fact that we all hold dear, the one rule, help. So while not all of us did not live here, all chapters are supported, no exceptions. This was now OUR neighborhood and we were not about to let someone else endanger it.

We sent Juan back to the car to report back to the chapter headquarters by our cars CB radio while Cleona and I made plans to get inside to see what was occurring. We figured it would take at least an hour or more before a sizable force could arrive. We could spend our time usefully while waiting to get additional information. We saw a door by the rear that we believed we could get in without being noticed so we quietly started working our way there.

One by one we slipped in and spread out. The warehouse was brightly lit so we had to find areas where we could conceal our presence. There were large air conditioner units that were placed every 30-40 feet around the perimeter of the warehouse that seemed to fit our need. There must have been something going on as the air conditioners were functioning and it was quite cool in the warehouse. We spread out and took stock of what was happening.

The warehouse was guarded by a group of armed men with another group of men and women in masks at the far northern part of the complex. They were working on some type of white/tarnish looking powder. Most of the rest of the warehouse was taken up by large bundles of green leaves wrapped in plastic on wooden pallets. Cleona and I rejoined behind one of the large pallets to compare notes. Cleona, who was from the local chapter and had worked with the DEA in the past, thought that the powder might be heroin or cocaine and the bundles were definitely marijuana. If so, what was contained in this warehouse must be worth several million. It must be the distribution center for the whole Southwest area. This was not something that could be allowed to exist.

We decided to separate again and stay put where we were until the reinforcements arrived. We hunkered down and waited. It was a different feeling sitting with a large group of heavily armed men walking around just feet from you who would like nothing better that put some lead into you. It is nerve racking and only through the rigorous training we had received kept us still when we wanted to stand, scratch an itch, sneeze, or just sigh.

It had been at least thirty minutes since we reported in when Cleona was noticed by one of the men in the roving patrol. Shots rang out and I tried to make my way over to support Cleona. Cleona was pinned behind one of the air conditioners and had no method of extracting herself.

I took a position near her and made ready to sell our lives dearly. Just as I was ready to rise up to get a little closer to Cleona, I saw a shadow go overhead. In the center of the warehouse, the glass panes of a skylight shattered and a man dropped down to land hard on the floor. The man was dressed the same as the guards, was not moving, and it did not look like he was about to ever get up again with his neck bent at the angle it was.

All activity stopped to see what was happening. While all attention was on the man that fell through the ceiling, another man all in black dropped through another skylight further down by about ten feet. Only this man did not land hard but softly and was firing two Uzi's each fitted with an oversized ammo magazine clip. I recognized Chris immediately even though he was all in black and a good distance from me. Recognition was easy since no one moved with such fluidity and cat like speed as Chris did. I could not see his eyes but I knew they would be deep red with black centers. The Uzi's laid down a lethal swath of death.

Chris was not sitting still though and was moving toward Cleona very quickly. Somehow, he knew where he was needed most. Chris jumped up and over the bundles or went around depending on the fire he was starting to take. I and Cleona came out of our stupor and opened fire in support. The volume of fire took the guards by surprise but they recovered quickly and still outnumbered us by around five to one. Unfortunately for them, not all the surprises were done yet.

Chris ran up one of the bundles in short little jumps and while diving down the other side threw a stun grenade toward the far end at the location we presumed was loaded with heroin. This set off a very large explosion that rocked everyone but Chris off their feet.

The blast of the stun grenade must have set off something used in making the drug as the blast was much larger than I had expected. At the same time, blasts hit several other entrances to the warehouse. The guards that were drifting to the entrances were blown off their feet, several never to rise again.

I started quietly laughing, yes I know that seems silly thing to do at the moment, but I had a good idea what caused those explosions. I would bet my next month's paycheck that Teja and Andrew along with the rest of the Protectors have arrived. The Protectors are never far from Chris, hence my silent laughter.

Meanwhile Chris had dropped the two Uzi's and pulled out two samurai swords that were strapped to his back. I now know enough about fighting that he was planning to do some real in close fighting and wanted something that did not need to be reloaded. Amazing what you can learn in a few years' time. Chris moved so fast it was hard to watch and I also had other things on my mind at the time, like surviving the next several moments.

It seems I was the closest to the largest group of guards and they were determined to clear me out of their way. I was being pummeled with shots that were only missing me by the merest of margins. Shots were pinging around my ears and I felt several graze my arm leaving trails of blood in their wake. I was firing as fast as I could and knew that I could not keep this rate of fire up much longer before I ran out of ammunition. Not that I was not taking some of them down but there were a half dozen of these jerks in my area.

I was down to my last magazine having burned through five clips in a matter of a minute or two when I saw out the corner of my eye Chris running quickly through the bundles toward me and silencing anyone foolish enough to stand in his way. Chris was running while twisting and thrusting at such a high rate that I was concerned that he was going to lose his footing. There were slugs smacking into the bundles Chris just passed and you could see they were trying to trace his progress will lethal lead. A major problem for them was that Chris was never where you expected him to be. Chris would be going forward one moment, then left, then backward, then right, then up and over. It was hard enough to watch let alone trying to follow him with a gun sight.

I wanted to yell at him to forget me and get to Cleona but I knew he would never be able to hear me. I did not want to be rescued at the expense of another. Here in the midst of a battle where my life was in extreme danger and could end at any moment, what came to my mind was how much life had changed for me. I was no longer afraid to die. I did not want to die but it just did not control me anymore. I had full control of my fears. I smiled as I yelled and let loose with my last clip.

Then it happened. I thought the sound of gunfire was loud before, now it took on a sound of its own. Through most of the entrances men and women poured through and charged directly at the remaining guards firing on full automatic. As one emptied, they would move aside and another would continue, then another. At the same time, two heavily armed bodies dressed in black dropped through the ceiling glass panes.

The roar of gunfire, broken glass, groans and screams was intense. I saw Andrew and Teja come through the entrance closest to me with Juan right behind them. I saw Caleb come right though the solid section of cement blocks behind Cleona. Now I knew why Chris had turned toward me. First there was a small blast and then Caleb came through the cement blocks like it was balsa wood. Caleb reached Cleona and pulled her behind him. Then he let loose with a 12 gauge automatic shotgun being sure no Brotherhood members were around. That cleared the immediate area whereupon he dropped the shotgun and pulled out his trusty pistols. With Cleona safely behind him, he patiently waited for reinforcements, which did not take long to arrive.

From the number coming through the entrances and the ceiling, I guessed correctly that both the Protectors and reinforcements had arrived together. The Brotherhood then showed what all the training was about. Each fighter paired up and spread out. They moved quickly around the bundles and air conditioners. No one had to be given directions; each knew what they needed to do. One by one the remaining guards were taken down.

I saw Yoshe Sun and Brandon Hall, members of the local Brotherhood, come upon several guards coming around the corner of an air conditioner. Brandon braced himself on the unit and grabbed Yoshe by her hands to swing her feet first around the corner into the guards. Yoshe while still holding onto Brandon's hands opened her legs wide while in motion twisting herself to gain a lot of momentum where she then used that momentum to slam her bootheels, which were now close together into one of guard's chest. As he tumbled to the ground, Yoshe landed, planted herself firmly and still holding onto Brandon, now swung him around the corner where he used his bulk to slam into the other guard. As the guards were trying to rise up off the floor, Brandon and Yoshe each pulled a knife, which they shoved into each of the men's chest. Needless to say, they would not be rising again. This all occurred in less than a four or five seconds. Brandon and Yoshe did not stop to admire their handiwork but continued swiftly on to find their next target. You could tell that these two had worked together and practiced this many, many times. Watching them was like watching poetry in motion, deadly poetry, very deadly poetry. But they were not the only ones I saw in the battle that followed.

I saw Noah and Wilson, a pair of Lord Protectors, slam into another pair of guards by grabbing the end of a bundle and swinging themselves fully up and over the bundle to land just behind the guards. They looked like professional acrobats they did it with such grace. The guards never got a chance to recover and turn fully around to meet this surprise attack. Noah and Wilson when they landed never slowed and continued in a roll toward the guards. Noah had a blade around eight inches long that looked like a half moon with a handle on one end. The blade was held in reverse so that it rested on his forearm, which he used to power into one of the guards neck. The man did not know what hit him and fell quietly with only a small death gurgle. Meanwhile Wilson was carrying a wicked looking knife that had a handle with metal spikes coming out it. I believe it was called a Cobra Extreme Spiked Dagger but it was too far away from me to be 100 percent sure. Wilson pushed it in the back of the other guard's lower back and sliced upward until it emerged from his left shoulder. The man looked down at the damage with surprise written all over his face before dropping motionless to the ground. Both men never slowed and continued to the next bundle to see what they could find there.

Most of the Protectors did not use handguns when in close unless needed to make sure they did not cause any friendly casualties. As I said before, we were very safety conscious, even when in battle. Besides, this was close in combat and there was nothing better than a trusty dependable sharp knife, blade or sword.

The firing continued for a few more moments and then stopped with a deafening quiet. Except that was from the groaning and crying from the men and women that had been working on the heroin or cocaine. Those individuals had been hiding under the tables when Chris threw the grenade. Several were wounded but I was not sure if any were dead. All the visible guards were down and I doubted any would rise again. It was just not our way to fight a war twice with the same person.

I looked toward Chris and saw him standing over several prone bodies. Chris was covered in blood and it was impossible to see if any was his own. But based on prior history, Chris did not get away unscathed.

I looked toward Juan and saw that he was still up and moving. Scanning the area, I saw several had minor wounds that did not look too serious except for Cleona. Cleona had taken a bullet in her upper right arm and in the fleshy part of her left leg. But when she smiled at me I knew she would be okay. That was typical of members in the Brotherhood. They smiled when others would cringe. Maybe that was our way of letting the tension out, who knows for sure, but it was sure good to see her smile.

No one relaxed until all the bodies were checked to be sure we would not hear from them again. While most were stationed on alert, others interviewed the people still left alive. It seemed they had been forced to come here to make heroin for a large drug cartel in Mexico to sell in the United States. They indicated they lived several hundred miles away in Mexico and had been bused here several weeks ago. All they wanted to do was go home to their families. Several of the

Brotherhood went to check out their story while others kept watch on them and tended to any that were wounded.

I started to make my way toward Chris and as I expected, saw that he had also taken damage in the lower right side of his chest. It did not look serious, more of a scratch, but without further examination I could not tell for certain. Curiously enough, Chris's eyes were still red and he was still on full alert. Chris was perched on a bundle and scanning the area. I started to ask what he was looking for when he signaled quiet.

Chris then hopped off the bundle and motioned for Caleb to join him. Caleb reached him in short order and Chris asked if he thought it strange that they had seen a lot of guards but no one that seemed to have been in charge. Caleb agreed that seemed odd when Chris pointed to a depression in the ground. I was surprised as I had been here for a while but did not see the depression until it was pointed out. I then noticed the way the bundles were placed so as to make it very hard to see unless you right on top of it. In fact one of the bundles may actually have been over the depression the way it was now placed. No wonder I had not seen it. Whatever was down there was meant not to be seen.

"Caleb my friend, I will bet you that if you look more closely down there you will find a trapdoor. It would be no major leap of deduction that they probably jammed the entrance on the other side. I wish we had someone with such great strength that he could gain us entry. What say you Caleb? Know anyone that would be able to rip that door open?" Chris asked with humor in his voice.

Caleb smiled, got down into the slight depression and found a hidden door jammed just like Chris described. Caleb grabbed the metal door handle, lowered himself until his butt was only inches from the floor and started straightening his legs pulling with all his might. You could see all the tendons in Caleb's neck stand to attention, the muscles on his arms and legs standing out in large relief, the blood rushing to his face. I told you before that Caleb was huge, but now, he looked gigantic. Caleb looked like he could let the old Greek mythical god Atlas take a break from holding the world up his muscles were so pronounced. At first, nothing happened, and then slowly you could hear whatever was jamming the other side start screeching. Slowly the door started opening. Caleb continued to straighten his legs. The door suddenly flew off its hinges and went flying through the air with a great bang to land ten feet away. Luckily no one was hurt. A few had to move quickly to get out of the way but laughed as it landed at their feet. The door was metal and must have weighed over forty pounds. Caleb looked up at Chris and said with humor in his eyes, "Lord, I thought you were going to give me a challenge, surely that was not it?"

Chris just shook his head and laughed.

While Caleb had been opening the door, others had been searching the warehouse to make sure that there were no hidden surprises. That was when they found Jeffrey Martinez, a member of the Brotherhood for several years, and one of the initial members of the local chapter. Jeffrey was found dead behind one the bundles with a gunshot wound to the head. It was obvious he had been killed elsewhere and brought here. Jeff had left his home several days ago to go hunting and when he had not returned several days ago, no one was concerned as he was known to stay out longer if the hunting was going well. Looks like he had run afoul of this gang and had not come out on top.

We all bowed our heads in reverence for a moment as his death was felt deeply by all. Members of the Brotherhood are like family. Chris knelt at Jeff's side and slowly ran his hand over his open eyes to close them. Chris then put his hand on Jeff's forehead and said quietly with pain evident in his voice "Jeff, my old friend, you will be sorely missed. Your wife and children will be taken care, on that; I will personally make sure of. Go in the knowledge that you have not died in vain. Your family, friends and neighbors are living in a safer place only through your efforts and ultimate sacrifice. We will not relent until we have crushed this group and when we stand over the last of our enemies, we will make sure they know your name. Go in peace my friend, go in peace."

Chris told Adam Young who was the commander of the local chapter that the battle was not over and that we needed to take the war to the enemy. Chris, the Lord Protectors and the original group, minus Cleona due to her injuries, would follow the people who had fled through the tunnel until we located their home base and identified who they were. Meanwhile Adam was to complete the examination and destruction of the drugs here before following with all the resources he could gather.

Adam bowed at the waist and did something I had never seen before. Adam leveled out his M14 to rest in both hands and offered it up to Chris. Adam then loudly asked Chris "Lord, I am not fit to lead these brave men and women to war. A commander yes, a Warlord I am not. I do not have the needed experience and would waste lives I hold so very dear. As a commander in the Brotherhood, I have the right to ask you to be our Warlord. Your war prowess is well-known to all in the Brotherhood. Will you lead us in this war? We are not a large chapter being so new and few in number but you will not find us lacking. We will fight to protect what is ours. So Lord, I ask you one again, will you be our Warlord and lead us in the battles to come?"

Chris looked at Adam, slowly turned a full circle while looking each man and women there in the eye. "Is this what you all want? Do you understand the request you all are asking of me? You must all accept, not just Adam. If I accept this honored position, I will not relent until this is finished. No truce, no treaties, no surrender, no prisoners. This war will be fought once and once only. If that means we have to follow them to the end of the world. Understand what am I saying, we will not fight this war more than once. I will use each and every one of you as I see fit, even if that is to throw your life away just to gain a tactical advantage. Wars have causalities; it could be your neighbor, your friend, your wife or husband and possibly your son, daughter, granddaughter or grandson. Who or how is an unknown, are you willing to accept this?"

As one, all present, myself included, yelled out. "Yes, lead us." Not everyone said it the same way but there was no mistaking we all agreed to have Chris as our Warlord. Chris stepped up to Adam and took the M14, held it high and then handed it back. Chris placed his hands on Adam's shoulders and said loud enough for all to hear "My friend, you will need this as you fight by my side. All of you know this; you will not be going alone. I will be by your side and where I go, the Lord Protectors go. They may be a nuisance following me everywhere I go, and you can ask my girlfriend on how hard it is to have a private moment if you do not believe me"—Chris paused here to look around at the Lord Protectors who were all smiling and nodding their heads in agreement before continuing after some chuckled—"but at times like this, I cannot imagine a better group of men and women to have around. And remember, you are members of the Brotherhood. I may only be an honorary member but you are not. You are full members of the Brotherhood and now you will see what comes with that. The ruling Council of the Brotherhood has already been notified of the situation and are rushing resources here to assist you as we speak. Fighters, equipment, and much more has already been dispatched. This was done prior to our taking this warehouse as we did not know what we would find. You are not alone, not by a long shot. You have lost a wonderful person like Jeff, along with a lot of sweat, blood, and tears to become members of the Brotherhood and the Brotherhood has not forgotten. They are behind you in this war. Stand proud because soon your enemies are going to see that they have made a fatal mistake. They made war on you, us, and the entire Brotherhood!"

With that everyone raised their weapons and yelled "The Brotherhood" several times before being replaced that with "Lord, Lord, Lord." With that Chris accepted being Warlord of the Brotherhood. I could feel and hear the tremor in my voice while I yelled. My blood coursed hotly with the passion and conviction that if anyone would lead us to victory, it would be Christopher Wilson, the Lord Protector of the Brotherhood and now, its Warlord! Heaven help any who got in our way.

I remember wondering at the time if this drug cartel had any idea of what type of hell was coming their way. I doubt it—I really doubted it! But then I remembered several things that Chris said that bothered me. First, he mentioned not being a full member of the Brotherhood. How could he not be? The Brotherhood was based on his ideas. I needed to check with Caleb on that. And more importantly for me personally, Chris mentioned a girlfriend. Who was that? Did Tiffany know her? I loved Tiffany very much and believed she would be crushed when she found out. I believe she had hopes that she and Chris could be romantically sometime involved in the future. I did not relish telling her.

CELEB TELLS HOW HE MET THE LORD

While Adam managed the warehouse and directed the support already arriving from other chapters, we started getting ready to follow the ones who escaped. Chris needed to relax in normal mode for a bit; we all needed to renew our ammunition supply and to bind our wounds. The latter being so important as we have learned from past experience, that no matter how small the wound, infection does not take long to get take a hold of a person's system. And we needed to be in top form.

Of all the injuries, Cleona's was the most serious and I finally had an opportunity to make use of my limited medical knowledge. Roy was checking out her wounds and remarked they seemed to be non-life threatening, looked like tissue damage only. Of course, his judgment was limited without being able to take some x-rays. Roy thought that I would be able to treat Cleona with the medical training I had so far so he asked if I could treat her while he looked on. I was glad to see that my medical training may now be paying dividends. I finished removing Cleona's sleeve and saw that the bullet wound in her right arm looked like it was a clean wound in that it had passed through without hitting any bone. Her lower left leg had been hit by a ricochet fragment but had not penetrated deeply. Roy watched as I removed the shell fragments that I could see and delicately removed some fabric from the arm wound. I then gave Cleona a Tetanus shot before I tightly bound both wounds. We would need to take an x-ray later but this should do for now.

I was going to take a look at Chris but Roy first said we needed to look at the others before we could get around to Chris. I was surprised at that but Roy had been by Chris already so Chris must have already been looked at. We spent the next half hour checking and verifying that everyone with any wound, no matter how serious, had been looked at or had someone with some type of medical experience treating their injuries before we got back to Chris. I was surprised how quickly that review went and how organized this activity was. As we made our review, almost everyone who had any type of injury already had someone already looking at it. Even the very minor ones. I was impressed.

Roy and I then started to take another look at Chris. I was confused at first as it seemed Chris had not been looked at but I took it that Chris had told Roy he was OK and to see who else may need assistance. Roy laughed when I told him that. Roy informed me that Chris made it a point that unless he was so seriously injured as to be in danger of losing his life, everyone else was to be looked at prior to himself. Then they were to use their best judgment and work on the most seriously wounded first. With his constitution, he was better able to shrug off minor, even serious, damage. I shook my head in wonder as it reinforced what I heard from others as I had walked around checking on their wounds. While being checked over, they would speak of Chris with great admiration. They would talk about how a true leader understood and worried about their people more than themselves. And Chris was more than just a leader, he was a leader that lived and fought like they did. And most important, he was also their friend. How many other leaders can say the same?

I was a little nervous even though this is exactly why I went into the medical field to start with. I had Chris remove his shirt and I was shocked by the number of scars on his body. I could hardly find a spot that is not covered by either an old or recent scar. How had he survived half of these I have no idea, some looked horrendous. My already high estimation for this man went higher even more. I decided then that I needed to add plastic surgery to my list of training. Chris may not care about the scars but I did not like to leave a mess behind. The wound was not too deep and looked like it was just a graze by a bullet. It took only a few stitches and I covered it with a clean bandage that should not fall off with the strenuous activity we would soon be in. Chris had me forego any drugs to help alleviate the pain while I did the probing and stitching as he did not want to impact his clarity when he went back into enhanced mode. It was amazing, here I was stitching away, and he calmly held a conversation with Cleona who looked like she was in heaven. Cleona, shot and in pain, sat chatting away with a look of such delight on her face that you would have thought she was at her senior prom dance. It was hard to tell from her smile and laughter that she had just been shot several times along with being in the middle of a warehouse where a major battle had just been fought with bodies lying all around. It looked like my sister was not the only female infatuated with Chris. Chuckling I just shook my head in admiration.

Caleb came and sat next to me and Roy while I worked on Chris. I asked Caleb how he met Chris. Caleb, smiled and said quietly in his deep booming voice, that it was he who made Chris the man he is today. Chris looked at Caleb with great fondness and said, "Eric, I agree with that statement. Caleb was my inspiration to learning how to protect myself. Life has mysteries that cannot always be explained. I knew when I first met him that he was connected to my future somehow. How? I did not know at the time, but now I knew. Today, I could not imagine my life without Caleb being a part of it. Caleb and I were meant to meet and become friends. Of that I have no doubt." They both looked at each other and smiled.

All conversations stopped. Everyone continued to get ready but all wanted to hear the story. Even though I found out later that most of the Protectors had heard it a thousand times, they never got tired of it. Caleb then went on to say that most of the beginning of what he was about to tell; he heard from Chris himself as he did not know him then, but since then, most had been collaborated by others. It seemed many years ago, in '64: when Chris was around eleven years old, he was visiting a used bookstore in the town of Upper Darby near Philadelphia. Chris was there to buy some used comic books or adventure stories. Chris had a whole ten dollars with him, a lot for an eleven-year-old at the time, and he hoped to get three to four books and several comics.

Chris's family lived in the suburbs, a place called Havertown, but they did not have any good used bookstores there so he had hitched a ride into town. In those days, hitchhiking was a common practice. Chris only got three books but found half a dozen good comic books with enough change left over to get a Philly pretzel and a root beer soda. Not the wide ones you see nationally nowadays but the Philadelphia style that were long thinner pretzels being thick in the middle with lots of salt. As Chris once told Caleb once "A little yellow mustard on them and aahh… they are so good." It is amazing what you remember when some dramatic event occurs in your life.

When Chris left the bookstore, he heard a very low noise coming from the alley next to the store. It was very light and hard to hear but it sounded like a dog whine but very soft and far away. Intrigued, Chris looked into the alley but could not see anything. Other than a dumpster and some trash, there was nothing else present. Chris moved further into the alley and the whining got a bit louder. Chris followed the whining and soon identified that it was coming from the dumpster. When he opened the dumpster, he saw a burlap bag on top of the garbage and food leftovers that moved like there was something in it. The dog whines came from inside the bag.

Chris opened the bag to see a tiny black-and-white puppy with an umbilical cord still attached. No sign of the afterbirth, but the umbilical cord looked like it had been chewed at the end of it. The end of the umbilical cord had a rubber band tightly wound around it so whoever dumped the puppy at least had done that. The puppy had the features of a beagle and looked to be no more than several days old. The puppy was curled up at the bottom of bag shivering. Whether the puppy was shivering from being cold or frightened was beyond Chris at this moment. Chris dropped his pretzel and soda in the other end of the dumpster and picked the puppy up. Chris carefully held the puppy to his chest. He could feel the puppy's heartbeat beating a mile a minute. It was an amazing feeling. Chris told me that when he looked at the puppy's closed eyes, he swears that they moved below the lids and would swear they looked right at him into his soul even through the closed eyelids. A shiver ran through his whole body the feeling was so strong. He knew he had to do something to take care of this puppy. How did the puppy get here? Why? Was it an unwanted puppy? If so, where were the rest of the litter? Was this one considered unfit, a runt?

Chris did not know the answers to that but knew he had to do something. With his mind made up, he proceeded to wipe the puppy clean as much as possible with the bag and was quickly able to identify the puppy as a male. And with that identified, the name Snoopy popped into his mind. Chris had told Caleb that when he started calling the puppy by the name Snoopy, the puppy stopped whining and started licking Chris's finger. Chris said he knew he had found the right name for his puppy. Yes, his puppy! Caleb laughed and said he joked with Chris when being told the story that he was sure that the yellow mustard and salt from the pretzel on Chris's finger had nothing to do with the puppy's enthusiastic licking. Chris had laughed but said that was when he swore to himself that he would do whatever he had to, to raise this puppy on his own.

That was not as easy as it sounded as his mother was extremely allergic to animal hair and dander. Chris was very close to his family and the thought that he would make his mother uncomfortable was not something he would even consider. Chris could not bring the puppy home so he had to come up with something else. But what? Chris spent the next hour sitting on the curb in that alley thinking on what he could do before he came up with a plan.

Caleb started laughing while telling this part and said, "Can you imagine, it is the mid-1960s and a boy finds a puppy? Oh yeah, what would a child know about the real world and the impact his decisions were going to make on many more than just himself and a puppy. "With this Caleb then said very quietly "And this boy at 11 years old, swore to himself that he was going to raise a puppy on his own. Do any of you understand the obstacles in front of him? I do. I was one of them. In fact, I was the major one." With that Caleb went on with the story. But as he continued, we could all see Caleb's eyes moisten. No one thought less of Caleb; we all knew there was a special bond between Chris and Caleb that nothing but death could part. I was about to find out what that was.

Chris took the books and comics back to the book store to get a refund as he knew he needed money to get some food for the puppy. The clerk knew Chris as a steady customer and refunded the money without the usual mark down even though he wondered why since Chris had just purchased them. And where did he get the puppy? Chris just shrugged his shoulders and said an emergency had come up.

Chris took the puppy to a local Acme store where he spent a half hour talking with the staff to understand what he needed. Fortunately there was a man who worked behind the service counter that raised puppies as a side business so Chris was able to get some good recommendations. Chris picked up a two cans of puppy formula, which the store only had two of as it there was no real demand for it, a baby bottle with several replacement nipples, a water bowl, a box of wet wipes, and several cheap blankets. Chris was short several dollars when checking out and was going to have to leave behind several items when the cashier seeing his consternation, asked him if that was his puppy. When Chris explained how he found the puppy and that he planned to raise him, the cashier reached into her purse and pulled enough money out of her wallet to make up the difference. Chris was flabbergasted and could not thank her enough. The woman whose name was Diana, and one that Chris said he will never forget, told Chris she was glad to see a young man being so responsible. Besides, she had three dogs of her own and one was a miniature beagle, which she believed was part of the mixture of the puppy Chris had in his arms due to its size and coloring. Diana wished Chris the best of luck on his way out.

Chris stopped at the back of the Acme to clean the puppy. While Chris cleaned the puppy with the wet wipes, he reviewed what his plans were. Chris planned to find a park locally where he could find an out of the way location where no one visited. Chris was not aware of any in his immediate area that met this description but Veterans Memorial Park in Marple Township did. It was a close to Havertown and would allow him to visit frequently. Chris placed the puppy and supplies on the ground while he a grabbed several small boxes that were in a nearby dumpster. The boxes were just a little bigger than the puppy and should be good for keeping him secure and warm when wrapped in the blankets. Chris fit each box inside the next size larger until he had around four boxes in total. Then he put all the purchased supplies in the corner of the boxes. Then with great care, he wrapped the puppy in the two blankets and placed him snugly inside the boxes. Now Chris was able to carry everything without too much trouble.

Chris made his way to Veterans Memorial Park where he spent the next several hours searching for a location never visited by any visitors. Chris finally what he was looking for at the far end where it was overgrown with brush and old tree hangings that was a good way off the main path. Only after getting through the brush did he find a small clearing where he planned to keep the puppy. First though, he opened a can of puppy formula, put it in the bottle and after some fumbling bad starts, was finally able to figure out how to feed the puppy. While the puppy was sloppily feeding, Chris looked around the clearing to see how to secure the puppy so he would not be in danger of any wild animals or passerby's.

Once the puppy finished the bottle and half of another, Chris put the puppy who was now dozing down in one of the boxes. There was a huge old tree in the back of the clearing that would be perfect with its overhanging tree limps to keep the puppy covered when it rained. So Chris used this as an anchor to start building a circular wall about three to four feet high and ten feet in diameter made of broken branches and tree limbs that were scattered abundantly around the area. This took several hours, at which time it was starting to get dark. Chris made a covering with long branches that he held down with vines onto the wall. It was convenient that the wall being made up of branches had small offshoots that he could use for anchoring the vines to. Chris completed the covering with several layers of leaves.

Chris was a boy scout and had been in the organization since he was very young. Chris had tagged along with George, his brother, to George's Cub Scout meetings and events since he was a toddler as George and Chris were inseparable. It was here he had learned how to tie knots and the basics for building the pen. At no time did he ever expect to have to build one in real life. Chris had thought it was cool to know but would not be very useful outside of cub scouts. How wrong he was. By the time Chris was done with his puppy shelter, it was dark out and he needed to get home as his parents would be very worried. Chris was now sore along with his hands being cut and blistered as he had done all this without gloves. But he was satisfied that he now had a home that would protect Snoopy, his puppy. So after one final feeding, Chris gave Snoopy one final hug and made his way home.

Caleb now lowered his voice so that you could barely hear him. Everyone did but they had to strain over the noise from the activity of people reloading ammo clips with bullets, belts with ammo clips, sharpening knives, cleaning guns and so on. Caleb then spoke of something that was obvious it was very painful to him. It seemed that Chris had to pass through Caleb's neighborhood to get to see Snoopy. At first no one paid Chris much mind but after several weeks, Chris ran into Caleb and his boys. There were six of them, two of those boys being Caleb's cousins Tyler and Elijah. Caleb was thirteen at the time and already 6'2" of pure muscle. When Chris tried to walk around them, Caleb flattened Chris with a roundhouse you could hear all the way down the block. At this the rest of the boys beat Chris until he was just curled up in a ball on the ground bleeding profusely. After a final kick, Caleb warned Chris never to walk in their territory again. They left Chris without looking back.

How or when Chris got up, no one knows. Chris never spoke of it and just shrugs his shoulders today when asked. Unfortunately Chris met Caleb and his friends often in the next several months. And each time, Chris was mercilessly beaten. Chris was a mass of bruises and cuts each time they left him. Eyes swollen shut, fat split lips, black and blue all over his body and lacerations in his scalp. His teachers and parents were beside themselves with worry. Chris's parents, Mark and Ava, even tried to force Chris to stay home but Chris would always find a way to sneak out.

Chris repeatedly said he would get through this and to trust him. But Chris's father and brother were not people that could not sit idly by. Chris always seemed to know when his father or brother were following and lose them by cutting through people's yards. So they started driving or walking down the same areas that Chris usually went trying to find the culprits beating on Chris. Caleb saw Mark and George several times but never let on that it was he and his friends behind the beatings.

On the third month, since meeting Chris, Caleb noticed a marked difference. Chris did not just take it anymore. Chris was actually able to dish out some of his own punishment. Of course the numbers were against Chris and shortly he would be beaten down again. In the fifth month after Chris found Snoopy, Caleb decided to find out why Chris had to go through their neighborhood. Chris was also becoming a force to be reckoned with. Chris was holding his ground more and more and if not for their numbers, Caleb did not know if even he could take him by himself.

Chris's fighting skills had improved tremendously over the past several months. Chris was fighting back with some type mixture of karate or kung fu. Caleb also noticed that Chris eyes were now solid pink when he fought. The pink was evenly distributed across his eyes with the black iris at the center. Almost like pink eye but more solid. Was that left over from the beatings? Could be as Chris's eyes were surrounded by black and blue. But Caleb did not remember ever seeing anything like this before. So Caleb had the boys leave Chris alone one day so he could follow Chris. Caleb watched while Chris, still limping from a prior fight, make his way to Veterans Memorial Park. What was odd was that Chris was carrying a big bag of dog food. Caleb, with only his cousins following behind, trailed Chris to his secret location in the park.

Caleb then went on to explain how he watched Chris go to a pen made of branches where there was a black and white dog inside a large dog cage. The dog was panting loudly and his tail was wagging a mile a minute. You could tell the dog was excited to see the boy. The boy carefully opened the pen and let himself in by bending down and crawling in on his knees and elbows. Once in, the boy looped a vine on the inside around a hook inside to keep the pen door closed. When the boy reached the dog cage, he flipped so he was upside down, and then opened the dog cage. The dog jumped on his lap and licked his face with gusto. The boy, while scratching the puppy behind both his ears, chuckled and softly said, "I missed you too, Snoopy. I am sorry, but I cannot let you out today. My legs are very sore and I would not be able to keep up with you and I cannot have you go somewhere someone may see you. They may take try and take you away. Maybe next time, okay?"

Caleb looked around as he could not believe this is why the boy would be taking the beatings that he and his friends were giving him. For a dog? Get real—there must be something else. But what? Caleb and his cousins watched for the next hour or so as the boy and dog played together. There was no mistaking the love they had for each other. Many times the dog in his exuberance would jump on the boy and he would flinch in pain but never showed any displeasure to the dog. Exactly the opposite, he showed nothing by love.

It was when the boy was feeding the dog that Caleb and his cousins made themselves known. The boy upon seeing them crawled out of the pen and stood in front. From his stance, Caleb could tell the boy was ready to fight. The weird thing was when they had been watching the boy play with the dog, the boy's eyes were a bright hazel, now they had a reddish tint. Darker than a pink but not quite a full blood red. What that meant, Caleb had no idea. But he could tell that the boy was not going to run away, not with the way his feet were planted.

Caleb walked to within several feet of the boy and stopped. Caleb with a snarl asked the boy what was going on. What was with the dog pen and why did he keep coming through his neighborhood? This boy marked with black and blue bruises on almost all visible parts of his body along with lacerations, calmly said, "Only way to get to my dog with enough time to care for him, not enough time to go around." What amazed Caleb the most was the boy showed no fear, none at all. Nothing but determination was in his eyes. Caleb was impressed, deeply so. Caleb towered over the boy and yet this boy was not going to back down. Caleb looked at his cousins who looked at Caleb with puzzlement. What were they going to do?

Caleb walked closer so he was right in front of the boy and asked "all this just for a dog?"

The boy responded, "Yes, he is my dog, my friend, my responsibility. His need is greater than mine," Caleb said at that moment he was struck by the courage this boy had. The boy had been beaten many times severely and stood to be beaten again now yet showed no fear. Caleb looked at the puppy and all he saw was a puppy that wanted out so he could play with his friend. Caleb told us he that now saw himself for what he was. Caleb did not like what he saw, a bully, nothing but a bully. Caleb felt something he rarely did, guilt. Guilt for hurting a boy who only wanted to care for his dog.

Tyler and Elijah, who had been listening to Caleb telling the story, jumped in then to tell us that Caleb surprised both of them when Caleb walked past the boy and dropped to his knees next to the dog pen. The puppy came over to Caleb inquisitively and sniffed the fingers Caleb put through open slots in the branch wall. Caleb looked up at the boy and asked what the puppy's name was. When he was told Snoopy, Caleb laughed with a deep bellow and quietly whispered, "Snoopy, huh? That is a good name for a dog, a very good name." Caleb then asked the boy if it would be okay if he held the puppy. The boy in response opened the gate where the puppy ran out, circled the boy several times before he went over to sniff Caleb who had not risen off the ground. Caleb, who was not known to show his emotions, laughed when the puppy jumped on his thighs so he could lick his face.

Caleb sat back on his haunches and while scratching the tummy of the dog who had rolled onto his back, asked the boy what his name was. After Chris let him know his name, Caleb introduced himself and his cousins. Tyler and Elijah were surprised at the change in Caleb and looked at each other in puzzlement. Caleb asked Chris why the dog was kept here, why not at Chris's house. Upon hearing Chris's reason, Caleb felt even worse for having picked on this boy. All this so Chris's mother would not be impacted by her allergies. Caleb could relate as he felt the same way about his own mother. Caleb picking the dog up in one hand and rubbing the dogs back with the other, came over to Chris to stand by his side. Chris started to rub the dog's head. Tyler and Elijah were then shocked to see the both of them playing with the dog.

Caleb then asked Chris, if he did not mind, would it be OK for him to stop by and see Snoopy. Chris said that would be great as Chris could only get out for several hours a day and Snoopy was at an age where he needed more than a few hours. With that, Caleb looked over at Chris then to Tyler and Elijah whereupon Caleb calmly notified Chris that he would have no more issues walking through the neighborhood. Caleb would make sure everyone knew Chris was now under Caleb's protection. Tyler and Elijah were astonished but they took their lead from Caleb. So be it, if that was what Caleb was going to do, so would they. Of course Snoopy playing with them over the next several hours helped tremendously. They never had a pet and this was a real treat. So that day, unlike most days, for several hours, four boys were just boys having fun with an excited eager puppy.

Caleb had lowered his head when he told us this last part. Now he raised it and his cheeks were wet with tears. I then realized so were mine and along with several others. Caleb looked around and said at that moment, he had made a life changing decision. No one, not even his cousins were ever going to hurt Chris again. Caleb would make sure of that by watching over Chris himself whenever he was in the neighborhood. In fact, God willing, Caleb would like to become a friend of Chris's, if he could ever forgive him. Caleb became, unknown at that time, the first Lord Protector. Caleb's cousins, Tyler and Elijah, became the second and third. All three were now committed to being Chris's protectors. It was the start of the Brotherhood, they just did not know it yet. Caleb stood up, walked over to Chris and put his hand affectionately on Chris's right shoulder. Chris reached over his shoulder to place his hand on top of Caleb's. Caleb said it was a decision that he never regretted. Caleb then sat next to his friend and quietly continued to prepare for war. Then, and only then, did everyone start talking again.

ERIC BECOMES A MEMBER OF
THE LORD PROTECTORS

As I finished up stitching, Chris started laughing and said to Roy who had been watching from close by. "Roy, I do believe we have finally found someone that can grant you your wish and take your place as my doctor. I barely felt the stitching. Good job Eric, very good, indeed. What say you, you up to the task? You want the job?" With that Roy pumped his fist in the air and yelled over to me. "Eric, you have my blessing, I never had the skill required for handling Chris. Chris puts up with me because, heck, I was the only one at that time with any medical training, if you call being a medic in the army medical group actual training. Chris, with his stubborn loyalty, refused to let anyone else work on him. I guess he was used to my butchering by then and afraid that the next one would be even worse. Please tell me that you want the job. In case you did not know, that responsibility will come with some awesome perks. First perk being that you become a full member of the protectors and everything that entails. We know that is what you have always wanted. What do you say, here you can get all you dreamed on by just saying yes."

Now that was a bribe I could not refuse, but something in Roy's and Caleb's expression told me that there was more to this than I knew. But Roy knew this was my greatest desire and laughed when he saw my expression of exasperation. My warning bells were ringing loudly, and I knew that I should pay more attention to them. But this was my life's dream; that was why I had put in all the hours at school, all the training with the Brotherhood, all now just waiting on me to respond with one word. Well, I thought to myself, no risk, no pain, no glory. What the heck, how bad could it be?

With that I smiled and said, "Yes, it would be my honor." With that one word, Roy jumped up, laughing, and said now it was too late for me to take it back. I was stunned and elated at the same time. I was now a full member of the Lord Protectors. Of course I still had to finish school, but Roy would help cover for me during that time. I had made it; my dream had now become a reality. I was the personal doctor for the Lord Protector of the Brotherhood, my friend Chris, who also made me a member of the Lord Protectors. Tiffany was going to be so proud of me.

Only later was I to find out that I had no idea what I had just volunteered for. The training, the number of battles, the number of injuries that I would have to repair and also take, were so much more than I ever imagined or had experienced up to this point. But so be it, it was what I wanted to do more than anything else. I then thought of Caleb. What I was going to do had to be no more daunting than what Caleb had had to go through. Between Caleb and myself, we would do everything possible to keep this individual, the one we loved and knew as the Lord of the Brotherhood, alive. For now though, enough stories—it was now time for war!

Everyone was now ready. An hour had passed. Chris talked with Adam who was coordinating getting additional resources from the other chapters. It was amazing how many had already responded and offered their services. It was not a matter of asking for help in the Brotherhood—they all wanted to help—it was determining which group would be best for this situation.

Chris talked with the commanders who had reported in on where he wanted them to place their men. Chris was surrounding a fifty-mile radius from our location and working his way in with battle-hardened members of the Brotherhood. Based on time, speed, and geography, the ones who escaped were not estimated to have gone any further without having run into one of our patrols. While we had been getting ready, Chris had Teja, Andrew, and several of my old group follow the trail of the ones who escaped through the tunnel. They quickly examined the tunnel and found the exit. It ran underground and came up about a hundred yards out in the woods to the north.

While Andrew followed the escapees' trail, Chris had a few jeeps brought up along with several trucks. What was in the trucks, I did not know, but from what conversations I overheard between Chris and Adam, it was filled with some very special equipment. There were about a dozen Lord Protectors present. Most went into the trucks and jeeps while Chris and the rest led the way on Harleys, following Andrew's directions. It was something to behold. There were not a lot of commands being given; everyone knew what needed to be done, doing it efficiently and quietly.

Chris, at the last moment, had Juan and Cleona, along with myself, join him. I was surprised since we were not the most experienced. Tyler caught my surprise and quickly informed me why with several short questions. Who found the warehouse? Who was the first in battle? How would you feel if you were now regulated to the rear when ready to take the war to them? Do you understand now why Adam asked the Lord to be the Warlord? Most would have thought little of the original group, the little details. How do you think they feel now riding with the Warlord in the lead group? I never had to answer verbally, I think my chuckle was enough. Tyler smiled and said welcome aboard, time to do our job, which he guaranteed me would not be boring.

We were only several minutes behind Andrew and his squad. Andrew led us at a slower pace than the people we were tracking but we were not concerned about losing them. The noose was set and being slowly tightened. Chris was constantly making adjustments to the Brotherhood commanders to ensure there was no holes they could escape in. I also found out that Chris trusted his Protectors explicitly and kept no secrets from them. Even command decisions. All Lord Protectors were privy to the Warlords commands as you never knew when one would be told to split off and connect with one of the remote chapters. CB Channels could be switched if there was ever a concern one was compromised. The benefits of having the Protectors listening outweighed the risks. This was similar in all chapters. I had been given a Protectors helmet with a receiver prior to leaving so I could hear the com traffic. I was a little confused by Chris's commands as I did not fully understand what his ultimate goal was. I would soon find out.

Andrew and his squad finally caught up to the men being followed as they had reached their destination. Our destination was a compound about twenty miles to the Northeast from the warehouse. From the initial detail being reported back, the compound looked like it was heavily fortified. The compound was about 2x's a football field long and about half as wide. There were guard towers at each of the four corners along with one in the center on all four sides. Someone had planned well.

The Warlord signaled us to increase speed and we arrived on the scene in a few minutes. You could tell immediately they knew we were out there. The towers, which were built with strength in mind, were a mixture of cement and steel. Each tower showed they had sandbags for extra protection. They would be very hard to get past. We stopped outside effective gun range to reconnoiter.

Chris took a few of the protectors and made a quick circuit of the compound. Upon his return, he said this spot was as good as any and had the group in the tucks unload his surprise. What that was, I did not find out immediately as it was done with minimal noise and under the cover of the trees. Meanwhile the chatter in the helmet heated up and I could tell they were several other groups nearby. But where or in what force, I could not tell, I was not yet familiar enough with the code words being passed back and forth to understand all the commands being given. Nor did they ever show themselves, which I found odd. The only ones visible to the enemy were us. Strange, to say the least.

Soon we saw some movement in the compound and it sounded like they were going to make some sort of activity in our direction. The Warlord did not seem too concerned and just relaxed in a lounge chair that he had brought out. In fact most of us were sitting in chairs per his directions. There were even a few large tents setup with a cot, table and chairs inside with the flaps open toward the compound to let in the air. Almost like it was done on purpose to let anyone looking inside see there was nothing there. Chris kept giving directions calmly like we had all the time in the world. Caleb and Tyler were playing horseshoes while Andrew, Teja and several others were involved in a poker game. Are you getting the drift? I always thought war was all business and no time for frivolities.

I was getting concerned and ready to say something when Chris winked at me and said to relax, all the preparations were now complete. Very quietly, he arose and walked over to me. "Eric," he said, "not all battles are about throwing yourselves at your enemy and pounding your way through his defenses. Sometimes, if lucky enough, you convince them to come to you. Now if we showed all our cards and they could see we were well prepared, they would hunker down and let us spend our lives needlessly trying to get through their fortified walls. Who knows what tricks they have up their sleeves? So better to get them to come out and be in an area of our choosing. If that does not work, then we will find a way to pound our way in. So relax. I will bet before they come out in force they will send a messenger to find out who we are and how we are setup. Then they will come in force. Especially when the messenger relays back what we want him to relay. How unprepared we look, which will correspond with what his men are seeing though the high powered glasses that are located at each of the towers. We saw them when we first got here. Just stay ready and be prepared for my signal." With that Chris calmly walked back to his chair and sat down all the time chattering into a hand held radio. But if you were watching him, you would swear he was listing to some music the way he was moving around and swinging his arms. Strange, very strange indeed.

Sure enough, Chris was right. Several men left the compound in a golf cart and headed in our direction. There were four men, three heavily armed and one dressed in a snappy suit. The three armed men looked around at us and sneered in contempt. Being we had put away our heavy weapons and only the light hand weapons were visible, I understood their reaction. It looked like we came to fight a major engagement with the wrong equipment and treating it like it was a party. I wanted to smile because that was just the impression Chris wanted them to get.

The man in the snappy suit got out with the three bodyguards flanking him and asked who was in charge. Caleb responded while rising to his full height. "What can I do for you?" Caleb asked. The man said his name was Juanito and asked why we were here. Caleb laughed and said that there was a new group in town and there was not room enough for two, so one had to leave, guess who?

Juanito while standing still, looked around a bit before saying he had not heard of any new group in the area and that they were not going anywhere. But they were willing to work out a deal, as long as the drugs at the warehouse were returned. Caleb sat down and put his feet up on a stool. Caleb put the knuckles of both hands by the side of his head and seemed to give it some serious thought.

After several moments, while Juanito paced nervously, Caleb looked up at him and replied. "Nope, they are ours now. And if you want us to go, you will cut us in for 50 percent of your operations." You could tell they had not expected anything more and were here more as a scouting expedition than trying to make peace. With that Juanito snickered, looked at Caleb, and said, "You may be big, but you are not very smart. Look around. You are way outclassed in men and arms. Do you really think you can fight all of us with this little force? We will wipe you off the face of the Earth. I recommend you pack up and go back to where you came from. Just leave our stuff when you go."

Caleb just sat back, smiled, and then spit at the feet of Juanito. With that, Juanito and the three guards got back into the golf cart and left. But not before they took a last good look around. No sooner than they were halfway back that Chris made a signal with his hand. Several standing by the tents casually walked in and closed the flaps. Chris spoke just two words into the radio loud enough for all of us to hear "get ready." We all casually strolled around getting near where we had put our heavier weapons and helmets. Over half of the Protectors quietly disappeared behind the tents.

The golf cart with its occupants disappeared into the compound. At least twenty minutes passed when the main gates opened again and several pickup trucks with machine guns mounted in the bed appeared. Each gun was staffed by several men while there were several more in the cab. Along with the trucks were an equal amount of convertibles with several men in each. The car tops were all down, and the men were heavily armed. The men in the back seats used the top of the front windshield to lean their heavy weapons on. The cars quickly lined up with the trucks in the front. They moved slowly into line and seemed to be in no hurry. Just as I thought they would start coming toward us, another dozen or so armed men came out on foot to follow behind the cars.

Still they moved very slowly in our direction. We could also see movement in the towers closest to us. Maybe they were waiting to see what we would do. That was an awful lot of men and firepower coming toward us. Chris looked at me and smiled. He had got what he wanted. I was not too worried as we were not as meek as we showed and were a force to be reckoned with. But that amount of firepower would not be suppressed without cost. But I was ready.

We found what cover we could and prepared to meet the enemy. I positioned myself behind a large rock. On my left Tyler took the other side of the rock. I could feel the excitement in the air. I was surprised on how calm I was. My breathing was controlled, my nerves steady, my mind clear, and my heart rate only slightly elevated. I looked around and only saw around half of the Protectors that came with us visible. Where were the rest? What had been in the trucks? What surprise did the Warlord have in mind? I found myself smiling and looking forward to see the shock on the faces of the men about to attack the Brotherhood. Not only were they attacking in ignorance of our true strength, but they were attacking the best the Brotherhood had. They were about to learn a lesson that others have also learned the hard way. Do not mess with the Brotherhood, definitely not a smart idea!

The enemy formation slowly came forward until they reached about several hundred yards from us. That must have been the distance they had preplanned to make the rush at us because once they hit it, they started shouting, shooting, and gunning the engines.

Most of the fire we received was wild and not much danger to us. Most but not all. I saw some ricochets that were no more than several inches from Tyler's face. As if this was what Chris was wait-

ing on, I heard him say just one word, "Now!" With that, the gates
of hell opened up. The tent flaps were flung back and a very large
machine gun with multiple barrels opened up and started spitting
out death. I later found out that was a T171 Vulcan Gatling gun.
Along with that, a M29 mortar and a 50 caliber machine gun opened
up at the same time.

Now I knew where the rest of the Protectors went. And of course
the rest of us let loose. The Vulcan hit the enemy lines like a wheat
scythe. The mortar and the 50 caliber were not ineffective but they
did not hold the impact or terror like the Vulcan did. You could follow the trail of bullets that looked like a walking hell moving toward
one of the trucks, which it ripped into pieces along with the men that
had been riding in it. Have you ever seen what a Vulcan? They spit
out very heavy slugs at an unbelievable rate that never slowed. The
weapon alone was to be feared no matter how many men you had.
But with the other machine gun and mortar? Well, let's just say I was
very glad I was not in front of them.

The enemy was being picked off very quickly. In less than a
minute, at least a quarter of the enemy were down. The rest panicked and tried to turn around. Only the fire from the compound
towers continued at us while the rest were running for their lives. But
the towers were too far away to be very effective. The Vulcan never
slowed in its trail of death. It went from one vehicle to the next, not
caring if it was a car or a person, the bullets went right through it. If it
was a person, the carnage was terrific. The tracers, every fifth round,
glowing orange like a little bit of hell, showed the path of destruction.

Meanwhile the rest of us concentrated on the armed men. They
were running back to the compound but unfortunately were also in
the way of the vehicles that were trying to go the same way. Between
us and the vehicles, over half the walking enemy were down. About a
third of both the vehicles and men finally made it back to the gates.
They created a jam and everyone was screaming.

At this time the Warlord said forcibly into his helmet
"Gentlemen, your turn now." With that, from all around the compound, Armageddon let loose. A fury of automatic gunfire opened
up all around the perimeter. It was hard not to yell out in excitement,

I felt like I would burst from pride. I saw Adam there with his chapter, I even saw Cleona was here, wearing several bandages but yelling and firing all the same.

The Vulcan now concentrated its fire on the towers closest to us, which went up in flames one by one until there was no movement or return fire coming from them. The far towers were targeted by the brotherhood groups in that area. These groups did not have any heavy weapons to match the Vulcan or mortar but they had plenty of snipers with high powered rifles. It only took a few moments before the towers were quiet. The gate was pounded by the mortar until there was no more movement on this side.

I turned to look at the Warlord and he was already a hundred yards away running to the gate with all the Protectors except me. I had been watching all the other action so closely that I had not kept aware of my own surroundings. My instructors would have been deeply disappointed in me. Nothing to do but run to catch up. As I was running I could see that the 50 cal and Vulcan had changed targets and were now concentrating on any large opening to make sure whoever was inside did not get anywhere near the openings. As for the mortar, it was concentrating its fire on a middle section of the compound and was smashing into the walls to make a large opening. Half of the men concentrated their fire on any small opening so no one peeked out while the other half started making their way to the new opening being created by the mortar.

Chris was the first to enter the newly made opening and ran through without stopping. The bravery of this man was incredible. As I was running, I was thinking obout how we had just eliminated over a dozen men, smashed a half dozen guard towers and pounded a new opening in the side of a compound. The people on that other side were going to be a little scared and peeved off. They would be waiting for anyone trying to enter. And Chris just ran in. That was either just very stupid or very brave. I would never call him stupid so he must have believed that the enemy were in too much disarray to be ready for him to come in so quickly. I could hear gunfire and increased my speed. I was not going to miss being there, I am a Lord Protector and my job and desire was to be there by his side.

I ran until my lungs and legs felt like they were going to burst. I entered with the last of the Lord Protectors and the first of the supporting Brotherhood. As we ran in, we could see there were several buildings in the compound that had been targeted by our mortar but had little effect. The buildings were well built and still standing with minor damage. The last of the opposing men were just ducking in when I arrived. All except for a few as the doors were closed on them before they could enter by those already inside when we started shooting in their direction. The few men still stuck outside tried to take cover by the cars that were strewn around the yard but were being systematically gunned down one by one. Within a few moments, the gunfire lessened to just covering fire from each side to keep the other from advancing.

The Warlord was down by the end of the corner of one building taking a look around at what was left in the compound. His helmet was off and his red eyes were clearly visible. I did not see any wounds that would require my immediate attention. He did have a small blood stain on his upper right leg but I could not tell if that was serious or not. It did not seem to be affecting his movements nor causing any discomfort. But knowing Chris's pain tolerance and on how serious a wound he could take made my diagnosis a best guess only without being able to check it out more thoroughly. I started toward him to check it out but he waved me away when he saw what I wanted. It was funny how fast I assumed total ownership of that responsibility.

I smiled and thought about how Tiffany would respond. Tiffany never forgot that night in the Sears parking lot and I think still had a major crush on Chris. Every time we talked, she would always ask about him and blushed when I asked why. I bet she was going to make me my favorite dinner and desert when I got back home just so she could pump me for every piece of information about him dealing with this event. My sis was a great cook, so this was going to be fun. If I survived today—that is, the war was not over yet.

Chris asked Roy about the group's injury status. That definitely was something I was going to have to get a handle on. It looks like I was not just responsible for Chris but for everyone around Chris. I should have figured that one out. Roy reported that due to the total surprise of the attack and the overwhelming firepower, only several were wounded but none were life threatening. You could hear the men and women talk about how complete the surprise was. Where did all the hardware and men/women come from so quickly?

It was from these snippets of conversation that I learned it was Chris who remembered that there was another chapter just several miles away that was the central depot used by the Brotherhood for refurbishing the major weapons the Brotherhood recovered from Viet Nam. This included the Vulcan, which had been found on an almost intact US plane that had been downed during the war on the outskirts of Saigon hidden under a thick dense tree canopy. Chris had contacted that chapter on the way to the warehouse prior to the first battle even taking place. Once he had been told the number of visible guards at the warehouse, he determined there may be a need for heavy firepower. As he said to Adam when he asked for them to be sent ASAP, you never know, better to be prepared than regretting and paying the price in lives later.

And Chris did not just ask for hardware, he also had requested fighters. This was before he had even finished entering the first building for recon. But as we found out, these actions potentially averted countless deaths of loved ones. Chris had not even been asked to be Warlord at that time but then again, real leaders do not need that to take the necessary actions, do they? And you wonder why we admired this man? Why we followed him? Why we loved him?

Chris pulled in Adam and several other leaders of the Brotherhood and told them his plans to finish the battle. Adam then informed Chris that a member of his chapter back at home base found out that this group were an offshoot from a cartel in Mexico. This member had been in touch with the leaders of this group who disclaimed any relationship with the group we encountered. That they had actually been at odds with them and fighting between the two groups had existed for several years. That was why this chapter had come to America. The group we were fighting had wanted to setup their own drug cartel in an uncontested area. The cartel in Mexico said whatever actions the Brotherhood decided was OK with them. Adam said once we finished with the compound, the war should be over.

Chris laughed, grabbed Adam by his shoulders, and said good-naturedly, "Is that all my friend? They have several buildings with almost a dozen men in them. What do you suggest?"

Adam, having known Chris for many years, did not take this as an insult but as a serious question whose opinion would be appreciated. You did not get to be a commander of the Brotherhood by who you knew or how much you owned, there was only one way, it was earned.

Adam suggested, they bring their snipers in, keep the enemy restricted to the buildings while they cleared a path to bring in the mortar, Vulcan and 50 cal machine gun. Then when they were all ready, pound the buildings and when softened up enough, follow up with infantry. We could take our time as we now controlled all the entrances and exits from the compound.

Chris smiled and said, "Adam, again I am reminded why you were elected commander. Sound ideas that I totally agree with. Make it happen. I also recommend that you have the Vulcan setup in a location so it can sweep any building entrances in case they make a run for it. When they know they have no chance to escape, I expect they will make a rush at us. The Vulcan will discourage that. My friend, they attacked your brave men and women, let them man the weapons to end the war. You give the final orders. Sound good to you? I make only one request. When you start the final barrage, I want everyone to yell the name of Jeff Martinez. Our friend paid the ultimate price for us and I want the last thing the enemy to hear is Jeff's name. May his name bring terror to their hearts just before they perish."

Adam smiled and patted Chris on the shoulder while passing him to prepare for the final action. I heard him mutter under his breath as he walked away. "And the man does not understand why we would follow him into the depths of hell. He never forgets that the pride and honor of the men and women in the Brotherhood is so important."

Adam stopped when he saw me looking at him. He grabbed my sleeve and said, "Chris could have let the fighters who brought the equipment and have the most know how in using them, finish it. Instead he gives my chapter the honor and privilege of ending the war when he could have let his own men, the Lord Protectors get all the glory. He lets me give out the final plan and commands even though he could have easily done the same. When the Brotherhood history talks of this war, the main person they will remember is the one who gave the final command. How rare is it for a man not to care about his own fame but to care more about the men and women who follow him. Again I say, the man wonders why we would follow him to the gates of hell." With that Adam released my sleeve so he could finish this war, to give the final commands.

Everything went as Adam said it would. The sharp shooters kept the men in the buildings until the Vulcan, mortar and machine guns were positioned and setup. The group that brought in the heavy weapons showed Adam's chapter on how to use the Vulcan as no one had seen one before let alone man one. I was not surprised to see Cleona as one of those who were manning the Vulcan. The honor to finish this was for Adam's chapter alone.

The plan was that after the men were whittled down inside each building, Adam would send in men and women to clean the buildings out. There was no rush, no one was going anywhere. We had many fighters by now from other chapters so there was nowhere they could escape to. We found two escape tunnels and a few quick charges closed them off. No one was going to escape that way again.

They tried attacking from the buildings as Chris warned but the Vulcan made short work of those that tried. From earlier conversations with Cleona I knew she had known Jeff Martinez personally and babysat his children frequently. Even with all the racket that the Vulcan made, I could hear Cleona screaming Jeff's name as she cut down them down one by one as they attempted their counter attack. I saw Juanito and another large man that I took to be the cartel's leader because of the manner of deference Jaunito gave him, try to ask for parley early on, but that was not our way.

I was allowed to join in the final assault as I had been temporarily stationed here and had been part of the initial sighting. Cleona led the assault by concentrating her fire on one of the main doors where I and a group I was not familiar with entered the first building. When we got in; we saw several bodies with one injured leaning against the far wall. This man tried to raise his weapon but was cut down by several before he got a shot off. We split up with several going upstairs and the rest of us fanning out.

We were careful while we checked every nook and cranny while at the same time fast enough to not allow them time to regroup. We fired and fired until our barrels were hot and glowed. I saw it when Juanito perished in a barrage of gunfire, I should—it was my gunfire that finished him off.

It did not take long to complete clearing all the buildings. Once the firing stopped, you could smell the acid powder smell, smell our own sweating bodies, hear the deadly quiet, see and hear the huge amount of flies but most of all, smell the stink of the dead bodies overpowering all other smells. The smell was no worse here than at the warehouse but it just did not register as much as now. Was it because then we had to prepare for war and did not have time to let the normal smells and sounds register? Who knew but the smell was something you would not forget.

And then I found out something Roy did not tell me when I accepted the position to be the Lord Protector's doctor. As I went to check on Chris, I saw that the wound on his upper right leg had bled a lot since I last saw it. I could not tell if it was serious or just a minor scratch as Chris had wrapped a bandage around his thigh on the outside of his pants. But when I went to look at it, Chris laughingly informed me that I had to follow the same procedures as Roy and turned away from me.

Roy, who was nearby, hearing the exchange starting laughing and pounding his thigh. I looked around in confusion and asked, "What procedures?" Even Caleb started laughing and the rest, well, they did not hesitate to let me know I should have asked that when offered the job. The laughter got even worse when I put my hands up in the air and said again "what procedures? Will someone tell me what the heck you are talking about? No one told me about any damn procedures?"

With that Roy, who was still laughing and having a blast at my confusion, said that Chris required all others that were injured to be treated before him. That he was adamant on that as he did not want any special treatment when it came to medical care and this procedure enforced that to utmost. Until everyone else had been taken care of, he was off limits.

I looked at Chris with astonishment, the exposure to Chris's health was compounded to a point I could not see how he had survived to this point in time. I then remembered the fight earlier and how Roy had looked at everyone prior to checking out Chris. Here I thought that was because someone had already checked on Chris. Roy though still laughing, joined me, and said it was not as bad as I let on. Everyone had their specialty and challenge; this one was now mine. And everyone knew of this procedure, except for myself, it seemed, which helped explain the quick response to the injuries before. When I mentioned this to Roy, he shook his head affirmatively and started laughing again. Roy sure was enjoying himself at my expense.

So with Roy by my side, we checked out everyone prior to getting back to Chris. Fortunately, there were only minor wounds to attend to, mostly from the individuals that cleared out the buildings. Chris's wound was only a small gash, which fortunately did not require any stitches. It was already covered in dried blood and I did not want to stop the healing by opening it up again. We were lucky that no one from the Brotherhood was killed during this last battle. Losing Jeff Martinez was bad enough, losing one of your family was one too many.

But even more important, no one would forget what happened here. That the Brotherhood was not to be messed with. If you did, you better be ready and pray, pray that the Lord Protector is not available, because if he is, you have no idea how truly deadly he is. Have no doubt, he will bring all the fury of the Brotherhood down on you like your worst nightmare. I know, to that I can attest to as I have been a part of it—that I can promise!

CHRISTMAS DINNER

It was just under five years after first meeting Chris that I was invited to a Christmas dinner at Chris's family's house. I was now considered the personal medical caretaker for Chris but between school, training and sports, it was few and far between that I was able to spend any time with Chris. Roy insisted that I finish school before assuming the role full time. Roy left no doubt that he did not want the job and it was all mine when I was ready to take it on. I was not anywhere where I needed to be but everything I had dreamed of and been working for these last few years had paid off better than I ever hoped.

Chris had invited Tiffany and me over to his parents' house for an informal Christmas dinner. Chris lived in his own house about fifteen miles away and we had been there many times but family tradition dictated that every Christmas was spent at his parents' house. We had been invited the last several years also but our own family commitments precluded us making it. Tiffany was always very disappointed but being our grandparents were not doing well physically, we could not be present during Christmas. This year, they went to visit my Uncle on the West Coast so we were now free to attend with Chris's family. I joked with Tiffany I thought that we should just stay home. I was taken by surprise how she looked at me like I had hit her and said I could do what I wanted but she was going. It was the disappointed hurt tone that made me deeply regret the joke. When I told her I was only kidding, she put her head on my shoulder while gripping my arm and told me "we haven't seen Chris in months due to all our commitments. It will be nice to see him again." It was the wishful tone that Tiffany used made me wonder was going on between the two.

So to Chris's parents' house we went. It was a tradition Chris's mother insisted on and one that the whole family enjoyed tremendously. Tiffany came alone while I brought my current girlfriend, Amber whom I met the year before. Amber was a brilliant premed student in her own right and expected to graduate around the same time I did. I had hopes that we would continue our relationship after college and make it more permanent sometime in the near future. Ok, let's be honest here, I was madly in love with her. And it was not just because she was very beautiful as well as being super smart, although that didn't hurt any. Amber, Caucasian with a German heritage, measured 5 feet 8 inches in height and had long flowing golden tresses that went halfway down her back. Her figure was slim and toned from a steady regimen of running and gym workouts with a good size bust. But the best feature had to be she had the most devilish pair of green eyes you could imagine. They twinkled when she spoke and lit up any room she was in. You should see those eyes—when she was playing a joke or laughing, they sparkled so brightly. And her voice, it was so sweet and charming. Every time I heard it my heart would start to race. Oh, how I could languish for hours just listening to her tell me of her day and her plans for the future. As I walked toward Chris's front door I smiled remembering that many of Ambers future plans included me, in fact most of them did.

Tiffany, who could have brought any of a dozen men who were constantly asking her for a date, was even more beautiful than Amber. I know she is my sister and I may be prejudiced just a little bit, but Tiffany is the most beautiful woman I have ever seen, be it in life or print. Tiffany, now having turned twenty, had matured into a woman of incredible beauty. Her soft thick dark black hair reached even farther down her back than Ambers. It framed her body that was voluptuous while still petite. When Tiffany walked, her hair flowed around her like it was alive and moving with her. Tiffany was 5 feet 3 inches and weighed just over 110 pounds. Her body was well toned and though not too muscular was defined beautifully. Tiffany was not a member of the Brotherhood but did train with us often so her body resembled a sculpture of perfection. Her eyes were a deep blue topaz color that had a slight oblong shape that enhanced their mysterious looking effect. You could, and I have many times, gotten lost in them because of their clarity. Her olive skin glowed and was enhanced by her chest, which definitely did not need any man-made assistance. It was the whole package that just took your breath away. Even mom, who was beautiful in her own right, said Tiffany outshone anyone she knew.

But the best part of Tiffany was not her beauty but her compassion and energy. Tiffany had started going to college, full scholarship mind you, at Rutgers University for nursing. Tiffany was planning on going for her Doctorate at night while working at the local hospital near home. Her plans were all laid and clear in her mind of what her life was going to be like. Tiffany wanted to be able to help women that have been victims of violence. She had not forgotten how she felt after her ordeal and it was only through regular phone calls and constant visits by Chris to say hi, was she able to get through it all so well. Thinking on it, maybe Tiffany had more than a crush on Chris. Because since that night, I have never seen Tiffany date even though countless men have tried. Even several of my close friends have tried only to be politely turned down. No explanation but almost like her heart was already taken. Well, tonight should then be very interesting, to say the least, because I have heard rumors of Chris having a girlfriend but have never met her. If she was here, I am not sure how Tiffany would react.

So on a Christmas evening, with a light sprinkling of snow, I walked up to Chris's parents door with Amber on one arm and Tiffany on the other. How could it be any better? When I knocked, the door was opened by a dignified middle aged man in his midfifties, whom I had met many times before. Michael Wilson, Chris's dad attended a lot of the training sessions, not to participate, but to watch. Mr. Wilson was there in support of his son and I believe took great pride in seeing the positive impact Chris had had on others. At Mr. Wilson's side was a small but powerful-looking black-and-white dog, a miniature Beagle named Snoopy, whom I and all

119

knew. Snoopy was present whenever Chris showed up at our training classes.

From what I heard, Chris and Snoopy were inseparable. Chris does not take Snoopy with him when he does his night roaming after an earlier incident where he almost lost Snoopy. Snoopy was knifed very seriously trying to protect Chris. Since then, Chris leaves Snoopy at his home or his parents' house. More often here by express order from Ava, who had come to love the dog like he was her own. It was common knowledge that when Mrs. Wilson heard about Snoopy, she started taking shots to help boost her tolerance for Dog dander. Which was not surprising, knowing how close the family was. So here Snoopy stood.

Mr. Wilson bent at the waist while swinging his left arm underneath his chest and said he was honored to meet two such lovely women. Mr. Wilson straightened up and reached out his hand to Tiffany by her hand. "Tiffany, I have heard from Chris many times of your great beauty but up until now, I always thought he exaggerated. Until now I have not had the pleasure of seeing you except when you are in training, at the hospital, and rarely at dinner. But never when you are all decked like you are now. You impressed me then, but today, well, let's just say you are a vision of beauty. Please excuse my ignorance as now I must join my son's opinion. It is my honor to welcome you into our home." Wow, what a welcome. I could tell Tiffany was taken in by his charm.

Mark then said to all, "Please call me Mark. Mr. Wilson is so old sounding, and I am not ready to acknowledge I am that old." Mark then turned to Amber and said he must have a talk with his son as Chris did not tell him that there were going to be two beautiful women coming to dinner. With that Mr. Wilson poked me in the ribs and asked me, "Is she with you, young man? If not, I will have to ask Mrs. Wilson to place her next to me." As I sputtered in response, Amber laughed while hugging my arm close and said, "I am. And I am sure Mrs. Wilson will make sure you are placed where she can keep a close eye on you." With that, Mark laughed and looked at me with humor in his eyes while saying, "Eric, I like this young lady, she is quick and gets my humor. Tonight should be fun."

With that, Mark, leading Tiffany by her hand on his arm and with us following, was led into the foyer, where we gave our jackets to George, who hung them up in the closet. George, of course, we knew very well. I could hear from the loud voices, that we had been preceded by Caleb and his fiancée, Sophia, along with Tyler and Elijah. That was not surprising as it seemed most conversations' volume had to be higher than normal to compensate for the booming voice of Caleb.

George led us into the living room, where everyone was standing around with a drink. Mark asked us what we would like to drink. Sophia looked to be having eggnog, Caleb had some ale, while Tyler and Elijah each had a Pabst beer. Amber and I decided to stick with iced tea, while Tiffany was having a pink lemonade. Mark took our order and left to get our drinks but not before supplying us with drink coasters and napkins. The house was a large five-bedroom-split level common in that area. The furnishings were early American and very well-kept. Everything was polished without a mark showing on any of the wooden tables. I did not see any signs of dust that seems to be a consistent problem in every other house I have been in, so I was quietly impressed.

I did not see Chris but could hear his voice coming from the kitchen. Chris walked in just as I was being introduced to Mrs. Wilson with some ruffle potato chips and onion dip in a large bowl. I noticed that he stopped when he first came in and seemed to be looking for someone. When he saw Tiffany, his eyes opened up, and he smiled while giving her a small wave. When I looked at Tiffany, she had her head lowered a little like she was a bit embarrassed while at the same time twirling her hair with her two right fingers. I was a little surprised as I know she only does this when she was happily excited like when she graduated high school. Was there more going on here than I knew? But I had no time to ponder that without being disrespectful to Mrs. Wilson.

Ava, as she liked to be called, was a woman in her early fifties that had aged very well. Ava had brown hair with a wide jovial face that had an impish grin on her face at all times. And her energy! Now I knew where the Wilsons got all their energy and good nature from.

Ava was in constant motion, making sure that everyone's drinks were filled while chatting with everyone like she had known them all her life. There is always one individual at a good party who keeps you involved and feeling like you are special—that was definitely Ava.

After we had received our drinks from Mark, Amber and I moved over to talk with Caleb and Sophia. Sophia was dressed in a very nice cream-colored pants suit that accentuated her svelte figure and tightly curled hair that was elegantly pulled up on top of her head. Sophia was a beautiful young lady that was the exact opposite of Caleb. Where Caleb was a huge block of solid muscle, Sophia was a petite woman with soft, plush curves. But there was no mistaking the love these two had for each other regardless of the size difference. Sophia kept her hand and arm entwined in Caleb's lower right arm while her head rested on his upper arm. It was obvious to all that this was the normal position that each assumed and loved. Every now and then, as if by reflex more than thought, Caleb would reach over with his left hand to gently caress Sophia's cheek.

Tiffany followed us over and after saying hello, asked if she could speak to Caleb privately and pulled Caleb off to the side. They talked in low volumes and surprisingly, I could not make out what Caleb was saying. But I saw Tiffany start and wring her hands as if in anguish. Tiffany then looked over at Chris who was helping his mother and father as they put out additional snack trays for their guests. I could see the worry in her eyes, which were misting up in tears.

I was getting a little concerned and was about to make my way over when I saw Caleb look at me and shake his head signaling no. Caleb gently grabbed Tiffany and directed her toward Chris. I could see she was shaking and about to start crying. Her shoulders were shaking with the effort trying not to. Chris saw her anxiety and quickly took her off to the side, away from the general area. You could see Chris was getting anxious and very concerned himself with why Tiffany was upset.

All conversation in the room was muted as everyone was aware something was happening. I saw Sophia grab Caleb and gesture to him on what did he do. Caleb whispered into her ear while sporting a great big grin. Sophia, after hearing what he said, literally punched

122

him in his arm twice and these were definitely not love taps. Anybody would have surely felt it but I am sure it was just a butterfly tap to Caleb. After the punches though, I saw Sophia grin and bury her mouth in Caleb's arm so she would not laugh aloud.

Now I was really confused. What the heck was going on? I looked at Tiffany again and I saw that Chris was reaching for a chain around his neck. I could not see what he pulled out as both Tiffany and Chris turned and faced the wall away from all prying eyes. I looked over at Amber and could tell she was just as puzzled as I was. Amber may have been my girlfriend, but she had also become quite close with Tiffany, so much so that they called each other sisters and did many things together without me. So Amber was just as conflicted as I was by what was happening.

Suddenly, I heard Tiffany gasp and put her hands to her face. She looked sideways toward Chris just prior to wrapping her arms around his neck and planting a long passionate kiss on his lips. You could see Chris was surprised but definitely not adverse to what was happening. Chris grabbed Tiffany by her waist and lifted her in a bear hug while returning her kiss with equal fervor.

What the heck just happened? Caleb's laughter rang out along with Sophia's. Mr. and Mrs. Wilson both were hugging each other and chuckling as was George. They were all privy to something Amber and I were not. Even Tyler and Elijah must have known as they were high fiving each other. I went over to them and asked what was going on. Smiling, they looked at me and said it was something I should hear from Tiffany. That they could not do it justice nor would they want to take away her moment.

To say this was perplexing to me is an understatement. I looked at Amber and just shrugged. But it was obvious that whatever was happening between Tiffany and Chris, Tiffany was deeply happy. Tiffany now had her head buried in Chris's neck and had her arms wrapped tightly around his waist. Chris's one hand was buried in Tiffany's hair behind her head where he would raise her head every now and then to give her a long slow kiss. You could hear Tiffany sniffing and if not for the smile of happiness on her face, I would have been concerned.

George pulled me and Amber into the kitchen to get drink refreshments while everyone else went to talk and laugh with Tiffany and Chris. I almost told George that I needed to talk with Tiffany but I did not want to insult my guests so went with him without saying a word. Amber looked at me and chuckled. Just before I left, I saw Ava and Mark hugging Tiffany who returned the gesture with great enthusiasm. It seemed like everyone was aware of what was going on but me and Amber. Although I am not sure about Amber, she was smiling like she had an idea of what was happening.

Things went on like this for the next twenty minutes at which time Ava notified everyone to get ready as dinner would be ready in ten minutes. While I made my way to the rest room to get washed up, Amber made her way over to Tiffany while Chris and George went to help Ava set out dinner. Sophia joined the two women and all three huddled in the corner. I returned just in time to see Amber exclaim in joy and hug Tiffany. Sophia meanwhile was examining something on Tiffany's hand.

I was pulled away from my observation by Caleb who started asking how my training was going as we made our way to the dining room. Everyone sat down at the large dining room table with Tiffany flanked by Ava on her right and Chris on her left. Chris was flanked on his left by George with Snoopy in the middle of the two of them at their feet. It was not hard to see the affection that George and Chris had for each other. Nor their familiarity with each other's movements. When they did even simple things like passing a dish, they did so without even looking up from what they were doing. They just knew when and where the other would hand off at. I saw Chris do several complicated handshakes with George that had Tiffany laughing with pleasure at them.

And Snoopy was not left out. Chris, along with George, was constantly feeding him scraps off the table. Snoopy just sat with his tail wagging his pleasure at being so spoiled. And Ava joined in by slipping Snoopy a small bowl with some cut up turkey. Mark watched all this with a grin on his face and you knew that he would have joined in if he could. I knew that Chris and family were very close and it was so nice to see how much. And then surprise, Snoopy got up and walked over to Tiffany and put his head on her lap like he had done that many times. I looked at Tiffany who was scratching Snoopy's head while slipping him a piece of ham. When she saw me looking at her with surprise, she mouthed "he's my buddy." And that was where Snoopy stayed. I guess it must be Tiffany's long fingernails being so much longer than a man's make her scratching much more preferable. I know because I feel the same way when Amber scratches my head when I put it on her lap while watching TV.

We enjoyed a wonderful traditional Christmas dinner of turkey, ham, mashed potatoes, gravy, homemade cranberry sauce, corn, yams, and green beans. Ava had a right to be proud of her cooking because it was better than anything I ever had at any restaurant. Caleb, true to his size, had more than one huge helping. All during dinner it was obvious something more had happened between Chris and Tiffany than I was aware of due to the frequent whispers between Tiffany and Ava with Chris blushing frequently. After dinner, we all sat around the fireplace to enjoy some sumptuous almond butter cutouts with a hot cup of cocoa or coffee. I saw that Chris and Tiffany were sitting together with their arms around each other and both seemed to be oblivious of anyone else in the room. Yep, based on the look on Tiffany's face, she definitely had more than a crush on Chris and he on her. The ride home should be very interesting.

Several hours later we thanked our hosts, said goodbye to the others and made our way home. Tiffany sat in the front seat next to Amber who was snuggled up to my right side with a great big grin on her face. I started to ask Tiffany what happened when Amber put her hand on my lips and quietly whispered later. I saw Tiffany was holding her left hand tightly with her right hand like she had something she was afraid of losing. Something of great importance. Tiffany was staring out the window at the little snowflakes still coming down like she was in a world of her own with a smile on her face that was so contagious that I could feel myself also smiling.

Something happened back there between Tiffany and Chris and I was bursting with curiosity to know but knew now was not the time to bother her. I was going to take Amber home where she informed me that she was going to be staying at my house that night as Tiffany had asked her to stay over. I smiled at Amber who poked me in the ribs and looked at me so seductively that I secretly thanked Chris for whatever tonight was going to bring me.

We arrived home in short order and while I parked the car, Amber and Tiffany went inside. I came in to see mom hugging Tiffany and stroking her hair while wearing the biggest smile I have seen her wear in a long time. I looked over at my father on the couch who chuckled at me with a big grin on his face and shrugged. Amber was standing nearby watching mom and Tiffany.

Without thinking, I said out loud I sure wished somebody would let me in on the secret. Mom looked at me, shook her head, walked up to me and brushed my cheek like she used to when I was a child having a temper tantrum because no one was paying any attention to me.

Mom said, "Eric, my son, you are one of the most intelligent persons I know. At the same time, you sometimes surprise me by being so clueless of what is so obvious and sitting right there in front of you the whole time. Do not forget to pay attention to the little things as they may be more important than anything else." Then she grabbed dad and they made their way to their room hugging each other like long lost lovers. I must have looked startled as Amber looked at me, laughed and said it was time Tiffany and I talked. She would be in my room.

Tiffany, when we were alone, came up to hug me with the most wonderful expression on her face and said three simple words. "He loves me." Tiffany then fiercely threw her arms around my neck said, "Oh, Eric, he loves me. Chris truly loves me. He asked me to marry him. Chris said he did not want to be away from me anymore." Tiffany was crying with happiness while she told me this. The tears were flowing freely.

Tiffany then went on to explain what I had not known. That Tiffany and Chris had been seeing each other steadily for the last several years. I thought it was very limited in like lunches every now and then. But it had been much more serious. Chris, shortly after he rescued us, when asked by Tiffany for a date, refused. But not for the normal reasons. Chris did not want Tiffany to want a date with him because she was infatuated with Chris because of what had occurred but because she really had feelings for him. And when she asked how she could prove her love for him, Chris had said time and patience. When she gave enough time for her appreciation to wane and see Chris for he really is, not for what he did for her. Then, if she still wanted something serious, then he would be honored. So it was only after six months did they actually go on a real date.

After several years of dating, it was Tiffany who asked for more. Tiffany told Chris she was in love with him and did not want to wait any longer. That she was afraid she would lose him to someone else. Surely Chris would find someone else by that time with all the woman that he meets, like Teja. Chris had gently put his hand over hers, looked her squarely in the eyes, and said, "Tiffany, that is not something for you to ever fear about. I fell in love with you the moment I met you. I cannot explain why except to say it has only grown stronger every time we have been together and I have been honored with your presence. I have never felt like this in my entire life. All I know that my life without you would be very lonely indeed. That my whole being cries out for you to be in my arms so very much. I want to taste your lips and feel your breath upon my neck. I want nothing more than to hold you in my arms right now and say yes to whatever you want. So do not worry about me, I will be waiting for your decision. I do this for you, not me, so you are sure, that you have had a chance to meet others and decide if I am the right one for you. I know it is a lot to ask but you must know for sure. I hope you understand."

Tiffany was elated to hear of his love but conflicted at the same time because any time away from Chris was going to be difficult. Tiffany did not want to wait. Especially with the great love she felt in her heart for this man. There was no doubt in her mind. Tiffany looked at me as she said this and I cannot believe I had never seen it before. Mom was right. The longing I saw now in her eyes had been so evident in her eyes so many times before when she spoke of Chris and I had just taken that as a schoolgirl crush, even after Tiffany had grown into full womanhood. How could I have been so blind?

Tiffany went on to explain that her love for Chris had never diminished but had grown every time she met or talked with him. Frequently, in the very beginning, Tiffany and Chris would meet for lunch and hold hands. Nothing more, nothing less. They would speak of what happened in their lives with Tiffany doing most of the talking. Chris seemed more enthralled with listening and asking questions more than speaking of his own activities. Tiffany was sorry every time lunch was over and anxious for the next meeting. At times, she felt like she was going to faint when he put her hand in his. Tiffany had met plenty of men over the past several years but none, even though they were good men, never held her interest like Chris did. Chris was the only man she was ever romantically interested in.

It was then Tiffany explained what happened tonight. Tiffany was ready to ask Chris for more, the waiting period was over for her, enough time had passed. So tonight she would find out if Chris still loved her or is he had found someone else. Tiffany and Chris had been separated for months due to each other's personal commitments that she was concerned that he might have met someone else. Her heart had felt so heavy with dread when they had arrived at the Wilson house.

Tiffany decided to see if she could get a hint from Caleb, him being Chris's best friend and all. Had Chris found someone else? It was then that Tiffany looked at me very intently and said, "Caleb is one awful man, and you must promise me that you will help me get even with him someday. Oh, he has such an evil, mean streak in him."

With that she laughed and said Caleb when asked, said, "Tiffany, I am so sorry, but yes, Chris has fallen in love with a woman awhile back. I thought you knew that. Not sure when but he keeps a locket with her picture hung around his neck at all times. You should ask Chris to show it to you. She is a wonderful young lady, I know you will approve and like her."

With that Tiffany, with a broken heart and unable to keep the sorrow out of her voice or eyes, went to ask Chris to see this locket. Tiffany did not know of any picture Chris could have of her so it could not be her in that locket. Tiffany, because of how much she loved this man and even though it was ripping her heart apart, was going to congratulate him on finding his true love. But even so, she had to see who this woman was.

Chris was surprised at the request as he did not know anyone else knew of the locket as he always kept it under his shirt but due to the pain he saw in Tiffany eyes, pulled it out and showed her what lay inside. Tiffany then grabbed my hands and gripped them so tightly that I felt sure that I was going to have some serious fingernail marks on them in the morning.

Tiffany went on. When Chris had opened the locket, there was a picture of Tiffany from several years ago in it. Tiffany was shocked and looked at Chris who simply said, "My love for you has never diminished only grown. There is only one woman for me and I hope with all my heart that you feel the same. I do not know what life will bring me but with you by my side, I know I can bear it all."

Tiffany told me that without Chris quickly grabbing her, she would have fallen on the floor in shock. Tiffany then pulled me into a hug and whispered into my ears. "I kissed him there in front of his parents. Oh, Eric, how embarrassing now that I think of it. But I could not help myself, not after all this time. And Eric, the kiss was so wonderful that I did not care who was in the room. I wanted to do it again and again. I never knew that such a feeling existed. My love at the moment was so intense that I lost any awareness of any others being present. I wanted that kiss to last forever. More especially so since I could tell that Chris felt the same way. The man I loved also loved me just as intensely. And Eric, that was not the last surprise. The picture in the locket was from an extra Polaroid picture taken the month after we were rescued. It was from when we first signed up at the Brotherhood local chapter, and they took the photos for our badges for admittance to the gym. I thought they had thrown the extra picture out. Seems Chris knew they would take two as a matter of practice and had asked for the spare one. Who was going to deny Chris? The next surprise was when Chris removed that picture to reveal that the locket had a deep depression. The first thing I saw was were several strands of black hair. Eric, it was my hair. Chris told me that they were strands that had stuck to his hand that night so long ago when he had held me close to keep me calm. Chris told me he knew then that he had met the woman he was going to be with for the rest of life, if she would have him. The other item in the locket was a ring. An engagement ring, for ME!"

With that Tiffany raised her left hand and showed me what she had been holding onto so tightly earlier since we left the Wilson house. It was a solid gold delicately designed looking ring with an intricate scrolling that spiraled around the entire ring. There were at least a dozen small diamond chips surrounding a large Marquise that had to be at least 2 carats in size. The clarity and brilliance of the diamonds were of such a high quality that it was evident even to someone as I who had no skill at such things. The ring was breathtakingly beautiful. Tiffany held it up and said that the scrolling, if you looked closely enough, were the names Chris and Tiffany intertwined with each other. When I looked, I could not find any starting place or ending for the scrollwork. I could not imagine the amount of labor or skill it took to make that happen. I was unable to find a flaw in it. Per Tiffany, that was how Chris designed it. I was surprised to hear from Tiffany that Chris had made the ring himself.

Chris, years ago, had taken a good part of his savings, to buy all the materials from a trusted friend at cost. Then he had this friend, who was a jeweler, show him the tricks of the trade to make the ring. It took over a year before it was finally completed. Chris made the locket first to sharpen his skills and then finally the ring. The jeweler was impressed enough that he offered to purchase both items himself at a much higher price than what Chris had paid for the materials due to the items being of such high quality. In fact, the jeweler remarked that he had never seen a ring so painstakingly made with such an intricate scroll work before. Chris had told the jeweler, the ring was not his to sell. A very special young lady owned the ring and its container locket. Chris was just holding them for her. Tiffany had learned all this from Caleb later that evening. After she had hugged him for being so "mean."

Well, to say I was surprised but happy for Tiffany would be an understatement. It was quite obvious that Tiffany was in love and very happy. Tiffany then told me that everyone in the Lord Protectors knew. All—that is, except for me, but that was only because of my being her brother. No one wanted to be the one that leaked it to Tiffany.

The Lord Protectors had found out over a year ago when Chris was seriously injured during a fight. While they were treating him, he was clutching the pendant tightly to his chest even though he was unconscious. They did not know what he was clutching so they had pried it loose from his fingers to check it out. Chris must have grasped it just before he lost consciousness. Prying it loose was not as easy as it may sound. Chris did not want to let it go and Chris's strength was legendary. But they finally did and when they opened the pendant, they understood exactly what it was and why he carried it. They knew Chris liked Tiffany from the times they had seen them dating but they had not realized to what depth those feelings were until they had opened the locket. And of course Chris becoming very restless and agitated until they replaced the locket in his hand also helped them understand to what degree these feelings went. It was obvious that the locket and whom it represented were very special to him, even when not awake.

The Lord Protectors never mentioned anything of this knowledge to Chris but did take precautions to make sure there was always one or two of the Lord Protectors watching over Tiffany from then on. Tiffany had been under the Lord Protectors protection for a year without her knowing. This meant that I just found out she was also under my protection. How appropriately funny it is, that two of the people I care most about and would do anything for, are now under my personal protection.

It was with great affection that I congratulated my sister and gave her my deepest wishes for a long and happy life together. But then I remembered Mom and Dad, that they seemed to have been aware of this event before we had even come home. Tiffany laughed and said Dad had been aware for the past year, Mom from the beginning. Tiffany and I could not keep the secret of that terrible event from our parents forever and once they found out, had requested to meet Chris to say thanks. Through the years, they have met Chris several times at local functions so he was not unfamiliar to them. In fact, they thought he was a perfect gentleman and liked him a lot.

Chris had approached them over a year ago and told them he intended to ask Tiffany to marry him at some future date. Chris wanted to have their approval before asking. They let Chris know they would be honored to have him as a son-in-law but it was totally up to Tiffany to make that kind of decision. They would abide by whatever she decided. Of course, mom had told Tiffany earlier that night, they already knew what that decision would be as Tiffany could not hide the feelings she had for Chris. So tonight's only surprise was the timing of the question, not Tiffany's decision.

THE ROOM

It was no surprise that in the several weeks following, Tiffany moved most of her belongings over to Chris's house. I was only too glad to help. After the first week, Tiffany said she and Chris were going to take a trip to Vegas to relax and wanted to know if I would go. They would really like it if I could. I could hear a pleading note in my sister's voice, but unfortunately, I had an exam on Monday that I had to study for over the weekend. It was a big part of my quarterly mark, and I did not have the time to take a trip. I explained my problem and my regrets. I could tell Tiffany was greatly disappointed but she said she understood. Several times I think she was going to say something else but she just gave me a tight hug and said she would miss me greatly. I could not go but I did hear that both mine and Chris's parents along with George planned to go. And of course most of the protectors. At least Tiffany would have plenty of good company.

We stayed in touch daily and her happiness, if that was possible, increased. So it was with great surprise that after a few months, Tiffany called me, in a very serious tone, to ask me to come over as she needed my assistance. The tone did not bode well, so I let her know I was available now if that worked for her. It was, and within an hour, I was being let in the door to Chris's, and now hers, house. As we walked through the entranceway, Snoopy came up to check me out and be petted. I could see the furniture was mostly early American, similar in style to that in Chris's parents' house, with a few French antique pieces mixed in, of which I had seen before. French antiques are Tiffany's favorites and I correctly guessed they were her contributions.

I asked Tiffany if she was OK, if everything between her and Chris were working out. Tiffany hugged me and said it was like living in a fantastic dream that she never wanted to wake up from. Being with Chris was even more wonderful that she thought possible. Chris was romantic, thoughtful, caring, attentive and so very loving. With that last word, I got a wicked smile from Tiffany that I have rarely seen and brought a smile to my own face.

Tiffany suggested a cup of tea, which I readily agreed upon. Tiffany knows how to make a special tea combination made up of different types of tea that I love and could never quite figure out how to make myself. She had shown me multiple times how to make it, but I always screwed up the measurements somehow. It was made up with a mixture of mostly green tea but also had a little oolong tea and rooibos tea.

As we made our way to the kitchen. I looked around and asked what it was it like living with Chris. That I had noticed a few of her pieces in the hallway, and was that what she needed help with? Or did it have anything to do with Chris himself? Tiffany looked at me with those wonderful topaz eyes of her and said, "Tea first, my brother, let's get some tea first. It is so good to see you. I miss you so. Not enough to go home, but I sure do miss you so." I knew exactly what she meant. We were close and had been together since we were born. Home just didn't seem the same without her.

Tiffany prepared the tea while I sat at the kitchen table. Tiffany also refreshed Snoopy's water bowl. Snoopy, who had followed us in, stood there with his tail wagging, and panting while looking at Tiffany. Tiffany smiled and opened the cabinet next to the sink where she pulled out a dog treat. As she gave this to Snoopy, Tiffany chuckled while scratching behind his ears and whispered, "Oh, you sure know how to play me, don't you? You are just like Chris. And yes, I love you too." Tiffany said the last just before she gave Snoopy a great big hug.

I knew that it was always best to let Tiffany move at her own speed and work into what she required assistance with. A little while later, Tiffany with her tea nestled in her hands, told me that she had full run of the house. That's the moment she walked in the house, she found Chris's checkbook and finances set out on the table for her. She was informed to go to the bank at her earliest convenience as they were waiting on her so she could be added to the house deed and checking account. Tiffany was taken aback by Chris's generosity whereupon was told that he had waited years for this moment and if he was willing to spend his life with her, objects were nothing in comparison, so it was a very easy decision to make.

Tiffany sighed and sipped her tea while telling me of her trip to the bank at the end of that week. Chris was going to go with her but had been called into work as the mainframe had taken a power hit, and they needed assistance in getting all the CICS applications back online. Some databases had been corrupted when it had lost power so suddenly. Oh, in case I never mentioned it, Chris was a CICS programmer with Sears Roebuck and Co. Quite a good programmer from what I hear even though he had never finished college.

But anyway, when Tiffany went to the bank and let them know who she was, the manager came out to meet her. He shook her hand and told her he had been waiting to meet her for the past year. It seems that when Chris had made arrangements to get a loan to purchase a house, this manager was the mortgage officer at the time and had handled the transaction. He was told by Chris that he needed to purchase a house so he could make it ready for the woman he was going to marry. When the manager had asked Chris who that was, he said that it was Tiffany Davis but that he had not asked her yet. That it was not the appropriate time for that but he had hopes that she would accept when he did.

The manager, who had known Chris personally for several years and was aware somewhat of the Brotherhood, thought very highly of him and that he must have had a good reason for waiting. It was not his business to ask why, but whoever this Tiffany was, she was a very lucky woman indeed. Now that he had the opportunity to meet Tiffany in person, he told her Chris was a very lucky man. Tiffany asked when this occurred and was informed it was shortly after the first night Tiffany met Chris several years ago. The manager, then just an account manager, worked with Chris on a financial plan to work toward buying a house. That Chris said he had met the woman of his dreams, but it was only when he took out the house loan did he identify who that woman was. Tiffany was floored by this revelation. It only confirmed everything that Chris had been telling her.

Her mind was in a whirlwind of emotions to know that this man had truly loved her all this time. In fact, as Tiffany was talking with the manager, the word got around who she was. Most of the female staff and even some of the men then came around to meet her. It seemed they all knew about Chris's secret love and they all wanted to meet the lucky woman. They all thought very highly of Chris. Chris was always pleasant to deal with and even came in every now and then with homemade cookies, Ava's of course, for everyone. And being so handsome and buff did not hurt either, from the ladies' standpoint anyway.

Tiffany ended up being at the bank most of the day. It only took several minutes to sign all the papers, but the girls wanted to know the whole story of how they met and what was it like being with Chris. To say most of the younger women, if not all, were infatuated with Chris would be an understatement. Even a few of the older women were. Tiffany confided in me she now understood why Chris wanted her to wait a few years for her to make up her mind. If this was what Chris had experienced in his daily life, how could he be sure of anything when you rescued someone? Tiffany understood the reasons but still wished it could have been a lot shorter as she believes she missed some very exciting years. When she told me this she blushed and when I finally figured out why, I did too.

I then asked again, what was it like living with Chris? Tiffany dreamily talked about her life and how much it had changed since she came to live here. I was not sure, but at times, it seemed she forgot I was here and was just talking to herself. Tiffany said that after the first night she was here, she found a rose petal on her pillow. Just one petal. When she picked it up and was looking at it, Chris had come up behind her and gave her a great big hug. Tiffany held the petal up and asked if there was anything special about it. Chris told her that he had been told by his mother that a woman was like an onion. That you had to peel off several layers to get to know the person underneath. Each layer was different and exciting. Well,

Chris thought Tiffany was more like a rose, that each petal removed just showed more of the beautiful person hidden inside. Each one more beautiful and fragrant than the last. So hence the petal. And there had been one more petal each night he was at home since then. Tiffany had never been able to find where Chris hid the roses, but she loved the thoughtfulness of the gesture.

Tiffany spoke a bit on how Chris helped out in all areas of the house. Cleaning carpets, clothes, dishes and so on. And of course there was Snoopy. Snoopy stayed in the master bedroom with them. Tiffany had been concerned that Snoopy would come to resent her after her arrival but it was soon evident he was happy with the situation. Tiffany believed that was because Tiffany was around more than Chris and gave Snoopy another person to play with and spoil him. Tiffany laughed when she said this.

So Chris was great around the house, all except for cooking. Seems Chris never took much time to learn how to cook as, well, he did not have much time. Hot dogs, pizzas, and hoagies seemed to be the norm before she arrived. Philly cheese steaks with lots of caramelized onions being his favorite. Well, Tiffany, loving to cook and having someone special to cook for, let her talents lose. Every night was something special to her and she made the most of it. Spadini (Italian dish, chicken wrapped with cheese), champagne chicken breasts, and Fontina pork chop, to mention a few. And of course, she had to learn how to make the Philly cheese steak. Tiffany even went to Pat's and Gino's in Philly to see how they prepared it.

Chris usually left late at night not to arrive back until early morning. Going out, doing the thing that he would do. Tiffany worried about him while he was gone but understood the reason. Tiffany would never deprive someone of the same thing she had benefitted from, Chris's protection. But that did not lessen her worry for him. Many times he came home injured, but thankfully, it was nothing serious, so far anyway. Each time, Tiffany, in schooling to be a nurse after all, would bathe and bind his wounds while asking about Eric. Eric was with Chris most of those times but did not worry about the minor wounds as Chris was always anxious to get home. And with Tiffany there, Chris would get excellent care.

Then Tiffany's eyes and tone lowered and you could tell that I was far from her mind. She made one short statement that Chris was all man and hugged herself while blushing like a schoolgirl. Repeated once more "Oh yeah, all man." Then her eyes rose to mine and her blush became a deep red as she remembered where she was and who was in the room with her. With that, Tiffany giggled and reached over to put her hand on my arm.

The tea now being gone, Tiffany took me on a tour of the house. As we were walking through the den, which was almost all early American, I asked if she planned to make any changes here. Tiffany wrapped my arm in hers and rested her head on my shoulder. Tiffany said that at first she was going to but after the first evening that Chris left, she snuggled up into the big warm oversized leather chair that he had just left. She could still feel his warmth and smell his scent in the air. She had grabbed a blanket, snuggled and snoozed there until his return. Snug in the warmth and love that Chris seemed to radiate. Each furniture piece seemed like it was a piece of him and she was reluctant to let one go. She planned to add some of her furniture where they fit, more like a couple together, a piece of him here and piece of her there.

The curtains now, they were all going. Chris had no talent there. None fit the furniture. Ava was by frequently, being so close, and they had become great friends. They both made plans on how Tiffany could spruce up the place and make it more woman friendly without making it too feminine. One thing I could tell during the tour, the house was immaculate and knowing Tiffany, Chris's cleanliness. which matched Tiffany's, only made him more special in her eyes. Especially so with a dog in the house.

One thing that really stood out was the pair of axes hanging on the wall over the fireplace. They were all metal, except for the handles, and intricately carved being shaped almost like a half moon with a spike on the backside. The half-moons were not a solid piece but more like a wing shape where the center part of the blades near the shaft were narrow and then spread out into a half moon until it rounded back on itself. Each blade was delicately carved and polished to a high silver shine. The top had a sharp round spike with another square spike on the backside. The edges of the half-moons were lined with what looked like small diamonds. The handles were about a foot and a half in length covered in thick leather. The detail was exquisite and unlike anything I had ever seen before. The axes glittered brightly from the light being reflected from a spotlight in the ceiling that was directed toward them. If these axes were real, I could not imagine how valuable they were. I looked closely and saw a small stamp pressed into the metal on the backside that read carbon and stainless steel. I was about to comment and ask Tiffany if they real when she pulled on my arm to direct me elsewhere. I figured we could come back to them at a later date. They had to be ornamental only as they must have weighed twelve to fifteen pounds each. No way you could use them for any length of time. Just too heavy to use except for maybe for someone like Caleb.

Tiffany showed me all the rooms upstairs and then took me downstairs to the basement. We were looking over the furnished basement when I finally asked her what the help she needed from me was. Tiffany said in a moment when she took me to a desk in the far right corner. It was a heavy carved wooden roll top desk that showed a lot of use. She slowly ran her hand across the top as if it held a pleasant memory. Snoopy who had followed us down, sniffed the desk and chair. Then he laid down next to it like he did that regularly.

I was then informed that one morning she had smelled coffee brewing and when she came downstairs, she found Chris at the desk. And while most folks were probably still sleeping, Chris was down here writing to parents and children that had been impacted by Chris in some way. Most were thanking him for his help while some were just to say Hi with a few others who were sick. Seems Chris had a fan base that liked to hear from him every now and then and others to let him know that they had not forgotten him. Chris could not respond to all, but he made every effort to respond to all the people that were sick, most of the children and anyone whom he had helped in the last six months or so. The ones he could not get to, he kept stored in a box and pulled some out when time permitted. That was a lot of letters/cards, an awful lot.

Tiffany, who had volunteered to take over finances, now saw where he was spending several hundred dollars a month on. Stamps, get well, birthday cards, etc. Tiffany had smiled when she looked at Chris at the time while he was doing this. He was sweating heavily and panting just fresh from his workout. Well, she assumed that was why even though she never really ever saw him work out.

Tiffany then took me to a heavy metal door on the back left side of the basement. When she opened it, I saw a room about 8 feet wide by 8 feet long and 10 feet high. The room had very heavy leather pads on the wall, even the door had pads on the inside portion. There was a seat bench that was attached and crossed the back wall. All the pads were heavily sweat stained, some with light blood stains. I noticed on the left side there was a slender solid wood shelf about 7 feet up built at an angle that blended in with the pads. Maybe a shelf was not the right word. More like a solid block of curved wood with holes in it. In the wood were half a dozen holes facing up that were several inches wide and deep. In these holes were round wooden sticks about 8 inches long that were covered in the center with leather. Deep soft rich heavy leather that covered all the wood except for the last inch on each end. The leather was of top quality and several layers thick.

On the opposite wall about the same height and make was another piece of wood. But instead of holes, it had hooks on which each hook held a pair of leather harnesses. I took one out and saw that it was the type that was applied to a person for restricting arm and leg movements so he would not be able to move. They were made with easy connections so this was not made for someone that you did not want to free themselves. It would take nothing to apply or get free from, even yourself, with these harnesses so very puzzling what they were for. The harnesses were also much thicker than the normal ones I have seen before. I could not imagine who they were meant to subdue. The room and the equipment here in this room made no sense. I looked at Tiffany with puzzlement evident on my face.

Tiffany still with her arms entwined in mine said, "Eric, like Mother told you the night I got engaged, you sometimes never see or realize what has been in front of you the whole time. Seems like I

140

share the same problem as you to some degree. We, you and I especially, with all our medical training, should have recognized and seen this years ago." Tiffany looked up at me with tears in her eyes and said, "How could we have missed it? How could we not have seen it? It was hinted at many times and we ignored it. We have talked it over and thought how amazing it was and wouldn't it be great to have that ability. Do you know what I am talking about?"

I shook my head in confusion, I didn't have a clue on what she was talking about. And then she said the two words that made everything come together. "Red Eyes." I gasped and dropped to my knees when the realization of what those two words meant. Which all my medical training finally made clear in my mind. Oh, how could I have been so blind? All this now made sense. I looked at Tiffany with the horror that I was afraid I was going to hear. Tiffany nodded knowing I had finally figured it out. Tiffany sat on the ground next to me and put her head on my shoulder and her hands in mine. She turned to me with pain and tears in her eyes and on her cheeks. She then explained how she had learned of this room.

The room that was built to suppress the pain caused by one man wanting to help others. Tiffany in a tortured voice told me how when she first toured the house, she saw the room but took it as something used for training, strange but nothing more. Last weekend Chris had to go out to California and had not returned until early Sunday morning. Eric knew about this as he had gone with him. They and the Protectors had gone to help out a chapter that had a bad run in with a gang on the lower west side of Los Angeles. Chris was in the middle of it, as usual, and it had lasted several days. Eric had examined Chris thoroughly but upon Chris's promise to let Tiffany take care of him, had only done basic care only.

Tiffany noticed that Chris still had pink eyes upon his return, which was highly unusual, and when asked, Chris had only shrugged and said it had been a tough weekend. As Tiffany nursed Chris's injuries, several more serious than she had ever seen before, she noticed Chris was shaking a little. After several minutes working on his wounds, Tiffany went upstairs to get more bandages. Upon her return, Tiffany noticed Chris was a bit feverish and his eyes were a little pinker, more red, than earlier. Chris seemed better after relaxing a few hours and they then decided to go to bed.

Tiffany had fallen asleep and when she awoke, noticed Chris was not beside her and that his side of the bed was damp, like he had been sweating more than normal. Tiffany put her robe on and went in search. When she did not find him upstairs, she figured he was at the desk writing letters. But when she did not see him there, she became a little concerned. There was nowhere else in the house to look and he would not have left without telling her.

Then she heard a very faint groan. It came from the back left side of the basement. Tiffany opened the door to the padded room only to see Chris with one of the sticks in his mouth while both his legs and arms were strapped into one of the harnesses. When Tiffany looked in Chris's eyes all she could see was the horrible pain he was going through. As Tiffany's gaze slowly spanned Chris's body, she could see his muscles straining and spasm without letup. The foot and calf muscles, the front and back of the thigh, the hands, arms, abdomen, and the muscles along the rib cage. All the muscles were rippling at the same time. If not for the leather covered stick in his mouth, Tiffany believed that Chris would have bit his tongue off in the first second or two.

The harness kept him from causing more serious harm that would have occurred with all his thrashing about. And there would have been plenty of that. Tiffany could tell that easily by the strain on the heavy straps. Having seen some of the pain tolerance Chris had, the pain must be terrible. Now she knew why the harnesses were so heavy. Her nursing training and experience understood immediately what was happening. Muscle fatigue, overexertion, probably dehydration and more. When Chris went into enhanced mode, he was supplying enriched blood at a high level. But what happens when his muscles are no longer getting that enriched blood? How many have heard of the individual that only does limited exercises and warm ups prior to a weekend of flag football? Weekend warriors sound familiar? Well, when these weekend warriors first go home, they feel tired but no worse for wear. What happens the next day, several days later? When their muscles let them know the actual cost. Some can barely move. Others, who have more exercise in their normal routine, less effect but depending on how hard they played, are usually affected in some manner. What do you think would happen if you stressed your muscles to such a high degree that most could not dream of and then for a very long extended period of time? As had happened to Chris this past weekend. And to top it off, take away the blood enrichment that enabled that high level of physical activity in the first place.

Tiffany told me at first she was ready to panic but when she saw that Chris was watching her every movement with pain filled eyes, she knew that this was where she could be what he needed most, his nurse. Tiffany got on her knees and for the next half hour or so massaged every muscle that she could see having a spasm. Finally, with a loud sigh, the stick half crushed with the leather almost bitten through, dropped from Chris's mouth. Tiffany, with Chris's help, undid the straps and helped him to the couch. The sweat ran down Chris's body in rivers. Tiffany ran upstairs and got a pitcher of cold water, several glasses along with wet rags and dry towels to wipe him down.

Upon her return, Chris was now trying to move around the basement on his own, which was hard to watch and listen to. Whenever he moved, she could hear the sound of his cartilage cracking. Her mind reeled with what she just witnessed. How often had her love gone through this? How could any man willingly experience this level of pain more than once? How did he do it? Chris put his left arm around Tiffany and pulled her into a tight embrace. Chris, still weak from the last hour, held on tight and said the words that meant more to her than any others could. "Thank you, my love, you sure came at the right time. I love you so very much!" With that Tiffany hugged him closer and quietly cried on his shoulder. Tiffany, now that it was over, realized she had been more scared than even the night she had first met Chris. She was not scared for herself, but for Chris. She knew how easily he could have perished from the stress he was giving his body. His heart was not made for this type of stress, no mans was.

With this, Tiffany looked at me and told me with her eyes now as hard as marble and a voice that brooked no argument. "It was not until later that I realized Chris was totally defenseless during that time. If anyone ever found a way to get past the Lord Protectors, I am his last defense. I am useless right now in that regard. So the reason I called you here is that I need you to train me to be a Lord Protector. Eric, starting tomorrow, I want you, Caleb, Iwao, Teja and the rest to start my training. I may be small but I can learn to fight. Teja did, Andrew did, I will. Understand this, anyone that threatens my man, my love, my hus—fiancé, will have to go through me first. No one threatens Chris in my house, got it!" Oh, I did, I most surely did. If that look on Tiffany's face was any indication of the skill level she could attain, which I believe it did knowing her so well, God bless any fool dumb enough who entered into her house to do harm to her man. They would have to go through her first and that was not going to be easy, nope, Tiffany would be a force to be reckoned with, especially in her own domain.

CALEB'S WRATH

The next several months flew by. School was going great, no major events in the Brotherhood and Tiffany's training was going very well. Chris was a little surprised at Tiffany's sudden desire to learn how to fight but figured that it was natural given her closeness with himself. Tiffany never told Chris her real reason as she felt that he would feel guilty for putting her in peril because of him. Tiffany impressed even Caleb with how quickly she picked up martial arts. As always, when she put her mind to it, there was nothing that Tiffany could not do.

But it was the sniper rifle that was Tiffany's true calling. Iwao took Tiffany under his wing and said that she was a true natural. What took others years to learn on how to control their breathing, muscles, patience, and so on, Tiffany did it naturally. Iwao was also a natural but had also been doing it for many years. Iwao had no equal anywhere in the world as far as I knew. And this was not just my opinion but many of the top professionals whom I have met these past few years. Iwao had private competitions against the top snipers in the world frequently as he said this kept him sharp and allowed him to review what tricks other used. Iwao was not too proud to learn from others, and that was my belief on why he was so good. Iwao would test others' methods to see how he could use them or use a composite of both theirs and his own to make his shots more accurate.

One thing that seemed strange but which Iwao was adamant about was for Tiffany to keep a shooting log of the shots she took in practice. He explained that there were several reasons for this. How your rifle reacts from a cold barrel versus a warm or hot barrel. The logs assist with understanding what the temperature of the barrel was on a given shot, what direction the wind was coming from, humidity, where was the sun, etc. The logs also assists with the maintenance of your rifle. Tiffany found that this was especially true when training with Iwao. Iwao was emphatic on a clean weapon and was not averse to having Tiffany clean it after a certain number of shots even if her training for the night was not complete. Luckily Tiffany got along famously with Iwao and took his guidance very seriously. So even if Iwao said to clean her weapon after just several shots, she did so with deep respect as she knew Iwao had seen something that indicated that a cleaning was necessary. Tiffany had often seen Iwao do the same thing himself when he was doing his own training so she knew it was not done in jest.

What surprised me, but shouldn't have knowing how close they have become, was that Amber started taking training lessons as soon as Tiffany did. It seemed Amber thought she had the same responsibility but for me. Amber told me that when I was working on someone, I was not aware of my surroundings as I focused intensely on the subject at hand. Amber said she had plans on being my protector when she was around, and that happened more often than not. Did I tell you all how much I loved this woman? Could any man be luckier? Anyway, Amber found out that guns were not her specialty but edged weapons were. Surprisingly, Amber took to the daishō, the long and short swords of Japanese origin. The swords were similar in design but of different lengths. Amber told me they were known specifically as o-wakizashi and *ko-wakizashi* swords. All I know was that they looked very sharp and deadly.

For distance, Amber liked the Shuriken versus a handgun since her wrists were so slender. But she kept both on her person as you could not always control the situation you were in nor how far away the attacker would be. And if she needed something heavier than a Shuriken, she would have something available. Amber was fortunate that there was a very renowned tandem team in our chapter.

Raku and Masaie were transplants from Japan who came here after becoming acquainted with Chris during one of his trips overseas. I found out from Masaie that Chris did not limit his activities to just the USA but wherever he went. It seems his reputation and endeavors were also well-known in Asia. In fact, Caleb had started several Brotherhood chapters in Japan and Hong Kong a while ago. That was why Raku and Masaie were here in the United States. They wanted to be a part of Chris's life. How they met had never been discussed openly, but you could tell that both Raku and Masaie both deeply admired and respected Chris with something more thrown in that you could never quite put a finger on. Knowing Chris, it was not too hard to figure out how the couple got to meet Chris.

Raku was a petite beautiful woman in her midtwenties being only five feet tall but moved like quicksilver in almost everything she did. Her eyes were more black than brown and her skin was a porcelain white in color. Her lips were thin and usually quirked in a rakish smile. Raku had long black hair that reached to the bottom of her back. The hair length was not just for ornamentation but also had a specific deadly purpose. Her hair was divided into a half dozen braids, which at the end of each, there would be attached a little silver ornamented weighted ball. They looked like exquisite jewelry until you had a chance to see Raku use them used in training, or as I had experienced, in battle. They were very deadly when she swung them around with her long tresses, able to give them such tremendous velocity. Especially when that velocity was compounded tenfold when she was being swung by her partner.

Raku's fighting partner, Masaie, who was also her husband, was taller at five feet ten inches with long legs and wide shoulders. Masaie, closer to being thirty than midtwenties, had short brown hair, mustache, short beard, and matching brown eyes. Unlike Raku, Masaie had a permanent dark tan from constant exposure to the sun. You would not call Masaie handsome except when you saw his twinkling eyes, which you would swear sparkled most times, especially when he was looking at Raku. Masaie's features were more streamlined that blockish, but there was no mistaking the power he commanded when he moved. When you had seen the ease that he twirled and threw Raku, any doubt that might have existed that he might be lacking in strength would forever be eliminated. But what I found to be their most wonderful talent was watching them dance.

Watching Raku and Masaie dance was like watching a waterfall in slow motion. I do not have the words to give it proper justice. The one thing that I can say for certain is that the love these two had for each other was glorious to see when they expressed it in the closeness and motion of their dance. That was in comparison to their dance of death when watching them in combat or training. They were never more than a foot or two from each other, and the speed Raku maneuvered around, under and over Masaie, along with the way Masaie would swing or throw her, was something to see. Both were very skilled in both unarmed and armed martial arts, especially all edged weapons. Both carried a single holstered Walther P5 but used it rarely. Both were deadly with it but preferred edged weapons.

It was during one of their training sessions with the girls that I got a chance to sit with Elijah and relax with nothing pressing to do for the next hour or so while the girls trained. Amber and I had a double date with Chris and Tiffany for a drive-in movie date scheduled right after training. We were chatting about mostly nothing when I asked Elijah if he had ever seen Caleb get really mad. I had seen him fight many times, but all with controlled fury. And when he was with Sophia, he was just a giant teddy bear in her hands. Elijah laughed and said that was one thing that he admired Caleb for—his ability to stay calm on almost any circumstance. But yes, he had seen Caleb get mad, really mad, but there was one that stood out over all.

Elijah then proceeded to tell me of this event. Elijah said that when Caleb first said he would watch over Chris, he took his declaration to protect Chris very seriously but that did not mean he agreed or fully understood why Chris had to do what he does. At first it was protecting Chris as he went through the neighborhood. But then Chris had come upon a rape of a teenager by several men in their neighborhood. Chris arrived after the rape was over but came upon them as they were about to knife the young lady. Chris failed and was left for dead after he had been knifed several times. The teenager did not survive. Caleb, Tyler and Elijah came upon the scene just after the police and ambulance. Caleb was furious that he had failed and swore to find the men who did this.

It was touch and go for days before Chris was out of danger. When Caleb asked Chris why, Chris just shrugged his shoulders and said, "Her need was greater than mine. But I failed her. It will not happen again. And I will find these murders if it takes me years. They were covered in masks but I will recognize them by their movements when we meet next, that I promise."

Tyler said Caleb looked at Chris in the hospital bed all bandaged up and made a promise to him. "And I will be there with you. Count on that." With that, Caleb walked over to Chris to lay his hand on Chris's shoulder. "On that I promise. We will find these three, no matter how long it takes, and they will pay the price."

It was on a night almost a year after Chris started making his rounds that it happened. Chris, Caleb, Tyler and Elijah who now roamed the nights together were in the Philadelphia area checking some areas near where Celeb used to live. Caleb and Elijah's old area was a known dangerous section of town to avoid unless you were a giant like Caleb or as deadly like Tyler and Elijah.

Caleb was leading the way as Chris was recovering from several injuries he suffered the week before. Chris did not have the full ability like he does today in those days to sense when and where someone was in danger close by but relied more on roaming the more dangerous areas until he ran into it by chance. Hopefully, if he did find or hear something, he could be in time and be of assistance.

It was a midsummer night and very humid. All four of us had been trotting for the last half hour in a random sweep when a loud scream that was abruptly cut off rent the air. Everyone stopped to orient where the scream came from. There was an abandoned building at the end of the block that seemed to be the likely source of the sound so we headed that way fast.

Caleb pulled ahead of the group and was first in the building. The building was in great disrepair and must have been abandoned for many years. There was trash littered on the floors everywhere and the smell of mold and sewage was overwhelming. The building entrance let into a small entranceway that led into a very large living room with garish wallpaper that was now covered in filth. Someone had dragged a soiled mattress in here at some time in the distant past.

But on this night the mattress was occupied by a shapely young woman being held down on her back by two young men while another very heavyset man was on top mauling her body. The man was very portly but you could tell there was a lot of muscle underneath all the fat. The man must have weighed in at 250 pounds at a minimum. The woman's clothing was in tatters and her face bloody from being hit several times. You could tell she was groggy and not totally aware of her surroundings. Off to the far side of the room was a young man lying on his side not moving and it was obvious he had been severely beaten.

Elijah spoke quietly as in deep thought and proceeded to tell the story like it was yesterday. Here was how Elijah told it to me. "Caleb, when he first entered, paused to size up the situation. That was when me, Tyler and Chris entered. At that time, the men by the woman turned to face Caleb. I could hear Caleb say a profanity as if in surprise. Tyler and I were about to rush over but Chris grabbed our arms to stop our advance. We could tell something was up by how hard Chris was gripping our arms. We swung our gaze to Chris and followed his gaze to Caleb watching the other men in the room. After we had a chance to get a clear look at the man by the woman, I could feel Tyler's, who was no more than a foot from me, surprise and rage. It matched my own when we saw who these men were. Chris signaled to us that this was now in Caleb's hands and we would all take our directions from him."

Elijah went on with the story. Caleb had not moved for a good 30 seconds and you could see the anger on his face. There were other emotions also crossing his stern features, confusion and disappointment? The two men holding the woman let her go and backed up to the far wall with their hands up with their palms facing toward Caleb. They had recognized him. The man on top of the woman, slowly rose and pulled something from his waist. I could not tell exactly what it was from where I was standing but from the manner of his grip I made the correct assumption that it was a knife.

Caleb walked slowly forward until he was over the young woman and only a foot or so from the man with the knife. You could tell Caleb was grappling with something. We did not fully understand until Caleb spoke. You could hear the pain in his voice when he said, "Jamaar, why? How could you?"

Jamaar looked at Caleb and said, "Why not?" with a sneer in his voice. "Who are you to be so high and mighty? Aren't you the one who left the group to go following that dude like a lapdog? We take what we want! Remember our code? Best you leave now or I will have to whip your ass like I used to."

Caleb looked down at the woman like he was torn and needed to think on what he should do. That was when the petite woman opened her bloodshot eyes and said through a cough of blood, "Help me!"

With that, you could see the confusion leave Caleb's face to be replaced by a deep seated rage. Caleb bellowed at the top of his lungs just prior to grabbing Jamaar by his throat. Jamaar tried to raise the knife but any semblance of the young man he remembered whipping was long past. Caleb was now a fast, strong, deadly man, even at his very young age, that few could match.

Caleb slapped the knife out of Jamaar's hand so hard it went flying into the far wall from where it bounced to lay at the feet of one of the other two men by the wall. The surprise in Jamaar's face was evident when Caleb lifted Jamaar by his throat with just one hand. Jamaar struggled mightily to free himself but Caleb slowly tightened his hand grip around the throat. It was there that I really saw Caleb's strength. Caleb was lifting this large man with one hand and even though Jamaar was extremely big and struggled wildly, Caleb's arm was ramrod straight and barely moved.

One of the men at the far wall where the knife had fallen, reached down to grab the knife at his feet and made a dash toward Caleb. Tyler made to intercept until he heard Chris say "No, this is Caleb's play right now, he will let us know if he needs any help." Tyler stopped with great reluctance with his hands tightly gripped and the muscles bulging in his arms in frustration.

The man rushed at Caleb with the knife raised high. Caleb, maintaining his grip on the Jamaar, swung his right leg up in a smashing blow with the metal tip of his army boots into the onrushing man's face. The man lost his grip on the knife and screamed while grabbing his broken nose. Blood was rushing through his fingers when Caleb followed through with a powerful uppercut that lifted the man several feet in the air. Before he could hit the ground, Caleb twirled, and while never relaxing his grip on Jamaar, hit the man in the center of his chest with his right heel while carefully avoiding stepping on the young woman at his feet. The man flew to smash into the far wall only to slump lifeless to the ground.

The other man fell to his knees and pleaded for mercy. Even in the foul smell of the house, you could smell the man's urine as it soaked his pants. Caleb now standing tall and motionless, looked at Jamaar who had stopped struggling with pity in his eyes. It was quite obvious from the way Jamaar's head flopped around that his neck had broken during Caleb's confrontation with the other man. Caleb slowly opened his fingers to let Jamaar slip to the ground with a dull thud. Caleb looked like avenging angel that you hear about in stories. He was standing tall with his muscles standing out in stark relief while hovering over the young lady he had come to save. Only if you knew him could you see the deep anger and hurt that he was feeling.

Caleb looked over the cowering man who had crawled into the corner. The man trembled with fear when he saw there would be no mercy from this towering man. The man rose to his feet and attempted to run past Caleb to a side door. Caleb with a loud roar, quickly cut off his escape and grabbed the man by his arm to swing him back into his chest where he applied a powerful bear hug. All in the room could hear the man's bones cracking then breaking. The man screamed in pain prior to Caleb tightening his grip even tighter. The man looked at Caleb just once more before he slumped and stopped breathing in Caleb's arms.

Caleb let the man drop to the floor and moved back to the woman who had yet not moved. It was hard to believe it had been less than 10 minutes since we had entered the room. Tyler had gone to the man who had been on the floor when we came to check on his status. It was not good but if we could get him to the hospital quickly, there was a good chance he would recover. Caleb meanwhile had slowly walked over to the young woman. He took off his shirt to cover her nakedness as best he could. Then, with a tenderness in sharp contrast to all the prior events, lifted her gently up into his arms. The young woman, who had been semiconscious the whole time, moaned and covered her mouth with her hand where she took a ragged breath only to cough up a small stream of blood through her fingers. Caleb slowly took his big paw of a hand and smoothed the woman's long curly hair off her bloody face. The woman woke enough to look Caleb in the eyes before falling unconscious in his arms.

I had not moved until now. I walked slowly over to Caleb and placed my hand on his shoulder. I asked Caleb if he was OK. Caleb looked at me with deep pain in his eyes and said he finally understood why Chris does what he does. Caleb then looked again at the woman in his arms and slowly the tears started running down his cheeks. As he slowly wiped some of the blood from the woman's face, he said that it was not until she had looked at him and asked for help, did it hit him that if it had not been for Chris, that he could have turned out just like Jamaar.

When we had first arrived tonight, I had not recognized immediately Jamaar as being one of our original gang. Not until Chris had grabbed my arm did I take the time to look carefully at the men in the room. Chris who had paid more attention than I had, recognized him immediately and knew that Caleb needed to handle this himself. Jamaar was one that had beat Chris senseless with pleasure many times. I am not sure as to how close Caleb and Jamaar had been at the end but it must have been a shocker when Caleb first entered and saw what Jamaar, his old buddy, was up to. And to top it off, Chris let us know that these three were the same men that had raped and killed the teenager a year ago. The same ones that started Chris on his endeavor to stop it before it happened.

We took both the young woman and man to the hospital where it was touch and go for a while but both survived. Caleb took myself and Tyler aside later that evening while we were waiting in the hospital on their status as he wanted to talk to us in private. Caleb is not one to waste words so I was not surprised when Caleb wrapped his arms around our necks and hugged us close. Caleb was more than just our cousin, he was a very close friend, which meant even more.

"Thanks to Chris, he saved me from being another Jamar. And you too!" That was it, no more. Not Caleb's nor our way. We all understood each other like never before."

Elijah sighed just before looking at me and smiling. "Sorry, I let me myself get caught up in the remembrance." I laughed and said that seems to be a trait of a lot of the members in the Brotherhood when they talk about Chris. Elijah chuckled at this. I asked if they ever heard from the man and woman that Caleb had saved. With that, Elijah laughed heartedly. Once he was able to stop laughing, he said they did not hear from the young man after he recovered but that they heard from the young woman often. In fact, I had met her often. With all the ladies in our group. I would not be surprised to hear that the young lady was now a member of the Brotherhood. I asked who it was. Elijah said the young lady's name was "Sophia." Elijah laughed even harder at the surprised look on my face and when I choked on my next breath. "Yes," Elijah said, "that Sophia," enjoying my face turning crimson in embarrassment. Again, I was reminded that there was nothing ordinary in the Brotherhood.

Elijah then lets me in on some side information that he thought I might be interested in. Caleb happened to be a financial genius who was one of the main financial resources behind supplying a good many of the chapters with their equipment and special hardware like the Vulcan. Caleb learned the business from father and was the owner of a startup financial services company very popular in the Northeast.

Caleb, through his contacts, also worked on identifying sites to search for some of the weapons that were left behind in Vietnam either through abandonment or from being choppers or aircraft being shot down. There was a lot of military hardware that could be salvaged there than most would believe. It was just having the right contacts, resources and an awful lot of money to get them, let alone the repair. Caleb had the money and contacts.

Elijah could see the astonishment on my face and chuckled in amusement. "What you see Caleb use mostly is how everyone thinks of him. Caleb uses his bulk and muscles mostly since that is his biggest strength. And when people see all that bulk, they assume, mostly to their detriment, that he is just another false stereotype of large people and not very sharp. I can assure you, Caleb has one of the sharpest minds I had ever met, and I had met plenty. Caleb was fortunate to have a good father and mother. Louise and Earl had a hard life, but they did not scrimp on making sure Caleb got the proper education. Earl was a stockbroker with minor success. What he learned though he taught Caleb. Earl and Louise were ecstatic and so very proud of Caleb when he started his company. It was still in infant stages but had some important clients.

With that, Elijah and I watched the ladies complete their training. We also got to watch Caleb and Chris spar with each other. In fact, everyone stopped to watch as it was treat rarely seen. Elijah and I knew we were good but watching those two told us we had a long way to go to get even close to their level. It was awesome to watch such power and speed. Both Caleb and Chris, moving with deadly grace, never slowed nor relaxed, it was a constant attack on each other. Neither was giving much ground to the other but you could tell that Chris's speed and power were not being fully utilized and being held back to avoid any permanent damage.

But it was no cake walk for Chris. Caleb's size and power could not be ignored and it was only through constant vigilance that Chris stayed one step ahead. It lasted for a solid 30 minutes and both were dripping in sweat when they finished. The gym was so quiet when they ended their bout that you could hear both men panting loudly trying to catch their breath. They bowed to each other and left to join their loved ones. I looked at Caleb with new respect from everything Elijah had told me and smiled in wonderment as Caleb reached Sophia and hugged her close. Amazing, just amazing, who would have guessed. I looked over at Elijah who had been watching me. I could tell he knew what I had been thinking by the smile on his face.

DISASTER

Did you ever get the feeling that things were going too easy? The next several months were quiet, relatively speaking, no one was seriously hurt and nothing happened to speak of. Tiffany and Chris finally announced their wedding date and it was no surprise to anyone that I planned to propose to Amber and ask her to marry me on the same day. It just amazed me that everyone seemed to know that I would was going to do that before I did. Am I that predictable? I had already tentatively approached Chris and Tiffany several months ago asking about a double wedding and they were only too happy to have us join them. I could not think if anything being nicer than to be at my best friend's wedding to my sister, and marrying a woman I just adored and loved with all my heart at the same time. That was if Amber accepted my proposal of course.

Oh yeah, I had not asked Amber yet at this time. So there was that small matter to do. To say I was nervous would be an understatement. I knew Amber loved me, and we had talked often about getting married, but that did not change the fact that if Amber said no, for any reason, I would be crushed. Really crushed. I could not imagine life without her as she had become so much a part of my life.

So with trepidation, I made plans to propose to her on the steps of the Philadelphia Art Museum. And yes, I asked Chris, who I deeply respected, to be there to support me when I asked Amber. Chris said he would be honored and would bring Snoopy along in support. Who could resist when a happy dog was present? And of course I told Tiffany of my plans. Tiffany hugged me and said we would be perfect for each other and joined in my plans.

Tiffany would help by bringing Amber there herself and make it just look like a normal get together for dinner. Tiffany and I agreed for everyone to meet on the museum steps around 6:00 PM on a Saturday in early May. Wow, it was going on six years after first meeting Chris thinking my life was over and now, well, it just couldn't be any better. Tiffany laughed at my concern as she knew that Amber loved me and would definitely say yes. Tiffany was surprised it had taken so long but took that as part of my shyness. I wish I had her confidence.

Chris was his usual helpful self and helped me find a Diamond Ring I think Amber would love. Chris took me to the same Jeweler who had helped him out before and we found a beautiful 1 carat Asscher cut diamond ring. It was set in a solid gold detailed ring that shone with the same intensity that I felt toward Amber. Yes, it was expensive and only through Caleb's financial help and the big discount from the jeweler he gave me because I was a friend of Chris's, that I could afford it.

And yes, I know, the first few years were going to be very tough financially as we were both in school and only had part time jobs. But once I told Tiffany and Chris of my intentions, they insisted that we live with them until we got settled in our new careers. Chris insisted, saying they had a spare bedroom that was never used on the far side of the house so everyone would be able to maintain their privacy. And since I was now his doctor, what could be better than living with the patient. I was still reluctant until I saw the excited happiness of both Tiffany and Chris. They really wanted us there. So I agreed and knew that Amber, if she accepted my proposal, would also agree.

So with my ring in pocket, on a quiet Saturday evening in May, I was waiting for Chris and Snoopy to arrive. I needed their company to boost my confidence before Amber and Tiffany arrived. I was not doing very good. My hands were sweaty and my heart beating a mile a minute while I waited. I had actually arrived several hours earlier as I was afraid to be late, which shows you just how nervous I was.

It was around a quarter to 6:00 PM when I saw Chris and Snoopy arrive and start ascending the Museum stairs. Whew, what a relief, they were here before Amber. There were only a few others around, which would be perfect as I was not one to do these public personal things out in the open with lots of people around. Yes, I know, I am that shy one you always see and laugh at. Except with friends, which was why I was so glad that Chris and Snoopy were here. I knew that Amber would expect me to get on my knee as I proposed as Amber definitely believed in the old school romance so this was not going to be easy for me.

I waved and Chris was responding when disaster struck. Snoopy had reached midway up the stairs where he had paused to wait on Chris. Snoopy stood still while he raised his head to look directly at me. Just at that moment a loud shot rang out. I saw Snoopy's eyes open in surprise and pain while also being flung backward. Chris, with dazzling speed, grabbed Snoopy and wrapped himself around Snoopy close to the ground.

I heard several more shots and saw the impacts on Chris's back. Chris was shoved several steps down all the while still holding Snoopy close and not letting him be exposed. I could see blood in great quantities and frantically started running toward them at the same time as I looked around to see if I could pinpoint the shooter.

As I ran, I saw several men that were hunched behind the brick base by the flag pole. It was tough to confirm if they were the shooters as running and looking around while also watching where you were going does not give you much time for close examination. Well, that was true until they saw me running toward Chris and Snoopy. One raised up a little while bringing a rifle around to bear on me. I never slowed in my rush to get to Chris and Snoopy even though I knew I would be their next target. I would not abandon my friend for my own safety. It never even entered into my mind to slow down to try and evade.

It was with surprise when I saw the man with the rifle lift up and be flung backward just prior to hearing a loud gun report its discharge. I smiled knowing Iwoa must have shown up, that was one nice piece of shooting. But there had been two men and the second man wasted no time in picking up the rifle and swinging it back toward me. I saw and then heard a second shot that clipped the base of the flag pole, which caused the man to miss me by a hairs breath as I could feel the bullets passage close by my left cheek.

I had made it down the first of the steps when I heard another shot and had just enough time to see who had made the shot. A woman about 150 yards in front of me in a bright blue pants outfit was kneeling with a large rifle in her hands. The woman had long dark luxurious hair and if I did not know better I would swear it was Tiffany. And running past her was another woman separated by just a few yards with long flowing blonde stresses that flailed out in the wind dressed in a beautiful sun dress that allowed her long muscular legs the freedom to run freely.

This woman had a Walther P5 in her right hand that she started shooting in the direction of the man by the flagpole. In her left hand she held an o-wakizashi sword. That was Amber if my panicked mind was still able to see properly. But no matter, I looked behind me and saw that the second man by the flag pole was now down and not moving. I was thankful of that for when I looked again at Chris, who was only a few yards away now, he shuddered and rolled down to rest on the next step below. Chris never relaxed his grip on Snoopy but you could tell from the way he moved and from the amount of blood that I saw that he was losing the ability to control his actions. Under Chris I could just make out Snoopy and he did not look to be in any better shape.

I reached Chris where I started to take an assessment of damage. But before I had more than a second or two, Chris turned his head toward me. Chris looked me straight in the eyes with his bloodshot eyes that had a pleading look. I could barely make out Chris saying just two croaked words through a mouth that leaked blood "Snoopy first." I knew what he wanted and as much as I wanted to treat both, I knew I needed to stabilize one before working on the other. And Chris would never forgive me if I worked on him before Snoopy, even if he was hurt worse.

I know what you are thinking, Snoopy was a dog and Chris was a person. But you have to know what I and everyone in the Brotherhood knew. Snoopy was family to Chris. Chris loved that dog more than his own life and would never forgive me if I let Snoopy die because I worked on Chris first. So as much as I wanted, I could not do anything different.

So I carefully moved Chris to the next step down so I could check on Snoopy. I am not a veterinarian, but I could make some educated decisions. I cringed at the damage I saw on Chris when I moved him. Chris would be lucky to survive and without immediate care in the next several moments, he would not. But I bent to Snoopy and saw that the bullet had entered through his front left side but I could not see an exit wound. Snoopy had been in the process of climbing the stair and had his body turned. It looked bad and there seemed to be an awful lot of blood but one thing that I could not find were any bone protrusions or bone fragments. I could not tell whose blood was whose so it made it all the more harder. Chris's or Snoopy's?

All I could tell was that there was a good amount and if it was from mostly just one of the two, it meant that person was probably in a much more serious condition. I believed that to be Chris's based on seeing him jump several times like he had been shot multiple times but I would not be able to tell for sure until I looked him over. I was carefully feeling Snoopy's ribs to see if could locate the bullet, when he shuddered and stopped breathing. Amber arrived and stopped right next to me on my right hand side. Amber put her weapons down to help me. I placed my hands in a circle to make a funnel and tried to breathe in Snoopy's mouth. Meanwhile Amber tried doing CPR. We did this for a few moments but it was evident that Snoopy was dead.

I was devastated as I knew that Chris would be heartbroken. From the corner of my eye I could see Tyler had arrived so I was sure he had already called for an ambulance along for more Brotherhood support. I would not be surprised to see this area swarming with some very deadly people in a very short timeframe.

I looked over at Chris and saw that Tiffany had put her weapons down like Amber had but kept them very close at hand. Tiffany had removed part of Chris's shirt but one section seemed to be stuck in a gunshot wound on his back. No way that could be removed here without the proper resources, and Tiffany was already putting a bandage using the emergency kit that she also carried at all times. Amazing what medical supplies we almost all carried around without really thinking about it. From what I could see, it did not look good. The quick glance showed a very ragged wound. And there was more than one wound on his back. I started to get up to assist as there was no more that I could do for Snoopy.

Chris, who had never lost conscious, looked at me with a question in his eyes. I shook my head and croaked out that Snoopy had not made it. Chris closed his eyes and you could see his body relax, like he had given up. Tiffany looked at me at that moment and I could see the fear and pain in her face. And yes, there were tears running down her cheeks but she never stopped working. I am sure my face reflected the same concern and it was not necessary for me to look at Amber's to know hers would mirror Tiffany's.

It was then I saw that Tiffany was holding her left hand on the second wound on Chris's back and blood was seeping through in a steady flow even though she had placed several bandages on. Every now and then, I could see Tiffany's body shake and only through her strong will that she did not break down in heartbreak. From my vantage point, it did not look like Chris had much time left. I joined Tiffany where I took the bandages off the wound that continued to bleed. I started pressing down hard just proximal to the wound. It was too deep to see where the torn artery was from the skin surface, but feeling around for the pulsing, I was finally able to find it. While holding down on the area, we slipped in some bandages. The bleeding seemed to have lessened greatly.

Just then several ambulances and cars raced up to the bottom of the Museum steps. Out stepped Caleb and he was followed by several middle aged individuals dressed in surgical gowns. I recognized one man of them being Dr. Ben Sternson who was probably the best Surgeon in the Northeast area. I had been fortunate enough to have been to several of his seminars so I did not know how Caleb was able to get him here so quickly, but we could not have asked for anyone better to have on hand at this critical time.

Dr. Sternson rapidly moved toward Chris. Dr. Sternson put his hand on my wrist and let me know I had done real good, very good, in fact. If Chris survived, it would be because of my efforts. Dr. Sternson must have seen the concern and worry on my face. Any other times, I would have been honored but right now, I was barely holding it together. Amber walked with me as I moved away from Chris to allow the second surgeon, Dr. Hudley, access to Chris.

Amber had rearmed herself and was intensely scanning the area. It would have been comical at any other time as there were now at least several dozen Protectors around who were armed to the teeth. But one look at her face left no doubt in my mind that she was not going to relax for the foreseeable future. Amber stuck to me like glue. Dr. Hudley stapled the wound in Chris's back in an attempt to stop the blood flow. Dr. Hudley also had started a blood infusion line while Tyler was pressing on the pint to add a little pressure to speed up the blood receipt. I did notice that the pint was emptying a little faster than normal and Chris's eyes, under his twitching eye lids, were now a very deep blood red like he was assisting in the blood infusion. I found that odd as it did not look like Chris was even conscious though he still gripped Tiffany's hand in a tight grip.

In short order, Chris and company were in the ambulance. I expected Tiffany to also require a ride to the hospital but to my surprise they found room for her. It seems, even unconscious, Chris would not release his grip even though they did try for a minute or two. Tiffany looked at me just before they closed the ambulance doors and my heart lurched to see her in so much pain. Tiffany's eyes were so bloodshot from crying that it almost looked like Chris's eyes did though hers were pink vs. Chris's red.

I turned to be confronted by Caleb. Caleb rested his large hand on my shoulder and said that Chris was lucky that I, Tiffany and Amber had been around. That I was not to give up hope as this was a very tough individual and as small as his chances of surviving looked, he had a chance in part due to my efforts. That might have helped me feel a little better if Caleb's eyes did not mirror the despair that I felt in my heart.

Caleb said for me to go with Tyler to the hospital and that he would be along presently. Right now, he had to see what he could find out about what happened and why. The tone in Caleb's deep voice made me shake a little bit as there was no mistaking the threat in his tone. If this was not a lone attack but something planned by someone or a group, well, let's just say I would not want to be whoever they were for anything in the world. Because if Caleb found out who it was, vengeance would be swift and total, of that I had no doubt, no doubt at all!

MIRACLES

Well to say the next several weeks were rough, would be an understatement. But even through all the pain and danger, there were still times that were uplifting and inspirational. Chris had been shot several times and the bullets had not only hit some arteries but also fractured several bones. If not for his level of fitness, it was doubtful he would have even made it to the hospital. Chris was in surgery for twelve hours upon his arrival and many more were planned. Outlook was not good.

Tiffany, who had never left Chris's side, was the first to feel his heartbeat settle down just a bit. Enough to tell Tiffany that something had changed. Tiffany had not slept in several days and was at the end of her endurance when this occurred. Since Chris's arrival, he had been through more than a half dozen surgeries, and enough blood transfusions for over a hundred individuals. The ICU was crowded with volunteers from the Brotherhood for blood donations for Chris.

I had never seen nor expected to see anything like what happened. Chris would take the rich red blood in and eject a worn out looking maroon color liquid. It looked like any trace left of nourishment had been sucked out. This went on nonstop for four days and vast quantities of blood were used. And it was miraculous what occurred. Chris shattered bones, which had been reset, healed faster than normal, not fully but enough to start the "bonding process" much more quickly. Same for his blood vessels. Shortly after Tiffany felt the change, Chris opened his eyes, smiled and reached up his right hand to caress the side of her cheek.

How do I know? Because, like Tiffany and most of the protectors, I had very little sleep and had been pacing between Chris's room and the break room. I happened to be with Tiffany when Chris opened his eyes. Chris looked Tiffany in the eye and asked "Snoopy?" Tiffany, caressing Chris's face while weeping, said that Snoopy did not make it. And now comes the inspirational part. Chris must have been exhausted and in great pain. But now no more than an hour after having woken up, made to get up. The nurses were pleading with him to stay in bed, that he was too weak and needed to wait on the doctor's OK before getting out of bed. Chris just smiled and even though you could see the great pain and effort it took him to move his legs, did so.

No one in the Brotherhood said anything nor attempted to help as they knew he would do what he believe he had to and would have asked for help if he thought he needed it. Needless to say everyone present would have been honored to carry him where ever he wanted to go. But all knew that Chris wanted to do this on his own. Chris slowly pulled his covers back and swung his feet over to the floor. Chris did not make a sound but you could see the pain and anguish in his face. His pallor went bone white and the nurses were frantic. But Chris politely waved them aside just as the attending doctor showed up. Chris then spent the next several minutes trying to raise himself onto his feet while politely pushing the doctor away who was trying to get him back on the bed with the nurses' help. The doctor and nurses pleaded with him to at least get in a wheelchair. But Chris, looking at Tiffany the entire time, declined. Once Chris was on his feet, his color returned a little, enough to tell you he would not fall immediately, and proceeded to disconnect all the pads attached to his body. Tiffany assisted and then they both walked out of the room very gingerly.

I believe to this day that only Tiffany would have been allowed to assist him due to the great love he had for her. I also believe that her assistance kept Chris from falling and maybe doing some irreparable damage. But then maybe that was how Chris had planned it, who knows, but I did notice how Tiffany fears seemed to fade from her face just a little having Chris in her arms once again. The walk to the break room was slow going and very crowded. Everyone—the great number of visitors, nurses, doctors, etc.—was grouped around and ready to lend a hand if needed. There was just enough room for Chris to take the next step with Tiffany pulling the rolling stand that contained the drip bottles that were still connected to Chris. When Chris finally reached the break room, he was sweating profusely and his pallor was now white as new fallen snow.

I now believed more than ever that he did the walk vs. wheelchair for Tiffany's sake. Tiffany needed to see he was improving. Again, I am reminded of the lengths Chris will go for others. After a few moments, Chris's strength seemed to return just before he stood straight and looked around at all in the break room. "Thank you all, without your support I would not be here. But I am here and I need your help again. I know it may sound silly but Snoopy was family to me. I cannot rest until he is avenged. I am not asking anyone to risk themselves for Snoopy, I only ask that you help me find out who did this. I will take it from there. So again, I thank you. You have no idea how much I appreciate all your assistance and concern. Now go home and see to your families. I will be fine. Love you all!"

With that, Chris slowly made his way back to his room and in bed. You could tell that the walk had taken everything out of him. Chris looked at Tiffany and patted the bed next to him. Tiffany very carefully worked her way onto the bed and lying on her left side snuggled up against Chris. In short order Tiffany placed her head on Chris's shoulder and fell asleep in just a few moments. I was not surprised as I knew just how tired Tiffany was. Working with the doctors and nurses, I helped them check on Chris's stats. I know, I am not licensed but Caleb and Tiffany made it quite clear that I was to be given full access to Chris.

I know, the normal thing would be that everyone went home and everything settled down. Yeah, that might have been the normal thing to do but not in this case. This man meant so much to so many and they were not going to relax until this entire situation was over. And the search for who did this had already been started. Hundreds, if not thousands, were already on the prowl. Caleb was leading that effort and he was relentless. And the people stopping by to see Chris only increased as people that were further out now had time to get here. It was getting very crowded in all the local hotels. It was something to behold. Every day, hundreds came through. Most with flowers, cards, anything to let Chris and Tiffany know they cared. And they were not wasted. All the flowers were passed out to the other patients and it was in short order that every room and patient had multiple vases of flowers. As Tiffany, who organized it said, it was kinda like sharing the well wishes for Chris in all areas of the hospital, not just his room. And everyone was more than happy with the solution as they knew there was no way Chris's room could hold all the flowers. And if it brought happiness to the patients in those rooms, the more flowers, the better.

After Chris's walk, the rooms and hallways were abuzz with whispers on what they just observed and joy that it looked like Chris would survive. But under all that whispering there was also a very dark menacing tone, discussions of justice and retribution, one they all wanted to be a part of. I being one of them.

The next several weeks were still touch and go. Many times Chris was placed back on the critical list when his blood pressure would drop and his temperature would spike. But each time, Tiffany would lean in and while holding his forehead she would whisper in his ear. Sometimes Chris responded in a few moments, other times it would be several hours. Tiffany never relaxed nor stopped her whispering until Chris was out of immediate danger. Three weeks after the day of the shooting, Chris was pronounced out of danger though he needed time to recover. The doctors were amazed at the speed of Chris's recovery. They thought Chris would require hospitalization for at least several months but were ready to release him in just over four weeks.

Chris had continued doing the blood transfusions and was rapidly regaining strength. In fact, it seemed that he was building more muscle than he normally carried. One ominous sign that worried both Tiffany and myself greatly was that the normal jovial Chris now very rarely talked or smiled. Chris seemed bent on recovery and was pushing his body to the maximum to make it happen sooner than later. Why? What was he planning? Why the need for speed? No one could get to either Chris without going through a very tight security screen. So Chris's silence was troubling and one that we feared meant that something was in the air and that we may not like the outcome.

Caleb, who came by often, spoke quietly with Chris but never loud enough or where anyone else could overhear. And it seemed to be a one sided conversation. Caleb would speak to Chris but Chris would rarely respond, just listen and nod. We all knew Caleb was leading the investigation on who had orchestrated the assassination attempt and we would have loved to be privy to those conversations.

It was a week after Chris was diagnosed out of danger that Chris made plans to leave the hospital. I found that odd as I thought there seemed to be an urgency to his departure. Caleb also seemed more agitated than normal and that had me getting more concerned. This was not lost on Tiffany and Amber. Both expressed their confusion and concern on what was happening. Even Tiffany could not get anything out of Chris on what the meetings were about nor what his plans were. But we all knew that Chris was planning something and it had something to do with what Caleb found out. Tiffany, knowing Chris best, was getting worried as Chris was still doing the blood transfusions and she could not remember when was the last time that Chris's eyes were not deep blood red. One benefit was that his wounds were almost all healed but she had major concerns on how long he could continue in this fashion.

It was early on a Saturday morning five weeks after being admitted, that Chris left the hospital. Chris did not go home but went directly to one of the larger gym's we trained at. Chris started exercising and it was evident that he was stiff and experiencing pain but he continued on for the next several hours with an intensity that spoke volumes.

Tiffany was beside herself with worry as she and I finally came to terms with what he was doing. Chris was getting ready to meet the individual or group that had planned the attack. We did not think he was ready for this, not for several more months. His body needed more time to recover after the extensive damage it had just suffered but we knew that there would be no talking Chris out of whatever he planned.

So we did what we could do best to help Chris, we trained with him because wherever he was going, we would be there too and needed to be on the top of our game. After an hour, the gym was packed as it seemed that we were not the only ones that wanted to see Chris. I was exhausted after the first thirty minutes as I had not been through this type of extensive training in several months. Training with Chris was definitely not for the timid.

Tiffany and Amber were just as exhausted and we all sat on a mat dripping sweat and catching our breath. While resting, we watched Chris who had not stopped start another session with Raku and Masaie. The intensity between the three was amazing to watch. Raku and Masaie moved with such grace and deadly precision that it was hard to believe any one individual could last long against them. But Chris not only did, he had them on the defensive the majority of the time and it was evident that he could have finished it several times if so desired.

The speed with that Chris moved was hard to comprehend, let alone watch. Raku and Masaie spun around Chris like a pair of deadly snakes. Striking here, feinting there, jabbing here. Masaie at one time swung Raku so hard overhead just after a block by Chris on a Masaie kick that observers gasped in concern as they could not see any way for Chris to block Raku's feet from connecting with his chest and sending him flying. But Chris with an instant recognition of the attack flattened to the floor with just his hands keeping him just inches off the floor mats and when Raku's feet swept by just an inch or two from his head at a high rate, he used his hands to twist his whole body in a half circle to swing his legs at Masaie's planted feet. It was only with great expertise that Masaie was able to back step quickly enough while still holding onto Raku avoiding Chris's legs. This maneuver forced both Raku and Masaie to be on the extreme defensive for the next several moments. I believe that Chris deliberately let Raku and Masaie recover so as not to end the session too early.

It was evident Chris could have used his greater strength to overwhelm the pair at that time but he seemed more interested in training on blocking and avoidance than ending the duel. Why, I cannot say for sure exactly, but I had a feeling that Chris was preparing for something that involved fighting multiple individuals at the same time. And if you were planning for that, Raku and Masaie would be the best to train with. After watching this session, there was no doubt in anyone's mind on why Raku and Masaie were considered one of the very best tandem fighters in the world.

During their session everyone had stopped their own personal training to watch the match as it was something that you may never see again. This session went on for twenty minutes of heart stopping action with no pauses for catching their breath. This was unheard of and only the very best fighters could maintain fighting at such intensity for so long. And it also showed how much Chris had recovered from his injuries. It ended with no victor but by all three just backing away and signaling it was time to rest. There was no doubt to any who would have won but it was just another trait that all admired in Chris. It was a training session that no one present would ever forget.

Afterward, all three sat together and reviewed their session. All three were drenched in sweat and sipping on water when Tiffany and I joined them. Raku and Masaie were in the process of confirming what I had suspected, Chris could have overwhelmed the pair several times but had held back so as to allow them to recover. You may think that they would have been insulted at such actions but you would have been seriously mistaken. They were ecstatic that they had lasted as long as they had and gave a good accounting of themselves in the process. Chris had been hard pressed many times and that spoke volumes of Raku and Masaie's expertise. And no one present could miss the affection Raku and Masaie had for Chris. It was also evident from their conversations that they had no intentions of leaving Chris's side until the current crises had been resolved.

It was just after the session review that Caleb, Elijah and Tyler entered the gym. The serious look on their faces quieted all conversations. Caleb talked with Chris privately in the corner where Chris lowered and shook his head like he was agreeing to something. Chris finally looked up at Caleb, at which time he said loud enough for me to overhear him say, "Four weeks, Caleb, I need four more weeks. Buy me four weeks, can you?" Caleb grabbed Chris's arm and said in a very serious tone. "Chris, whatever time you need, we will make it happen. You tell me four weeks, four weeks it is. We will be expecting you then." Caleb, Elijah, and Tyler then left with a purpose in their steps and expressions that you knew something was up.

The tension in the gym was very high at this point. It went even higher when Chris looked over at Tiffany with obvious pain in his eyes. We could all tell that something major was happening when Tiffany who had been watching all this broke down in tears. Tiffany grabbed my arm for support and looked at me pleadingly. I knew my sister and she was not easily frightened. There was only one thing that I could come up with to make her react so. Something in that look from Chris told her that Chris was about to embark on a course of action that he did not believe he would return from. My heart was in my throat as I grabbed Tiffany and held her close. Her sobs were like daggers ripping my heart apart. Chris slowly made his way over and pulled Tiffany into his arms. Tiffany and Chris left the gym together with no other word spoken.

I turned and you could part the air with a knife the tension was so thick. Masaie looked at Raku and very forcibly said, "再び発生するつもりはありません." Then switching to English he looked around and said, "Not going to happen again." Raku looked at Masaie with tears in her eyes and concern on her face. Very quietly she asked Masaie what we all wanted to ask. "Caleb has found out who shot Snoopy didn't he? Now Chris is making plans to fight this alone. No different than when he saved my sister and mother. Chris almost died then and now it is happening again."

It was the first time I had heard anything about how Chris knew Raku and Masaie. Masaie took Raku in his arms and just repeated saying 再び発生するつもりはありません over and over again. Masaie looked at me and it was evident that this was not something said in jest. And it was not something lost on me and all present. We all looked at each other and made a silent agreement. When Chris went to wherever he planned to in four weeks, we would be there with him, this was not an option. Chris was not going to fight alone. As Masaie said, that was just not going to happen.

171

PREPARATION

The next several weeks went by fast but stressful. Everyone knew something major was going on and all wanted to be a part of it. But it was not to be. Only certain individuals were pulled out and who or why was a mystery. But it was common knowledge that Caleb was making the decisions and call ups. More and more of the protectors were being drawn off every day until there was only enough to cover their security details by going to 12 hour shifts.

But it was not only protectors being called up and not only from our chapter. I am proud to say that of the twenty or so that were asked for, not one, not a single one turned it down. The requests were not an order but just that, a request. We are not the military and everything done in our chapters are done on a voluntary basis. It was not unusual to have someone who could not go at one time or another either due to family or work commitments. But in this case, each and every one not only accepted but was grateful for the opportunity. You could tell that from the responses to the individual making the request that being usually Tyler or Elijah. Usually it was with words of thanks, a gripping of the arm, or just the smile on their face was enough to tell you what they felt. Where they were being sent or what their duties were no one knew.

Security was tighter than I have ever seen. Not even the protectors left behind were being informed. I know, I was one and it was one reason it was so stressful to not being involved. But a pattern did start emerging by who was being pulled. A good many were good long shots with a rifle, not snipers like Iowa as there were very few that were that good, but individuals that could hit a small target at five hundred yards accurately most of the time. Then there were those individuals who have spent a lifetime hunting and able to track or see signs of someone passing where you would swear no one had been by in a hundred years. And finally, the few we had that used to be sappers in the military at one time or another. Some of the very first requested in our chapter had been sappers during World War II and/or the Korean War. I have seen these guys do amazing things in engineering that backed up their otherwise unbelievable stories of what they did while in service. It was a puzzle we hoped we would know about soon enough.

I knew why I was not included. I was here for Tiffany. Chris personally asked me to spend more time with her, especially when he had to be away from her side, which was more and more often. As each day passed, you could see the stress building on her. I spent every free moment with her I could and would bring along Amber along if she was available. Amber shared my grave concerns also as we have never seen Tiffany so distraught. I have lived with Tiffany the majority of my whole life and we had been so close for so long that I knew her better than anyone, except maybe now Chris.

By the way Tiffany was acting when we were with her, we knew that there was something she was not telling us. Something I could not put my finger on but something that kept whispering to me that I should know. At the same time, from her actions and words, I had a feeling Amber knew more than she let on and maybe, just maybe, she had a hunch of what it was. But no amount of prodding from me would persuade Amber to either tell me or confirm she had an inkling of what it was. And with Chris stepping up his training and silence, the stress levels for all was rising every day.

Three weeks after Chris asked Caleb for four weeks, Chris asked me to meet him at a local restaurant on a Saturday evening. It was strange in that he asked that I come alone. I met Chris at a Howard Johnsons around 6:00 PM. Chris was there when I arrived, and we sat in a booth in the rear where we could have some privacy. It was hard to describe how Chris looked. I had never seen him in such good shape physically. The muscle definition was tremendous yet not too bulky. It was the eyes that still haunt me to this day. They were, and it took me only a moment to identify it, haunted. Chris's eyes were bright hazel, but the white were crossed with red lines and the skin around the eyes were dark with deep shadows like he had not slept in a very long time.

Chris opened the conversation with small talk on how everything was going with Tiffany. I figured correctly that he was waiting for our food orders to be taken prior to getting to why he asked to meet. Once the waitress had dropped off our drinks and taken our orders, Chris's volume and tone dropped where we would not easily be overheard.

"Eric, I am glad you could join me tonight. I desperately need your assistance with a personal item I would not be comfortable to give to anyone else except maybe Caleb, but he is not available," said Chris. With that Chris reached behind himself to pull out a large yellow envelope that had been tucked in his flannel shirt that I had not noticed. Chris placed the envelope on the table between us and looked at it with eyes that were tightening up. With his eyes that were bunched up like he was in great consternation, Chris looked at me and said in a strained voice "Soon I will meet the individuals that shot Snoopy, my friend, my family. When I do, I am not sure how it will all go down." With that, Chris puts both his hands on the envelope and pushed it toward me while saying "I am not sure what will happen but I will not leave my loved ones without all the legal documents necessary to proceed on without me. Tiffany is worried about me and does not want to go over this with me at this time. She feels that I am saying good-bye. Eric, believe me, I have no intention of letting these creeps take me out but there is no certainty in this business as you are well aware of. That is the basis of all the training we do so you can deal with it as best you can especially when your friend next to you buys it. A novice with no skill can take out the most skilled person if the conditions are right. It all depends on what is happening at the time and in the fog of battle, there are no guarantees for anything. So I need to be sure that the proper steps at home are taken care of."

I could see the pain on Chris's face and hear the anguish in his voice. Chris's hands were trembling a little when he looked pleadingly in my eyes and asked would I help him. Would I take the envelope and go through all the documents. But open it only if something happened to him. They contained titles to the house, the few valuables he had, life insurance policies, stocks and bonds, bank accounts, pension plan, and an inventory of all his personal items. They were all bequeathed to Tiffany and any future children. I silently sighed as the stress must be telling on Chris. Usually Chris was so accurate when he spoke, it was one of his known traits. I was not sure Chris realized he had said future children. He would have to have survived to have future children and hence this packet would not be needed. But with all that was going on, I could understand the lapse.

There was one particular item that Chris said was worth more than all the rest. It was a gift that Caleb had given him several years ago. It was a pair of axes hanging on the wall above the fireplace. When Chris said that, I remembered the axes I saw when Tiffany was showing me the house many months ago. They were extraordinary and if what Chris said was true, they must be real and worth a small fortune. Chris said he planned to use those axes soon as they were fully functional but wanted to make sure that I recovered them if anything went wrong. Caleb would know what to do with them.

Chris closed his eyes for a moment, which caused several tears to slowly roll down his cheeks. In all the time I have known Chris, I cannot remember when I have seen him so upset unless it was when he was holding a recently departed friend or not arriving in time to protect an individual. Never when it was just the two of us out for dinner. It was very unnerving and frightening, to say the least. I cannot tell you how much I loved and admired this man and here, unless I am mistaken, he was preparing for his passing and asking me to be the conservator of his estate. It brought to my mind the picture of how distraught Masaie and Raku had been just recently and their comments. Everything was pointing to them being right about Chris's plans. I swore to myself, again, that this was just not going to happen, no way. Not even if it meant losing my own life, it was just not going to happen.

Chris slowly opened his eyes and repeated his question, "Would I help?"

"Of course," I answered, "whatever is needed. But understand this Chris, that I plan to give these back to you unopened once this is over. I met a man once who told me I was a brave man. I remember that day and how it changed my life. I would have been too timid then to tell him what is on my mind but he has shown me that is not the way to go through life. I have also since that day seen how that man has positively and dramatically changed so many lives that I have lost count. I am not sure what your plans are but there are many people that care, love and need you. My sister being one of them. So you better make sure your plans include your survival if you care anything about all the men, women, children who have come to love you like the close friend you are. Do not let this turn from justice into revenge that becomes all consuming. Promise me that."

Chris looked at me solemnly and said that he was doing everything he could to minimize casualties. That he was working with Caleb on all possible strategies and Mason on the odds of success with all the knowledge available. Mason was jokingly called our bean counter. Mason would take all the details like the area layout, personnel involved, weapons being used, the time of day, and many more items to supply a detailed judgment on the odds of success, injuries or even possible death. Mason was very good and had been highly accurate.

Normally that would have alleviated some of my concerns but now, it even elevated them even more. That was because anyone who knew Chris knew that he would not ask anyone to go where he would not. That if he was trying to minimize casualties and this being so personal to him, how that would that impact who or how others would fit into his plan. The only comfort I could come up with was knowing that Caleb was involved in the strategy. Caleb would not sit out no matter what Chris wanted. Caleb's, along with Elijah's and Tyler's, devotion to Chris was legendary. They would laugh at any request for them to sit out no matter who asked, even Chris. Of that I was positive so why did I still have that feeling that something was different this time around.

I talked with Chris for a bit more and I made sure he was aware that I would make sure Tiffany would be okay, that I would follow any instructions he provided in the envelope. Chris and I finished our meals and made our way to our cars. Just outside, Chris turned to me like he wanted to say something more but shook his head and said, "Thanks, Eric, you have no idea how much it means to me to be able to talk with you and you being here when I need you most."

Chris grabbed my hand and pulled me into a big hug. I hugged back and when we separated, he saluted like old with a smile on his face. I felt like a weight had been lifted from my shoulders when I saw that smile. But again, something kept bothering me, that I was missing something. It felt like it was right there before me, something so obvious, I was missing something important, really important, I could feel it. Something I needed to know, that I should know. But what could it be? I left there more worried than when I arrived.

RAKU AND MASAIE

The next day after meeting with Chris, I went to the gym early as something told me I needed to get some additional training in. Amber had a class so she could not join me. Raku and Masaie were already there ahead of me along with most of the remaining chapter members. They must have been there for several hours already as they were all drenched in sweat. I sat with Raku and Masaie to see if they had any further insight on the plans for the coming week. Masaie just grunted no but said they would be ready.

I then asked Raku the question that had been bugging me for the past month, how had they come to meet Chris? Raku looked at me like she was making up her mind if I deserved a response or not. After looking over at Masaie, who shook his head yes, Raku then told me their story. Raku said that the first part of the story was relayed to her by Tyler after they met and got to know each other in Japan several years ago.

It seems when Chris was around sixteen, just after he saved Tiffany and myself, he, Caleb, Elijah and Tyler had saved the daughter of a prominent Japanese businessman named Hideo from a group of young hoodlums on the east side of Philadelphia. Hideo, after hearing from his daughter, Kiyomi, of their martial prowess, had invited all of them to visit his family in Japan. Hideo wanted them to meet some very good friends of his who were Karate masters and ran their own martial arts schools. Chris was going to decline but Caleb though it would be a good for Chris to get away and get some much needed rest. The last several weeks had been very rough and all were in need of some downtime. Chris reluctantly agreed but was secretly pleased to be able to visit Japan as he had never been there before.

Chris and friends did not normally accept gifts from persons they helped but Hideo and his daughter were very insistent. Hideo thought that his friends could improve the group's martial skills and that only could be good for all of them. So everyone packed their bags and headed to Tokyo to spend several weeks in Japan.

The trip was exciting and very relaxing for all the first week. The days were spent at the martial art schools while spending the evenings with Hideo and Kiyomi exploring Japans historical sites like the shrine at Tōshō-gū and the temple complex of Naritasan Shinshō-ji.

The martial art masters were very impressed with Caleb, Elijah and Tyler's skills. Caleb, Elijah and Tyler were told that even though they did not have any professional training, they were very skilled and it would be hard to find someone in their age bracket that could compete at the same level, even here in Japan where the martial arts were taken much more seriously than in the United States. As for Chris, they were just floored at his skill. Tyler told Raku that watching the masters spar with Chris was one of the most amazing events he had ever seen. Here was a sixteen-year-old sparing with someone in their midthirties that had grown up living and teaching the Aikido and Taido styles of martial arts.

Raiden was the name of one these masters and after working with Chris for a few days, had asked him if he would mind sparring with him this coming weekend, he was that impressed. Raiden was around five feet, seven inches and 170 pounds of muscle. There was no fat on his stout frame and he moved with a solid lethal fluid grace. The second master was Takeshi who was taller at five foot ten inches and weighed about 165 pounds. Though not as solid as Radien, he moved more swiftly and more prone to defense vs. the more aggressive attack style that Raiden preferred.

Both were considered two of the best martial art champions in Japan and after watching and working with them for a week, it was easy to see why. The spectators that weekend were mostly from the students of these two masters but not all. The masters were famous in Japan and rarely ever held a personal competition from someone outside of Japan. When word spread of this match, a few of the local dignitaries also came to watch. Of course all expected the match to be short and overwhelmingly won by Raiden.

Tyler smiled when he had told Raku this part of the story as Raiden was very skilled and normally should be able to deal with Chris easily but he knew something the spectators did not. Both he and Elijah took full advantage of that knowledge by taking all the bet's they could find on Chris as they got some really good odds. Some odds were as high as a fifty to one. No one besides themselves believed Chris had even a remote chance of defeating Raiden.

Tyler told me they laughed each time they were able to find another bettor, at which Caleb shook his head in exasperation as he thought they were taking advantage of their hosts. But they could not stop smiling as they pictured in their minds what they knew and the others did not. They have seen both Chris and Raiden in action while the rest mostly had only seen Raiden. They knew who was better.

Chris moved with a speed and power that was not so obvious when you looked at him standing still. Tyler said there was one exception to all the betting being placed. It seems that Kiyomi also believed in Chris now as she also bet against Raiden even though she had known him all her life. And she was shameless in that she would shyly tell the odds makers that she knew Chris would lose but after everything he had done for her, she could not bet against him. As Kiyomi told them with humor in her voice while batting her eyelids, "What else can a little woman like herself do? I owe him my life." Kiyomi was given even larger odds than Tyler and Elijah were able to get because of sympathy.

Kiyomi and her father joined Caleb, Elijah and Tyler just before the match started. Hideo laughed quietly when Kiyomi showed her father all her betting slips and admonished her saying she should not take advantage of her friends in this way. Kiyomi smiled while saying "But Papa, as you have told me many times, a sucker and their money are soon parted so who better to lose it to than me?" Both laughed, and Tyler knew that Chris had a few more individuals that had come to believe in him.

The match was held in the courtyard of Raiden's school in an area that was around 40 x 40 square feet. The arena boundaries were marked by tile markers buried in the ground with the spectators standing just outside these markers.

The match started off slowly with both circling each other when Raiden unexpectedly came charging toward Chris. Raiden, now in the air, was swinging his left fist in a chopping motion toward Chris right side was at the same time had bent his body and was swinging his right foot toward Chris's left leg. You could hear everyone draw in their breath in as most thought that there was no way Chris could avoid both blows. And if either one landed, it was going to hurt and put Chris on the defensive. But if both blows both landed, this match would surely be over before it even began.

Gasps were heard when Chris with speed and agility that only those who have seen him in action would believe. Chris literally jumped fully over Raiden while twisting onto his left side to avoid both blows. And while passing over Raiden, it was not lost on anyone there that Chris could have retaliated as he tapped Raiden on the back with the flat of his hand.

Chris landed smoothly and swung around to his right and took off on a quick run that caused Raiden to temporarily lose his balance trying to keep Chris in his line of sight. Raiden recovered quickly and sprinted toward Chris. Both met in the middle and everyone was then shown what a duel between two masters was like.

Raiden was relentless in his attack, which was done swiftly and with power. A chop here, a sweep of the legs there, and all with power and agility. But each attack was met or avoided and it seemed to be a stalemate between two equally matched opponents. It went back and forth across the arena all the while fists, legs, arms were wind milling at an awesome speed that was hard to follow. Both fighters were sweating profusely but neither showed any indications of slow-ing down.

Up to this point, everyone was amazed at how intense the match was progressing. Usually the matches at this level of intensity would end in just a few moments. But unknown to most of the spectators, it was obvious to those who knew Chris that he was holding back. And they knew why. It was not Chris's way to embarrass his host if possible. But if you watched closely, there were several times it was obvious that Chris could have gone on the offensive when Raiden was out of position.

Raiden and Chris were moving so fast it was hard to pick out what opportunities each had unless you knew what to look for. Caleb smiled at Kiyomi once when after a particularly tricky move that Chris did to avoid an upper body attack, Kiyomi whispered to her father that Chris had just passed up on a chance to take Raiden's feet out from under him. Kiyomi looked at Caleb, who shook his head in agreement and said as quietly as he could, "Chris admires and likes Raiden, so he is not about to show him up on his own turf. Once he determines that there is no doubt of Raiden's skill in everyone's eyes, he will go on the offensive and put more pressure on Raiden."

Almost as if that was a signal, Chris who had been moving with a swiftness that was already hard to believe picked up his pace even more. The whole match up to this point had been Raiden mostly on the offensive with Chris matching move for move with defensive action. Chris's eyes were now a light pink in color. Chris all of a sudden stopped being on the defensive and went on the attack. It was like a light switch being turned on it was so sudden.

Chris started with a series of swift counter moves that pushed Raiden back to the edge of the arena. Raiden was obviously surprised and now having great difficulty meeting each attack without stepping out of the arena. You could feel the tension in the air as the awed spectators were watching one of the greatest matches they have ever seen.

Raiden, about to be pushed out of the arena, tried to go back on the offensive to gain some space with an overhand swing when Chris stopped short, braced his feet and met Raiden's hand with a return blow. You could see the surprise and pain in Raiden's eyes. Before Raiden could get his hands back up, Chris swung both clenched fist straight at Raiden's chest only to stop short just before connecting.

Both fighters stopped moving where Raiden looked into Chris's eye, glanced down at Chris's bunched fists, then looked behind himself. All there knew that Raiden would have been flung out of the arena if those bunched fists had landed. Raiden then bowed in recognition of his defeat. Chris returned the bow with his back straight and his hands stiffly at his side until he was parallel with the ground. Both were then surprised by the loud cheering and clapping of hands by all the spectators present. It went on for a good five minutes and when it finally subsided, all the spectators, including Caleb, Elijah and Tyler, bowed to both Raiden and Chris to show their appreciation for a match that had no equal in their experience.

Suddenly there was a chant from the crowd. "Musha" was being repeated over and over again. It was being directed at both Raiden and Chris. Hideo explained that the word meant warrior. Kiyomi, whom many here knew and how she had come to meet Chris, started yelling out to Chris, "プロテクター." This was then picked up by others until most were yelling at Chris "Purotekutā, Purotekutā, Purotekutā." Kiyomi, in between her chants, informed them the word stood for protector. Caleb, hearing the chant, remarked to those near, "you know, I like that. Protector is a good name to describe Chris, a real good name." Kiyomi was overjoyed and hugged Caleb. Caleb was a little flustered as he was not used to endearment demonstrations of this nature, at which both Elijah and Tyler broke out laughing.

After the match, everyone settled up on their bets where to Tyler's surprise, the losers were only too glad to pay up as they considered the match to be something so very unique it was worth every yen. Raiden, who was as gracious in defeat as he would have been in victory, invited Chris to dine with him and his family later that evening. Raiden said he would be honored to introduce Chris to his three sons and wife over some authentic homemade Japanese kaiseki ryori as only his wife could make. Chris was only too happy to accept and notified Caleb of his plans. Caleb and the rest were going to go celebrate all their winnings by going to the best Kabuki theater in Tokyo. Elijah laughed and told Chris most of the winnings would probably go to pay for Caleb's food bill as he seems to have grown fond of trying every fish dish in Japan, regardless of expense.

Chris, after cleaning up, left with Raiden and had a wonderful time meeting Raiden's wife and children who were all under the age of six. Takeshi with his wife and daughter had also been invited and present at the dinner. All had a great time and a little after 9:00 PM, Chris took his leave as he wanted to explore Kyoto where Raiden lived. This was where Raku said her story started.

Kyoto was a very traditional town and where Raku had grown up all her life. Raku and Masaie had known each other all their lives as their families were not only neighbors but were partners in a thriving trucking business. Masaie had always been Raku's guardian as long as she could remember and been a martial arts student since he was three years old. Raku, who said she knew that Masaie was the person she wanted to spend her life with since she was eight years old, made the decision at that young age to be a tandem fighting partner with Masaie. Masaie, who very rarely talked, smiled and said Raku only knows one way of doing things, all out. So it was only a few years later that they became one of the top tandem martial arts team in Japan.

Raku and Masaie were out that same night with Raku's younger sister, Atsuko, and mother, Mi, attending an Aoi Matsuri festival. It was a majestic time and the festival faithfully observed ancient traditions. It was while they were walking past a darkened alleyway on their way home that they were accosted by a group of twelve to fifteen armed men. The weapons they were carrying were varied with some being the traditional bow and arrows, swords and others being equipped with modern handguns.

The men were not interested in taking their valuables but were going to take Raku's sister and mother along with them to ensure a business deal. They were informed that a local gokudō, organized crime lord, wanted their fathers to pay protection money for their trucking business. Once they agreed and made the first payment, the women would be released unharmed. Any attempt to contact the police now or even after the deal was done would mean retaliation against the two families.

Raku and Masaie attempted to try and prevent the kidnapping at this time only to be injured in the attempt. They were able to injure a few of the kidnappers but the numbers were just too much against the teenagers. Masaie, took the most serious injury with a slight gunshot wound to his left ankle and a flesh wound to shoulder while Raku took an arrow to her upper thigh. The injuries were not life threatening but did limit their mobility. The kidnappers left with Raku's sister and mother in tow while assisting the three of their members hurt during Masaie and Raku's attempted defense.

Shortly after their departure, Chris who had heard the gunshots, came onto the scene. Chris, introducing himself while bandaging up the pair with strips of his shirt, was told what happened. Chris asked if either of them knew where the kidnappers would likely go. Masaie and Raku had an idea of the vicinity where they may go but no exact location. Chris said he must then hurry to try and track them before they went underground where he would most likely lose them.

Masaie and Raku said there was no way a teenager was going to be able to do anything once he did catch up with them. If anything, he would get himself killed. It would be best that they wait for their parents to show up to make a decision on what to do next.

Masaie and Raku looked at each other while Raku told me this part of the story. They seemed upset at something at this part of the story but did not elaborate. Masaie said they noticed that Chris's eyes had changed color from when he first arrived. Chris's eyes had been a bright hazel but now were almost all a light red. And they noticed that he seemed to have physically bulked up some. They were puzzled but were surprised most by his response to their suggestion on waiting. Chris looked at them smiling and said he could not wait, that "their need was greater than mine." With that Chris took off running.

Masaie and Raku hobbled together to the nearest phone booth and called their parents. Masaie attempted to follow Chris but the injury to his ankle made that impossible. Both thought that Chris would have to be very lucky to find Raku's family and if he did, there was not much he could do once there. As they said to each other many times in the next half hour waiting for their parents, what could a teenager do against a group of armed men? Chris was definitely brave but very foolish.

It was about fifteen minutes later that their fathers showed up. Raiden and Takeshi, along with a half dozen their older students, were with them. Raiden and Takeshi were personal friends of Kenta, Raku's father. Since they both lived in the immediate area, they were the first ones Kenta thought to contact for help since he did not want to go to the police at this time.

When Kenta relayed the story told to him by Raku about an American boy who was going to follow the captors, Raiden and Takeshi had a good idea who it was. There were not many Americans in this area of town. Everyone was armed in some degree with an assortment of weapons that almost matched the kidnappers. Even Daisuke, Masaie's father, and Kenta were armed with their service pistols and swords from WWII.

After a quick explanation of what had occurred and the visit by the American boy, they set out to see if they could track down the kidnappers. It did not take long before they found out that the way had been marked for them. Seems that someone had left a mark on at least one corner on each of the streets that they passed. Nothing much, just a fresh slash as if made by a knife while running past. Raiden was the one that noticed the mark and pattern after he saw the second marking. It was not really obvious until you actually looked at it closely. The slash started at the beginning of corner and went in the direction they needed to follow. Raku still remembers to this day Raiden muttering, "simple but very effective, very smart. Lead us on Chris, lead us on."

As they proceeded, all now knowing where to look, could see the markings that Chris made so they were able to pick up their speed even though still limited due to Masaie and Raku's injuries. There had been some talk of leaving them behind but this was discarded as there was a serious concern that the kidnappers may come back and find them alone.

After going another dozen blocks with several twists and turns, they heard a loud shout yelling Raku's name. There, a block away, was Atsuko. Atsuko was running toward them crying and yelling Raku's name. As Atsuko got closer, they could see that her white dress was splattered with blood, a lot of it. Raku gathered her sister up in her arms while her father checked her over to see where she was injured. It only took a few seconds to realize that Atsuko was not injured and all the blood was someone else's.

Raku looked at Masaie and her father with dread in her eyes when she asked Atsuko where Mi, her mother was. Atsuko pointed up the street and said through tears "hurry, please hurry. He is dying." Takeshi was the first one who voiced who "he" was by just saying one word "Chris." Masaie asked Atsuko, while moving as fast as he could, how her mother was. Atsuko said she was okay but had stayed behind to try and help the American boy. Mi told her to find help fast.

Atsuko led them all back up the street for several blocks to a large house on the right. The house had an oversized double door entry that had been forced open. The lock was hanging from the door like some battering ram had hit it. Just inside, there was a large entryway where on the left side was a beautiful wooden spiral staircase that led to the upper floors while the main tile foyer continued into the main living room just beyond. There were three bodies visible.

One body was just inside the smashed doors in the hallway and you could see a small amount of blood leaking from his eyes, nose and ears. What caused this required a more thorough examination than was available at this moment. The second body was located at the bottom of the stairway and it had an obvious neck fracture from the angle the head was in relation to the body. The last of the three bodies was draped over the stairway railing near the top of the stairs with a knife handle protruding from an eye socket.

As they went further in, they came to a large family room that contained another four bodies. Two were slumped over a couch in a fashion that indicated their deaths were sudden and violent. No indications that a weapon was used but they were definitely not alive. One of the two was on his back and the face held a look of surprise on it. Another body was lying in the middle of the room and looked to have been almost cut in half while the fourth looked like he had been run through several times with a sword.

Raiden makes a quick comment upon seeing this "Chris was able to arm himself with some of their weapons, he had nothing but a hunting knife when he left my house." They reached the kitchen where they found another three bodies. They were located at the back end of the kitchen near a stairwell leading to the basement. The bodies were positioned such that they indicated they had been guarding the stairs. It was obvious that two of them had been cut down with something very sharp while the last one had a crushed nose that had been pushed so far back into his face that it was difficult to even identify it as a nose if not for knowing where it should be. The power behind such a blow made even Raku flinch.

Atsuko led them frantically to the stairwell leading down to the basement. Atsuko had to step over a body found slumped over the railing midway down where the ceiling no longer obstructed the railing. His back looked to have been crushed based on how spongy he moved when Masaie had to lean on the body to get past with his bad ankle.

Atsuko, once she reached the bottom, ran to a small woman at the far end of the room who was leaning over a figure that was propped up against the wall. The rest looked around at the scene of carnage around them. There were another five bodies scattered around the room in all types of positions. Raku, though injured, ran to her mother, screaming out, *"Mama e, mama e."*

Her mother, Mi, turned to look at her daughter with tears running down her face without rising. Mi, no bigger than 5 feet and less than a 100 pounds, had both of her hands on the prone figure's chest where blood was still seeping through her fingers even though she had ripped off her blouse to use as a bandage. Her body was covered in blood and no one could tell whose. "He is dying, please, I cannot stop the bleeding, please help me!" Masaie's mother pleaded.

Raiden and Takeshi were by her side in a moment and gently eased her away from the pale bloody figure they knew was Chris. Kenta grabbed his wife in a huge embrace and asked if she was OK. Raku and Masaie joined them. Mi, while still weeping, looked up at her husband and whispered "I am okay, but only because of this boy. Oh, Kentu, you should have seen him. We were held down here where we would not be heard or seen. I never thought we would see you or Raku again. I was so very scared. Then when we thought all hope was lost, we felt the walls shake just before we heard a loud commotion upstairs. At first I heard shots and screams that seemed to be far away but they kept coming closer. You could tell that whatever was happening was coming directly toward us. I heard the men upstairs yelling, sounds of fighting, the sound of someone running toward us. The men down here with us were screaming at each other while one or two kept yelling upstairs asking what was going on. They were scared, really scared. One started going upstairs only to meet whoever was coming down the stairway. That man started yelling only to stop halfway through. We could liberally hear his bones being snapped by whatever/whoever was on the stairway."

At this time, Mi turned to look at Masaie and Raku with wonder in her eyes. "A man came flying around the stairwell much faster than anyone could imagine. The men who had gathered by us started shooting and yelling. One man, who had been laughed at by the others earlier because he was a kyudo expert and only carried a large bow on him, was more patient than the rest. While the others were shooting randomly, I saw this man put an arrow straight into the man's chest as he came toward us. It did not help the kyudo expert much as the man without slowing yanked the arrow out of his chest only to reverse it and use it to shove it up under the kyudo experts chin until the tip appeared out of the top of his head. The man then laid into the others with his fists, feet and sword. It was horrible. The man was so very fast while being so lethally brutal. The other men were laid out in short order. After he finished off all the last of our captors, he turned toward us. This man was covered in blood and body parts of the men he had just killed."

Mi shrugged off her husband's arms and grabbed Raku so that their faces were just inches apart. "Oh, Raku, I was so very frightened. I thought this terrifying man was going to attack us next. I had my eyes closed in terror and was praying that he would make it quick. Just let this all end quickly. I was shocked when I heard a pain filled voice that gently said, "Raku and Masaie will be so very glad to see you. They are very worried about you. They should be here soon'. I opened my eyes and finally saw who was standing in front of me. Masaie, he is just a boy, just a boy. I could see many injuries on him, the chest wound from the arrow, what looked like several gunshot

It was Chris's daring attack that caught them away from the passage. They dared not hurt Mi and Atsuko until they knew the strength of the attackers in case they could be used as hostages."

Tyler started laughing, whereupon he said, "And when they saw a boy, just a boy, they did not take him seriously. Well, they found out he is much more than a boy—he is a man to be reckoned with. A very deadly and determined young man."

Raiden, who was sitting in a lotus position on the floor in the corner, piped in with "I guess we were lucky they did not attend the match between Chris and me, huh?" At which all laughed and agreed with the assessment.

It was then that the doctor and nurse came in to let them know that Chris had a good chance but would not come out of medication for several hours. The nurse said she would have the staff call them once Chris awoke. You could imagine the nurses surprise when all proceeded to get comfortable to wait. Not one had made any attempt to leave. Caleb smiled and when asked by Mi why he smiled, replied. "Chris has this type of effect on people. Everything else can wait while they wait to see him get better. No thought of leaving or even taking in their immediate surroundings. As I said earlier, this is not the first time my cousins and I have been in this type of situation, we have seen this before. Even up to the point that you, nor anyone else, has noticed that you are still without a blouse."

Mi bushed scarlet as she realized that in all her worry for this boy, she had forgotten that she had been walking around without her blouse and only had on a bath towel that barely covered her bra. The nurse, who had not left, said she would get a dressing gown for Mi. Raku got up and walked over to Masaie to lean her head on his shoulder. She then turned and asked how they could thank Chris for all he had done for her family.

Tyler spoke simply, "Chris expects no thanks. But we have found that he believes he can never have enough friends."

Masaie, stood up straight and proclaimed with a broad smile, "Oh, we can do more than that, much more." Masaie whispered in confidence with Kenta who exclaimed loudly that was a great idea and that he would make all the arrangements.

Masaie then gave me a quick summary of how in a few weeks after Chris recovered and was released from the hospital, he was granted full family membership in the Montoku Heishi (瓶史文徳) clan. Kenta and his family were direct decedents of the fifty-fifth emperor, Montoku. The ceremony was ornate, to say the least. Kenta, Mi, Raku, and Atsuko wore traditional outfits from the appropriate time period as did most of the many brothers, cousins, uncles and other relatives that came out in droves. And of course, Chris's family who had been flown out the day Chris was hospitalized, was in attendance. Per Masaie and Raku, Chris was now considered family with all the family rights and obligations of the Montoku Heishi. Caleb, Tyler, and Elijah were granted honorary membership but not family rights. That was a very rare and unique privilege afforded to Chris only.

Raku saw that Eric had a puzzled expression on his face and asked him what was bothering him. Eric looked at Raku and Masaie and said one part of the story confused him. Chris had gone to Japan only shortly after Tiffany had first met Chris. Did Chris actually say the name Tiffany to Raku's mother Mi or did Raku and Masaie just assume he meant Tiffany. Masaie then confirmed that Mi was very specific with the name Tiffany. Tiffany was not a name they heard very often, if at all, so it was one that stuck in their minds. That this Tiffany must have been a very special woman to make such an impression on this brave young man.

Eric laughed while shaking his head. "Tiffany loves Chris so very much and I know this will make her very happy to know that he felt the same so early on in their relationship. In fact, if I work this right, I may be able to get her to make me one of her famous Philly cheese steaks sandwiches in return." Eric put his arms around Raku and Masaie's shoulders' and in a conspiratorial voice said, "You two want in?"

Raku and Masaie looked at each other with a big grin on their faces. "Wouldn't miss it. Never had one and we hear Tiffany has taken making one to the extreme as she knows that is Chris's favorite sandwich. Count us in. But that will have to wait as we have some other business first." And with that we shook our heads in agreement

193

and made plans to train together the next several days. Time was getting short and we were not going to not be ready. When Chris met the people that attacked him and killed Snoopy, we were going to be ready and by his side.

TIM AND MOLLY

That Tuesday, we were informed that the coming Saturday was the day Chris would go to meet the people that attempted to assassinate him and killed Snoopy. It was several days of tense training and speculation. We were all informed that anyone that wanted to participate, needed to be at the gym by 4:00 AM on Saturday. The destination was several hours away and we would be given directions that morning. It was all voluntary but I had no doubt that every individual would be there. And based on the comments I heard the next several days only confirmed what I believed. Everyone was excited. They all wanted an opportunity to help this man that had done so much for them. Training was extensive but you could tell that everyone was being very careful not to push it to a point where they may injure themselves. No one wanted to let an injury take them out of action. Not this time.

And even though everyone was tense about this coming Saturday, I was proud to say that it also pulled everyone even closer together than ever. Chris was one that everyone admired. And because of their concern for him, they knew if they wanted to assist him, they needed to be in top form and that included working closely with others in the Brotherhood. So it was a long week but also short at the same time. If not for Amber's massages after most training nights, I would have paid a heavy price.

So on that Saturday, I was at the gym by 3:00 AM. I checked with Tiffany to see if she needed a ride but she was going with Chris. I asked about going with her but she wanted the time alone with Chris. I could tell from her voice she was not taking this very well. I thought Amber would go with me but she left at 1:00 AM to go meet Tiffany. The surprises just never seemed to end this week. So at 3:00 AM I went there alone but I was not alone for long. Everyone had decided to make it early, they were not about to be late as they knew no one would wait. Most were here from the night before.

We all boarded pickups or cars that were carpooling at least five to a car. The ride lasted close to ninety minutes. It was located close to Blue Marsh Lake. The area was secluded and away from any population centers. We pulled into a parking area that already had quite a few vehicles. I saw Roy, Teja, Andrew, Iwao there along with many more. Even George and Mark were there. They were armed and looked like they intended to join in even though they were not members of the Brotherhood nor as well trained.

I watched Iwao for a moment who was sitting on a truck bed cleaning one rifle and had several more in the bed of the truck. It looked like he had been here for several hours already based on the food and drink wrappers piled up in the trash can nearby. I think his deep concentration matched everyone else's at this time. But there was something off with him that I could not pinpoint.

I noticed that this area was in a depression that could not be seen unless you were on top of the hill to the east. I also saw half a dozen protectors stationed here in pits that were heavily camouflaged with heavy duty binoculars looking through the slits that had been carved out in the ground. These slits allowed viewing without being seen. I stopped by one pit where I looked out one of the binoculars. In the distance, about eight hundred yards away, was a large mansion that looked like it had at least six or seven bedrooms besides all the other rooms of a building of that size. I could see armed people strolling the lawns. I counted at least six walking around and another several on the open porches that were located around the house.

I asked Melinda, whose pit I had stopped in, how many people did they believe were in the mansion. Mel said they estimated around eighteen to twenty in total. There could be additional people if they had not shown themselves outside since the Brotherhood found the place a little over four weeks ago. Mel shrugged her shoulders and said they had been unable to get any information about who or what was inside the mansion. The people there were on alert, and Caleb believed they knew they were being watched. Up to this point, that was all the Brotherhood had done.

I left Mel who went back to monitoring the mansion. And you could tell she took it very seriously. Especially today now that everything would be decided in the next few hours. I walked over to talk a bit with Teja when I saw Amber, Tiffany and Chris sitting off to the far side by Tim.

Tim was a gentleman that Chris had helped out early last year. Tim and his sister had been set upon just like Tiffany and I had been. Chris along with the protectors, had stopped the planned rape of Molly, Tim's sister. But unfortunately, Chris did not get there until after Tim had already been shot several times. One of those gunshots had caused permanent damage to his spine. Tim had no control of his movements from the waist down.

Tim had been so grateful and impressed with Chris and the Brotherhood that after he recovered, he joined the organization. Tim, just getting used to not being able to walk, was surprised that the Brotherhood accepted him with open arms and expected him to train just like the rest of them. Tim found to his delight that the protectors were not concerned that he could not walk. They worked with him to see where he could be most effective. And like Tiffany, he found that he had an affinity for long distance shooting. Tiffany had done training with him in the past and thought he was in the top five in the area, which spoke volumes of how well he had progressed in such a short time. Tim also trained in hand weapons, where he also excelled in pistol shooting. In fact, I could see that Tim had three hand weapons on his person currently. Two were shoulder holstered and one on the back near the middle of his waist. Tim was doing the same as Iwao, cleaning one of the three rifles he had lying on a blanket next to him while talking with Tiffany and Chris.

I walked up and sat next to Tim and Amber. Well, that was after I gave Amber a great big hug and kiss. Of course there were several catcalls after the kiss lasted a full moment or two. Jealous, they are just jealous. And if I had anything to do about it, there were going to have many more opportunities for a lot more catcalls.

Tim was just telling Chris how much he appreciated everything Chris had done for him and Molly. How kind the Brotherhood was to have taken himself and Molly in after the incident and treated both so warmly. That he did not know what he would have done since he could not have watched out for Molly in the condition he was now in.

Chris, whose head had been resting on Tiffany's shoulder, jerked up to look intensely at Tim. "What do you mean by that Tim? What did we do special for you or Molly? Are you referring to you having lost the use of your legs and Molly having Down's syndrome? Because if you are suggesting that anyone did anything special for either you or Molly, you are surely mistaken. I get the feeling you are suggesting that you and Molly have a handicap? Really?"

With that Chris stood up and called out to Daniel who was just passing by. Daniel was known for in close fighting but horrible at any long distance shooting. Daniel trotted over to ask Chris what he wanted. Chris told Daniel that he needed someone to cover him when he made his play. Would he be available? Daniel looked at Chris with horror on his face. Daniel said he would do whatever Chris wanted but he recommended that Chris gets someone that had the proper skill, like Tim there. Chris patting Daniel on the shoulder, said he agreed, while looking at Tim. Daniel sighed and walked away in relief.

Chris went back to sit next to Tiffany where wrapped her up in his arms and had her place her head on his shoulder. Chris then asked Tim "Daniel has great reflexes and coordination but sucks at judging distances. I guess Daniel is handicapped too, huh? Tiffany, maybe you should let Daniel know since I doubt he is aware of his handicap, what do you think? And then there is Caleb, I better tell him he is handicapped too as he cannot run as fast as I can. Wow, is he going to be crushed."

Chris looked at Tim who was now looking chastised. Chris continued on with "Do you remember when you first came to the gym? Do you remember the tension, the arguments? How everyone was trying to get so much done that even though they respected and loved their friends, the stress was getting to them? By the end of the night, tension was so high Caleb had to make sure that there were extra personnel around to make sure things did not get out of hand? Remember that? And do you remember what happened in just several months after Molly showed up? People are now laughing, more encouraging, just plain happy now even after a long night of training. How the numbers at the gym have increased once the word got around? Do you know why?."

"Well it was Molly. Molly's constant cheerfulness and attention to everyone is the reason. Molly never gets upset, never tires, makes sure everyone has water, always ready with a bandage when needed, laughs easily and very often. Caleb has to force her to leave at night and you know as well as I do, Molly just waits for Caleb to leave and comes back. Molly loves it there and they all love her. Same as I and Tiffany do. So my friend, do not tell anyone else that Molly is handicapped, they may not take it so well because only you seem to think she is."

Chris with his head pressed against Tiffany's was running his left hand through her hair like he was trying to imprint the feel of it in his mind told Tim, "Everyone has some area where they are not as good as the next person. I have no skill at cooking and Tiffany demonstrates that every night so effectively. Caleb has no patience with sloppiness. Eric does not always recognize what is there just in front of him. But each has something unique that contributes to the whole. Caleb, well, he brings planning and coordination and of course, he is immensely powerful along with a great intelligence. Eric's secret is that even though he may not recognize what everybody else sees right away, he takes it all in. He does not forget anything. And when the time comes when it needs to be understood, it all gels together for him and there is no one else you want to have by your side at that critical time. It is like his mind prioritizes what is important and stores the rest. I know I am glad he is my physician even though he is still in school. I cannot imagine anyone else doing the job. Tiffany, long distance shooting, intensely dedicated and well, you have to admit her cooking is second to none. And of course, she has the patience and love to take care of a man that would be lost without her."

At which Tiffany lifted her right hand to caress Chris's cheek and saying, "And you are so loving and kind to everyone. Especially to me my love." Chris kissed Tiffany before continuing, "So, Tim, you may see that you cannot walk like normal where we see a man we can count on to guard us when needed. And one other thing since you seem to have some of the same attributes as Eric. I do believe that you may soon find out that Molly is about to become engaged." With that Tim, who was now startled, looked at Chris in amazement before saying, "Huh? Who? When? What?"

We all laughed at Tim's confused expression. Chris pointed out Conrad who was in the middle of the camp walking hand in hand with Molly. Conrad was carrying a jug of water in one hand while holding hands with Molly with the other. Molly had paper cups with her other hand, which she was using to give water to all that wanted some. It was so obvious that they were sweet on each other as Molly would hold a paper cup while Conrad would fill it before Molly would hand it off. Then holding hands all the while walking to the next person. Not during the whole time did they release their handhold.

We laughed even harder with the surprise that was now evident on Tim's face. Chris still laughing, said he would not be surprised if Tim heard from Conrad shortly about Molly. And if Molly's expression when she looked at Conrad was any indication, the feelings were mutual. Chris did not recommend that Tim tells Conrad that his future bride was handicapped. Conrad was very skilled in armed and unarmed combat and was known for his acute protective streak of his family and those he loves. Nope, that would not be a good idea for Tim to mention Molly being handicapped to Conrad even if she was Tim's sister. Nope, not a good idea at all.

With that, Chris and Tiffany left to talk with Caleb. I snuggled up to Amber who hugged me before disengaging. "I have to go my dear, Tiffany asked I stay with her. You understand, she needs me right now. I will catch up with you later." With that Amber kissed me so deeply that the catcalls died out before she was even done. Wow!

But looking at Tiffany as she walked away, I could tell from the way that Tiffany clutched at Chris that the time for action was upon us. I saw George and Mark walk over close to Chris. Just before I left, Tim asked me while looking at Chris "He has no idea, does he?" I looked at Tim with a puzzled look. Tim glanced at me then back to Chris when he replied to my look. "I could tell you were surprised he knew you so well. You were, weren't you?" Tim was right, I was surprised, very surprised. Only Tiffany, Amber, and my parents knew that uniqueness about me, at least I had thought that up to now. It was not something you would tell someone, who would believe you. I truly believed they alone knew me to that degree. I guess I was wrong.

Tim continued, "He has no idea of the impact he has on people or how he changes their lives. How by just being who he is, enables people to be so much more than they would have been without him. Or how much we all love him for all that he does. Not just the saving part but just being himself. Does he?" Tim looked at me when he asked the last question. I knew what he meant as I had thought that same thing myself so many times. I also knew Tim was not expecting an answer.

FAMILY RIGHT

The time finally arrived for the big event. We were all ready. We found out that Caleb had been using the sappers to slip in at night onto the grounds searching for any booby traps. They found plenty. The sappers, living up the high reputation we held them in, disarmed all they found while leaving them where they were at looking like they had not been touched. And they did this all under the watchful eyes of the people on the porches who stayed on watch twenty four hours a day. Was it easy, absolutely not! It was amazing the degree of camouflage they prepared themselves with. It took several hours to complete with many others assisting. These sappers took great pride in spending hours squirming agonizing so slowly to their objectives. And then disarming the trap or explosive under the very noses of the guards who sometimes were only a few feet away. How they could sit so still for so long while a guard was just a few feet away having a cigarette was beyond me. Did they get them all? It was doubtful, but Caleb had the sappers concentrate most of their efforts on the path to the west side entrance, where the main entry attempt into the mansion was going to be made. So it was hopeful that this area had been adequately cleared. Caleb had also not forgotten to have the sappers check for tunnels but thankfully none were found.

Along with the sappers, Caleb had the pits dug that I described earlier. These were not only for watching the mansion bit also doubled as a sniper pit. Iwao was in one with his three rifles near at hand on a towel. Cartridges were lined up in several containers of fifty each point up just next to the slit where he would rest his rifle. Tim was spaced another twenty feet to the right of Iwao. Tim had his rifles and cartridges laid out similar to Iwao. That was expected as Iwao had been Tim's instructor. I was surprised to learn that Tiffany was going to be in a pit directly in the middle of both of them.

There was something wrong though. I could tell from Caleb's expression that he was greatly conflicted. This was also true for Tyler and Elijah. All three looked anxious and angry, yes, very angry. Like something was about to happen that they did not like but had no control over. And when I looked around I noticed it was not limited just to those three. All the protectors were showing some sign of distress. Iwao was fidgeting and anyone that knew Iwao would tell you, that he never ever fidgeted. Teja and Andrew were nervously pacing. Raku was clutching Masaie's arm in almost a panic stricken grip. Roy was looking at me like something big was coming. And Tiffany, how can I tell you how my heart broke when I saw her. She was crying in Chris's arms and I doubt that there was a person there who was not ready to join her. George and Mark could tell something was wrong but were looking around more confused than anything else. Something was happening that I doubted I would like. But what?

It did not take long to find out. Chris pried Tiffany from his arms and looked at Caleb who came by his side. Caleb went to one side of Chris while Tyler and Elijah went to the other. The rest of the protectors started lining up on each side, myself included. That was when the bombshell that the other protectors must have deduced came.

Chris swung his arms wide while saying loud enough for all to hear. "Caleb, it is time, now it is time to end this. With that, I formally claim the Brotherhoods rule of Family Right. Being an honorary member of the Brotherhood, I am allowed to demand the right to be the first and only one to take the fight to the people that took an action against my family. That family being myself and Snoopy."

I was floored and I definitely was not the only one. But you could tell most of the protectors already knew and they were not happy about it. Tiffany sobbed and asked Chris "Please my love, do not do this. Do not make all of us who love you so much watch you go into battle by yourself. For our sake, accept the help all here are prepared to give." Mark ran to his son and told him "over my dead body are you going alone. I am going with you." George who had followed his father, repeated what his father said. They were adamant they were going.

I told you before that Chris's family were close. Chris's father and brother must have known they would be in great danger and of all here, the most likely to get hurt or killed. Yet they did not hesitate to put themselves in harm's way. There was no doubt to anyone present they planned to be by Chris's side. To see such family loyalty and closeness was inspiring, to say the least.

I was stunned though. Really stunned, my mind was in a turmoil. No way, not after all this was I going to let Chris go alone. I looked at Masaie and Raku and you could see how conflicted they were. They had accepted membership into the Brotherhood and had to abide by the rules. But you could tell they did not like what they just heard any more than I, and I would not be surprised if they ignored it. But then again, knowing Masaie's commitment when he gives his word, he would not break his vow. Doing something like breaking his word was foreign to him. And Raku would not do anything without Masaie. I thought about it but knew I would not, could not, break my oath. If I did, what would my oath ever mean to anyone in the future or theirs to me?

After completing his proclamation, Chris walked over to give Tiffany a final kiss and hug. Chris raised Tiffany's face to look directly into her eyes. Chris then told Tiffany, which we all heard even though he spoke softly, "Tiffany, I cannot tell you in words how much I love you. From the day I met you until now, my love for you has grown to where I cannot imagine life without you being in it. But that is true for all here, they are all family to me. If I take them with me, some will not make it. And that would not lessen any of the risk to myself, in fact, it would be the opposite. Mason has been running the figures for me as soon as we knew what we were dealing with. Mason?"

With that, Mason, our bean counter, spoke up and it was obvious he did it reluctantly. "Tiffany, based on there being an estimated eighteen to twenty persons in the mansion, Chris's odds if he goes alone are between fifteen to 20 percent of surviving. If the Brotherhood went with him, the odds reduce to less than 2 percent.

Chris, when with others, will worry more about them than himself hence putting himself more at risk. Tiffany, I ran these numbers a thousand times and wanted, oh god, I wanted to get different numbers but they always came out the same. Let the Brotherhood and/or the Protectors go with him and he will not survive."

Melinda, who had given up her pit to another sniper, asked, "And what if there are more than twenty down there?"

At which Mason puts his head down and said the odds for Chris went to almost zero. More than twenty and Chris, whom Mason expected to be seriously wounded by that time, would not be able to take on the additional combatants.

We all looked at Chris who said we have to deal with what we knew. That there was no advantage to having the Brotherhood risk their lives. Besides, he already lost one family member to these assholes and he was not about to lose anyone else. Not if he could help it. When he said this he turned to his father and brother and asked them to abide by his decision. They meant the world to him but this was something he needed to do alone. He needed the freedom of knowing that he did not have to worry about others. That was the only way he would make it through this. Mark and George looked at each other and you could see the despair and hurt in the eyes. They did not believe Chris would make it back. The odds were just too great. Both gave Chris a hug at the same time while Mark asked his son to promise him not to take any foolish chances. If he needed help, he was to yell and let them know.

With that, Chris went to the back of one of the pickup trucks and pulled out the two axes I had seen in his living room. Chris gripped one ax in each hand. Most would have had problems swinging just one of them due to the weight but Chris swung both around like they were as light as a feather while he was getting the feel of them. The normal pistols and other fighting equipment were also on but I could not see how he could use them with an ax in each hand. I knew that to him this was going to be a personal and up close battle.

I stood there in shocked silence while Chris walked to the ridge. Caleb, Tyler and Elijah also went and stood there on each side of him again. You could tell they were going to go with him no matter what

Mason or the Brotherhood oath said. They had been through too much with him and would not let him do this by himself. Tiffany meanwhile had crawled into her pit and checked her rifle out. Tiffany may not be able to go with Chris but damned if she was not going to do what she was trained to do. And doing so, maybe increase Chris's odds. Tim and Iwao were already prone and ready.

Chris, put his arms out to each side with the axes blocking their movements. "Gentlemen, we have discussed this before. I need you, friends that I have counted on all these years, to protect those that mean more to me than life itself. You promised me that. You promised you would stay here to protect my loved ones whom I love so very much. Do not fail me know. Let me go knowing that my loved ones are safe and in your protection."

With that, Chris took off on his usual fast run. And Melinda was right. They knew we were there. The guards outside withdrew inside in short fashion. But then I was amazed at what I saw. All around the bowl, men and women moved into view. All members of the Brotherhood. I saw Adam and his chapter and that was just one of many. There had to be several thousand at the minimum. And they all yelled. Nothing specific, just a yell. I know they had heard everything that had just gone down. They were as frustrated as we were. So if they could not go with him, at least they could distract by yelling. Anything to grab attention away from Chris. And yes, I joined in.

Automatic weapons opened up on Chris before he had gone very far. Chris was doing his normal thing and was spinning the axes so fast they were like shields being carried in front of him. You could hear the pings of the bullets bouncing off the axes. Tiffany, fired just behind Iwao and just ahead of Tim. All three hit their targets based on the excited yells from the spotters. And that was repeated around the bowl. This lessened the fire Chris was taking but not all. Tiffany yelled at Tim "See Tim, I guess Chris was right about you huh? Now help me protect my husband and the father of my son."

Husband? Father? My mind, which had been struggling with everything that happened that day, finally did what it was supposed to do. It put all the pieces together. In just a few seconds, everything made sense. The slip ups when they both talked with me. The Vegas trip. My parents, and I believe Chris's, would never have been comfortable with Tiffany moving in with Chris unless they were married. It would have been Tiffany's call as I doubted that Chris would mind it either way. Hence the trip both families took to Vegas just after Tiffany moved to Chris's house with the protectors that I could not make. Finally, Chris asking Caleb to wait four weeks. I bet Chris needed to wait four weeks to know what sex the baby was in case he did not make it. It now all made sense. And then the final piece that made me burst out laughing. While smiling I took off running toward Chris as fast as I could. I was glad I had not put any of my weapons down as I was going to need them all very shortly.

Caleb, standing on the crest took a grab at me as I passed. Only to hear me say in passing, "Family right. I claim family right to go with my brother-in-law." I heard Tiffany yell, "Go, my brother. Save my husband!" At that moment I felt before I saw two others that joined me in that dash to help Chris. Masaie and Raku were next to me yelling "Family right, Chris is a family member of the Montoku Heishi clan and we go to join our brother in combat." I heard Caleb yell at them to go give them hell.

I saw Chris stumble then recover quickly. I knew he had been hit. Nothing was coming our way, we were still too far away. I am sure that all inside knew what Chris looked like and how dangerous he was so all fire was concentrated on him. Not that there was that much gunfire anymore as you could see the sniper fire from the hillside was having a major impact. Several bodies were hanging on the balcony railing. But I could see no way Chris would survive going in the side door. They would be there in force waiting on him.

Then I saw that Chris must have figured the same and had a different entrance in mind than any would have thought of. He went up. Without slowing down, Chris when he reached the door, jumped and using the pikes on the back of the axes, climbed the side of the brick mansion in just a few seconds. It was hard to believe anyone could move that fast unassisted up a brick wall. Chris did not use his feet but would put one pike in the cement and use that to swing up where he would repeat the process. When he got near the balcony, he put his feet against the wall and pushed off to give himself some momentum. After the push off while swinging upward, he took both pikes and slammed them into the wood at the top of the top of the balcony where he then used the power in his arms and the momentum from the wall push to fly over the balcony straight into the open doors of the room above. In total, it was only a few seconds since he reached the wall that Chris was flying through the balcony doors.

We were still a distance away but we could hear the surprise of Chris's entrance just before the screams and gunshots started. I could imagine their surprise, who would have thought it could be done let alone so quickly.

The screams diminished in volume only to continue further inside the building. It was a very long minute before Masaie, Raku and I arrived at the side entrance. Just as we were about twenty feet away there was a flurry of shots directed at the joints of the side door from the hillside. I could actually feel them passing by my cheeks they were so close. They smashed at the door jambs in such quick succession that I knew that all three of the snipers that I left behind were involved. They made short work of the door and as it leaned inward Masaie showed his power by barreling straight through.

We were ready for a warm welcome but what we saw made us all stop in amazement and, I am not ashamed to admit it even now, queasiness. It took all I had not to lose my breakfast. Masaie did not seem to have been impacted at all but Raku was. Raku did lose whatever was in her stomach. The sight in front of us was gruesome and confirmed that Chris had been here. There were bodies that had great big slices through their chests, throats, arms, and blood everywhere. There had to have been a half dozen persons here and each had a gruesome wound on them. Not a one was moving. Blood covered the vast majority of the room. This was a sight I knew would give me nightmares for many years, if not for the rest of my life. It did not take much to imagine Chris using two axes with all the power that he controlled. And the sight here matched what I imagined.

We could still hear screams and gunfire along with running footsteps on the second floor. We passed a stairwell that must have been where Chris came down and moved into the next room only to find the same carnage but with fewer bodies. And this was repeated for the next several rooms we entered. I was starting to feel a dread come over me as I realized that unless I was mistaken, the body count was near twenty without counting the ones Iwao, Tim and Tiffany had taken out. And I knew that we had snipers from the other chapters doing the same from all the other three sides of the bowl rim. If the number of bodies inside was already near twenty, what Mason said came home to roost in my mind. Chris's odds of survival were nil. We had to find Chris ASAP.

We ran up the first set of stairs that we came to only to be met with what we saw downstairs. We could hear the sounds of fighting coming from further down the hall. We picked up our pace as best we could. We came into a large entertainment room that must have been used as their headquarters. There must have been close to twelve bodies here alone. Masaie and Raku looked at me with dread in their eyes as they came to realize what I had below. We had seen around twenty eight to thirty individuals so far. It was a conservative estimate as the manner of their deaths made it hard to confirm how many bodies were in a room as we're not taking the time to stop and count.

After we had passed another several rooms, each having three to four bodies, we came to a room where the door was closed. And just before we entered, we realized that there was now a deathly quiet. No sound at all. We cautiously opened the door and inside a very large bedroom we saw Chris leaning on the far wall with only one ax in his left hand. The other hand was pressed against a wound on his chest that was leaking blood through his fingers. That was not the only wound we could see. Even though he was covered in blood, I could see a knife handle visibly protruding from his upper left thigh. It was odd in that Chris looked relaxed leaning against the wall with his head hanging down and his eyes closed. Was he still awake? Was he alive?

As we opened the door further we saw that there were at least four or five men standing scattered around the room. Most seemed to have been injured in some way. There had to have been another half dozen bodies lying around the room but these were not in the same state as the others we had seen earlier. These seemed to be all in one piece with most just having a chest wound that left no doubt it was a fatal blow. But the men standing seemed dazed but moving like they were coming to their senses. We knew we had to move fast if we were going to save Chris.

All three us burst into the room firing the handguns we had cocked and primed just before we entered the building. Now was the time to see if all that training was worth it. I let loose firing all eight rounds in my magazine without pausing. I saw two go down from my fire. Masaie took one out and Raku took out one more. All four went down before they could get off a shot. But one man that was partially hidden by the large bedpost that missed our attention got off two shots. Both shots slammed into Chris and lifted him off his feet before dropping him to the ground in a heap.

Masaie and Raku went into a frenzy and I watched as Raku swung Masaie so her heels struck the lone gunman in the right side of his forehead. As the gunman was stunned and pitched sideways, Raku completed her swing around Masaie and continued on around with her back toward the gunman only to plant her feet while bending down at the same time pulling Masaie, who had pushed off, so that he went flying over her to land on the man's side. Masaie did not stop but continued his roll while at the same time entwining his lower legs around the man's neck. Masaie using the momentum he built up, grabbed the bedpost to use as leverage to roll in the air where he lifted the man by his neck using his feet only to slam him against the near wall where all could hear the cracking of the man's neck. Masaie stood over the man like a demon and would have done more except for the scream from Raku.

Raku and I had reached Chris and rolled him over. I barfed. The sight before me was horrific and it was my friend. He had multiple gunshot wounds and other serious wounds while being covered in the intestines of the people he had fought. I knew we needed to get him outside immediately. Masaie and Raku grabbed one side while I grabbed another. We carefully made our way to the main stairwell that would take us to the first floor. We were halfway down the stairwell when we realized there were still some of the enemy alive. Two stood, both injured in some way, at the bottom of the steps with guns pointed at us.

I expected to be cut down at any moment. I sighed and closed my eyes waiting for the end. I heard the crash of several pistols. I opened my eyes and was surprised to realize that none of us holding onto Chris was hit. Both of the men that had been at the bottom of the stairwell were now lying several feet away in a pool of blood. Standing at the door entrance was Chris's father and brother with smoking pistols in both hands. Mark looked at me and quietly said, "We have family rights too!"

Mark and George replaced Masaie and Raku, who then proceeded to be our guard while we carried Chris outside. What awaited us outside were, well, how do you explain it in adequate words, several thousand men and women standing there armed to the teeth just a foot or so from the mansion. It was a scary sight even if they were family and friends. And once we stepped through, dozens upon dozens went steaming onto the building to make sure there were no more surprises. There weren't.

Tiffany and Amber came pushing through the crowd with Caleb leading. And Caleb was not being gentle. Move or get pushed. In short order, Tiffany was beside me holding Chris with her hair flowing down to mix in the blood that covered Chris. Tiffany looked up at me with desperation in her eyes. "Eric, I need you, Chris needs you, save him. Please my brother, do what you must but save my husband."

Caleb who had taken Chris from our exhausted arms carried Chris to a medical tent that had been set up only a few dozen yards away. Where had that come from? Caleb, planning… Chris said that earlier… of course, he would have been prepared for this eventuality. Not just for Chris but anyone who may get injured. And there, all dressed in her nurses outfit was Amber. Tiffany ran to get sterilized and put on her uniform. Roy was already in his scrubs and waiting next to the tent entrance. Tyler and Elijah were waiting on me and assisted me getting cleaned up faster than I could imagine.

In less than a minute I was standing over Chris with a surgical kit along with Roy, Amber and Tiffany as assistants. Then everything settled in my mind and it focused on the task at hand. Chris was correct in that I never forgot anything. Not that I had a photographic memory, at least I did not think so, but everything I have ever read or experienced was compartmentalized in my mind somewhere. When I desperately needed it, like now, it all came together. While I had been cleaning up, they had taken off Chris's weapons and clothes before they scrubbed him as best they could without removing any of the bandages that had been placed on him to stem the flow of blood. There were quite a few. And of course, they had already started a blood transfusion.

As I stood there for the first second, my mind in the strange manner it organizes things, triaged the wounds. I started on the most serious but first I did a chin lift to open his airway and feed oxygen by a face mask. I saw a lot of organ trauma from the gunshot wounds. I did not suspect any damage to his lungs or chest wall so passed on a chest drain at this time. Tiffany and Amber setup ECG monitoring while I continued my exam.

I started a full exploratory laparotomy as he had several major wounds in his abdomen from both gunshot and knife wounds. I had Amber administer antibiotics while I started a fasciotomy to remove the shirts fragments and other clothing pulled into the wound along with any dead tissue I could see. In short order I was stitching this, suturing that, taking this foreign object out, repair this, repair that. I was sweating bullets already as I did this and deeply grateful when Amber wiped my forehead with a damp cold clean cloth. I knew Chris was up to date on his tetanus shots as we all were so that took one concern off my mind. I was also concerned about respiratory distress for one thing along with quite a few others like subcutaneous emphysema.

Chris was in a comatose state and no sign if anything was helping. But I went on and on to do what I could. All the times I had opened a medical book instead of going to a movie or on a date, came to my rescue. In the last few years, I have read thousands of books, medical classes, observation of Roy and others, all of which now came to bear on the next action I took. It did not take long before I was totally zoned out. I did not realize who or what was around me. All I knew was fix this, fix that, stop the bleeding here, clean out the wound there, until finally I realized that I had no more wounds to work on.

I looked up and standing there on either side of me were Dr. Sternson and Dr. Hudley. They both looked at me with pride on their faces. I checked Chris's vitals and they were still there. Not great but I could feel his pulse and his temperature was high but not where it would have alarmed me. Both doctors patted me on the back and said they could take it from here. As I was turning, Tiffany, still in her nurse's garb, flung herself in my arms. "Oh, brother of mine, I have never been so proud of you. You were amazing. I have never seen you so in control. You saved my husband, I know it. He needed you now more than ever and you came through. Thank you brother, thank you!"

With that, Tiffany went back to Chris's side, only to be replaced by Amber. Amber literally grabbed me by my shoulders and swung me around, where she gave me the deepest kiss of my life. As I came back down to earth, I stammered, "What? What did I do?"

Dr. Sternson, while still checking over Chris, said, "You performed a miracle young man. You operated on Chris like a man with fifty years of surgical experience. I have never seen the like before. Where you learned all the techniques we will have to discuss at some future time because even I could not replicate some of the ones you did here today. They were just amazing, just amazing. You saved this man's life, there is no doubt of that. If you had not been here, he would have never made it. Good job son, excellent job."

I looked at my hands in doubt. Did I really do all they said? It all seems a blur at the moment. I felt drained and extremely tired. How long had it been? In looking at my watch I saw it had been over five hours since I first entered the tent. What? No way, it could not have been that long. I looked at Chris and realized that my dream had come true. I did what I had promised to myself those many years ago. And I also knew that I had so much more to do in the future as this was only one day in many that would come along with a man like that. And I knew I was going to be there anytime he needed me.

So while the doctors and Tiffany watched over Chris, I left the tent with Amber snuggled in my arms only to be met with a deafening cheer. Around the tent stood or sat all the thousands that had been here earlier. And I am sure more had come and were still arriving. And all were yelling in jubilant shouts my name, "Eric, Eric, three cheers for Eric!" The noise was deafening. I was in disbelief. I had only done what I needed. Amber could see my confusion and whispered in my ear. "You just saved a man they love tremendously. Not only by risking yourself but also by operating on him at a much higher level than you should have been able to. I think they got it right, my love. Oh, and to assist you in being overwhelmed, yes, I accept your proposal for marriage. You forgot to ask me but I did not forget to answer." With that Amber leaned into me and showed thousands upon thousands that she was pleased with me, very pleased indeed.

As I sat on an overturned oil drum, they tore down the medical tent while at the same time getting Chris ready to be taken to a hospital in the care of Dr. Sternson and Dr. Hudley. I was told in no uncertain terms to get some rest as they could manage it for the next few hours. The doctors would meet me at the hospital later. Mark and George came over to thank me profusely, which was all starting to get to me as I really do not like being in the limelight. Everyone in the field wanted to stop by to congratulate me and thank me. Only Caleb, Tyler, and Elijah seemed to understand me as they stood by the side of Chris with great big grins on their faces as I sat in torment. All the while this was happening, my shyness was screaming at me to get the hell out of there.

They were still prepping Chris on the stretcher for transportation with Tiffany, Mark, and George standing next to it, when I saw it. I saw a slight movement of Chris's hand. It slowly rose to where his thump was pointing straight up. I would have sworn I was mistaken when I saw his lips curl in a small smile and his left eye peek at me from under hooded eyelids. I looked at Tiffany who saw the same and looked at me with such happiness it took all I had not to cry out in surprise then and there. Tiffany walked over and whispered in my ear, "Chris is telling you did great and it is your time now, Eric, it is your time. Enjoy it, you deserve it."

With that, I remembered what Adam said that day so long ago. Chris was allowing me the honor of the day. Chris could have shown he was awake and all attention would have been drawn to him. But that was not his way. Chris would rather sit in the background and let someone else get the acclimations. So again, I remembered Adam's final words that day: "How rare is it for a man not to care about his own fame, but to care more about the men and women who follow him. Again I say, the man wonders why we would follow him to the gates of hell." I cannot say it any better, so I will not try.

EPILOGUE

So as we ran to catch up to Lord Protector in Fairmount Park, I reflected back to those few months after that day when I saved Chris's life. It was several weeks later that Chris was released from the hospital. He was not in the greatest shape, but he wanted to recover at home, and no one could disagree that Tiffany was the best medicine for him. Amber and I officially announced our engagement, and I know I got the best of the deal. We still planned to get married with Tiffany and Chris, who wanted to hold a proper ceremony in a church after the baby was born. Excuse me, babies. It seems Tiffany and Chris were going to have twins in a few months. If the sonograms were correct, I will be the uncle to two boys.

To say both families were ecstatic was a given. Especially as this would be the first grandchild on both sides. Tiffany told me that Chris came up with the names, and she happily concurred. Alexander, after our dad, and Michael, after Chris's dad. I said that was awesome, both fathers would be greatly pleased. Then she told me the bombshell. Both boys' middle names would be Eric, after me. Chris came up with that, and Tiffany could not have been any happier. I said she should let George be the middle name on one of the boys. Tiffany laughed and said that George would be the name of their next boy. And Tiffany proudly proclaimed she planned to have many more.

So my life had turned upside down since that day I first met Chris, and I wouldn't have it any other way. I made good on my goal to be Chris's doctor, but I knew there was so much I still had to do for this man that had changed my life like no other could. I still needed to learn plastic surgery as I had not forgotten my promise to clean up his scars. Life was not easy but it sure was rewarding. So as I ran, I reflected on where my life would go. I knew one thing: it would not be boring. And that was confirmed as I saw Chris had finally reached his destination where I could hear a scuffle going on. So we all picked up our pace and did what we did best—protect the Lord Protector.

That is my story, for now anyway.

ABOUT THE AUTHOR

G. J. Moses is an information technology director for a medical imaging company. He manages during the day while reading and writing at night. Since he was a young child, G. J. has been an avid reader of science fiction, fantasy, and action/adventure. H. G. Wells, Edgar Rice Burroughs, and Isaac Asimov were some of the early authors that influenced his style. After forty years in IT, G. J. has taken on a new passion of bringing stories to paper.

He now lives in Texas with his wife, Melinda, who has been his greatest fan and motivator.

CPSIA information can be obtained
at www.ICGtesting.com
Printed in the USA
LVOW11s0803290617

539794LV00001B/79/P